BUT I LOVE YOU

A NOVEL

BY PETER ROSCH

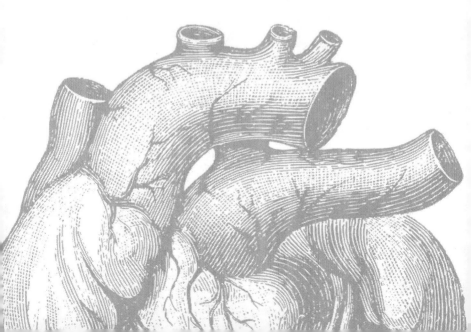

BUT I LOVE YOU

Copyright © 2014 by Peter Rosch

ISBN: 978-0692210925

Cover Art by Ariele Jerome
Rosch, LLC. • Books, Music, & Film •
To read more from Peter Rosch visit: www.level9paranoia.com

This book is dedicated to my dear mother. During my formative years and beyond, her endless warnings about strangers and their stranger-danger most certainly must have played their part.

Ariele made me do it.

Love is the ability and willingness to allow those that you care for to be what they choose for themselves without any insistence that they satisfy you.

—Wayne Dyer

WEDNESDAY
AUGUST
SEVENTH

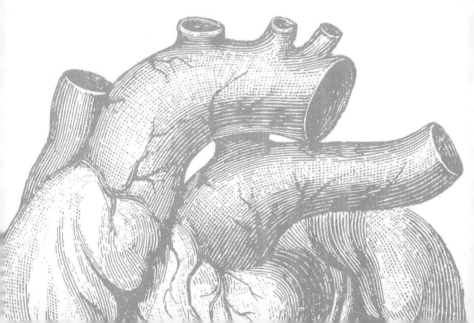

I am terrified by this dark thing
That sleeps in me;
All day I feel its soft, feathery turnings, its malignity.

—Sylvia Plath

Chris endured an uncomfortably long examination of herself by way of the treasured mirror over her bathroom sink. It was early, not quite six, and the sun had just begun its ascent, cresting over an eastern horizon hidden by endless Manhattan fabrications composed of concrete and steel. The last few semi-serene moments of a city night's attempt at stillness quickly dissipated with each new band of creeping natural light as they snuck their way into her SoHo loft. The same delightfully warm and varied illuminating hues that had contributed to the unit's coveted uniqueness, were now inhospitably threatening to force her to come to immediate terms with her latest reality. For a brief moment, her exhausted mind discarded the predicament and permitted a senseless wandering to the time when she had eagerly purchased the street antique now reflecting the disheveled, torn, and blood stained mess she was that morning.

The mirror had always held a special significance, because it had been the first purchase, the earliest of many made over the years, obtained with her own money—a paycheck she had earned. Like all upstate country junk for sale on the streets of Manhattan, it was aggressively priced and could have been categorized as too expensive for a young professional, only weeks into her first job out of school. The mirror's magnitude coaxed her out of half a paycheck; its ornate and aged frame, the multiple nicks, and the scattered scratches living delicately upon the reflective surface gave it a history that made the purchase feel legitimate. It was time to shed the sorority sister exterior she'd worn for four years. Chris believed obtaining this single asset would mark the start of a new act: that of successful graduate with a big-time job in the make-it-here-make-it-anywhere city.

Through a grating wheeze, the overweight gentleman hocking the barn finds had fortified the decision, assuring her, "This mirror is easily three times older than you good lookin'. An antique worthy of an old soul like your own."

She had recognized his flattery for what it was, an effective shyster's tool for securing a sale. Still, it worked. The prior six months of damning interviews it'd taken to find a clock to punch, during which she had heard nothing other than unbecoming assessments about her unpolished looks, rudimentary skills, and greenhorn abilities, had left Chris eager and at long last relieved to hear anyone suggesting she was deserving of anything. In particular, she fancied the idea that she was an old soul, and allowed herself to believe that the sweaty beast wasn't just trying to butter her up to take her money. She quickly parted with the last of the cash her first legitimate payday had afforded her, and walked awkwardly, but contently, carrying a mirror half her size and at least half her weight, back to her Upper East Side apartment some seventy blocks North and multiple avenues East. Back to the York Street two-bedroom she shared with three other recent grads.

The mirror was the only piece of furniture she still owned from her first year of urban dwelling. She'd gone to great lengths to ensure it would never lose its siren song, keeping its appearance identical to the condition it possessed the very day she'd obtained it. No new imperfections, even after ten years and four moves, two of which she had performed herself, and two made by paid professional movers who'd meticulously lugged it and all of the newer, fancier things she'd collected with the much larger paychecks she'd earned during a professional climb some might categorize as meteoric. The last team, a white-glove number based out of Red Hook, was responsible for the mirror's current location in the Crosby Street loft that she had called home for two months shy of a year.

Until that moment, the prized piece had shown no new scratches, nicks, scrapes or wear—preserved perfectly as a reminder of hard work and humble beginnings. But there was no denying the effect of the mangled mess it now carried within its hand-carved frame; the mirror felt cheap, used and broken. The purchase, the York Street hovel, the former roommates, and the young wannabe she'd been weren't themes Chris had bothered reminiscing about in ages, and the timing of their reintroduction seemed comically weak to her. She grinned the ill feeling away, stuffed it back into the deepest recesses of her *supposedly* old soul, and commanded her thoughts back to the murder.

In the few hours preceding it, Chris had become comfortable with adding the role of *planner* behind a murder to her growing list of unattractive firsts. It'd always been characteristically easy to compartmentalize all the negative baggage that came with unsavory deeds, but she'd surprised herself with how quickly she'd grown amenable to the potential pitfalls related to being the impetus behind removing someone from the world permanently. She had accepted the impending consequences of having someone murdered—that was something she believed she could live with. But owning the actual hands directly responsible for snuffing out and brutally destroying a human being, even the one she so desperately needed removed, hadn't been a scripted part of the plan.

Randy had dropped the ball. More accurately, Chris believed Randy *would* have dropped the ball. Her snap-deviation to their overall scheme had been predictably messy. Still, a life's worth of past snafus had always worked out swimmingly once the dust settled, at least as far as she was concerned. Chris didn't see any reason why last night's debacle would ultimately resolve any differently than those—with time, with extra effort, yet ending in her favor.

She began the arduous task of removing the dried blood from her face and arms, confident it was mostly the victim's.

Though it'd passed with an intense brevity, her altercation with Randy shortly after the finale of their shared crime had left physical consequences as well—minor cuts and scrapes that she adorned brightly against her pale complexion. True to form, little time was wasted in silently crafting logical excuses for them in order to stay the course.

No way in hell I'm missing tonight's event.

She was sure she could do a more than adequate job of hiding them with the dozens of cosmetic products lying around her bathroom. The role of Chief Marketing Officer at a major make-up brand had been good to her, monetarily speaking, and now even the infinite freebies seemed well worth the sacrifice of a ninety-hour workweek. They performed their concealing magic as she deliberated over a series of what-ifs regarding Randy and his steadfast commitment to her cause.

Chris stopped and stared, unblinking, deep into her own eyes to see how this accidental promotion to full-fledged murderer might have changed the twinkle that had lived there. It delighted her to find it still alive and well, in both, and possibly brighter than it had ever shown before.

"Why I thought this time would be any different is beyond me," she said softly aloud to herself. The last of the apartment's shadows then disappeared unwillingly to the smug satisfaction of the morning sun. "Want something done right Chris? You always end up doing it yourself."

FIVE DAYS EARLIER,
FRIDAY
AUGUST
SECOND

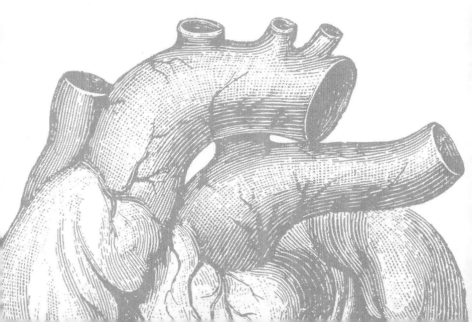

CHAPTER ONE

Profit is sweet, even if it comes from deception.

—Sophocles

"So, why *are* you the way you are?"

Alicia Lynn Wilde began her first interview of the morning like any other—with a far from accidental, overbearing emphasis on the word *are*, executed to deliver a deliberate subtext designed to rattle its victim. The purpose of the question in which that accentuated sting resided was crafted on countless hours of Alicia's own real-world experimentation. It had proven the perfect combination of words, effective for two reasons: it elicited the most pertinent details about an interviewee's charisma in the shortest period of time, but also, and more importantly, created the first of exactly three weeding criteria for admittance into Elite Two Meet. A trio of hurdles that had to be cleared, in person, even as the subject remained unaware of their existence, and all three completed within the first ten minutes of the interview.

A different, albeit similarly intentioned lead question had also been meticulously scripted for potential male members, but this opening query—by far—had proven the most successful in starting a revealing dialog with the female applicants, who outnumbered male candidates six to one.

If her question was bobbled, or went unanswered before the second sip of her Chai Latte, then Alicia knew she could wrap up that particular inquisition in just under two minutes. No point in dragging someone through the rest of the process—no point in dragging *herself* through the rest of the process—if at any early point she knew the applicant wasn't going to receive an invitation to become an Elite Two Meet member. After all, her time had become valuable. Though she often suspected the woman on the other side of the table—the same table in the same café where she'd conducted hundreds of interviews over the last three years—might also be of some importance in whatever world she inhabited, Alicia was quite alright with knowing full well that the only reason for terminating an interview quickly was because it meant she could have a few moments to herself, at least until the next *victim* arrived.

In its infancy, before Elite Two Meet had grown into a huge success, and before Alicia had been unofficially anointed "the Queen of everything a woman wants from life" by the story-starved media, she might have started the very same interview with a far more cordial and expected string of words. A traditional greeting along the lines of, "Hi, how are you?" Or a similar salutation that came only after a brief verbal blurb about herself, in which she'd try to set the applicant at ease with information on the humble beginnings of her matchmaking service, and how sincerely excited she was to be meeting so many interesting people, both women and men.

The polite Kansas rube routine had been delightfully effective in the early going. A sales pitch built around a bright-eyed, awe-shucks persona that successfully charmed; potent in recruiting members for her fledgling club, in securing funds from investors, ensuring commitments from eateries and bars, and unexpectedly advantageous in giving her a slight edge over the three or four possibly smarter, but far colder East Coasters who had designs on launching very similar mingling singles enterprises. She'd won that battle being everything they were not—and yet now, one would be hard pressed to find a single difference between Alicia and those also-rans. Her accent, once a delightful differentiation in a part of the city filled with near-cyborg like humanity, was dead. She doubted she'd ever be able to find that subtle drawl again, even *if* she made a trip back home, which hadn't happened in nearly five years and didn't seem likely to occur over the next half of a decade either.

Excellent answers to the first of her many queries were happening with far less frequency in the last few months, but if an applicant responded favorably, Alicia still only ever gave any human being, regardless of gender, a total of eighteen minutes to make their case for entry into her extraordinary VIP pen of eligible bachelors and bachelorettes. An entire interview would be over in precisely twenty minutes, with the final one hundred and twenty seconds spent delivering a painstakingly crafted synopsis of the next steps. If an applicant was hearing that synopsis, it meant Alicia had already decided to permit them access to Elite Two Meet. *Access*, not membership. A membership wouldn't be granted until the successful completion of a newbie's initial event. It was a secondary vetting conducted by Alicia in real-time, a final estimation of any first-timer reached via her own observations of their interactions with existing members and other novices hoping to perform well enough to obtain a full-blown membership, even at the going rate of eighteen hundred dollars a month.

On the surface Alicia's summation of what lay ahead for a qualified interviewee may have seemed casual, but of course, it was worded in such a way as to keep that soul guessing whether or not they had survived the preliminary cut at all. After her creation of that primary question, the additional two hurdles, and the twenty-minute limit to all interviews—male or female—not a single person who'd made it that far had ever been denied a chance to attend at least one function—save for one gentleman who had bent the truth considerably on the already lengthy written application required to even get an in-person interview with Alicia in the first place. Since then, identifying registered sex-offenders had become no more difficult than locating a cup of coffee, and she had added a few more required details to the application that thus far had achieved the desired effect of preventing anyone with even a juvenile misdemeanor from ever hearing her next-steps synopsis, let alone having the pleasure of her acquaintance.

"I want to thank you so much for going out of your way to meet with me today. I'm sure your time is as valuable as you think it is, and that's probably part of the reason you'd like to join Elite Two Meet. Busy, productively fantastic lives aren't always conducive to meeting that special someone, and that tragic fact was the impetus behind my creation of Elite Two Meet. I'm happy, why shouldn't you be? Right? *So…*"

The special emphasis on the two letter word *So* was also very important, because without some illusion of cognitive dawdling, an applicant might realize that there was nothing casual about any of the process, and might leave wondering if they'd be better off with one of the other latest professional singles services that had positioned their strategies as more relaxed alternatives to Alicia's supposedly rigid program.

"I want you to know that I really enjoyed meeting you, and I'm going to take a good look at the rest of your application, which is something I wouldn't do if I didn't already at least think you'd be a great new addition to our little group."

This was a lie—two lies actually.

Any person meeting with Alicia at that café, at that very same table, had already had their application punctiliously reviewed and then starred by all three of her screeners. People she trusted to do the homework for her, three younger women who, as is typical of the large-ego-set, had reminded Alicia of herself before her big city socialite transformation.

The second lie began with the word *little* and ended with it too. There was nothing little about her operation anymore. Alicia had nearly eight hundred clients, and while those individuals never numbered more than twenty at any particular event, it was very likely that if you became a member, you'd meet many of that eight hundred over the duration of a year's worth of events. Carefully scripted mixing and matching of different souls to be each event's attendees, enforced with the express intent of not letting anyone get to know anyone too quickly—at least not if Alicia and her team could prevent it. Helping people find that perfect match was the stated goal, but the basic internal rule of thumb was not to let that special connection happen until at least three months of dues had been paid.

If a couple took their fledgling relationship out of the Elite Two Meet construct quickly, so be it. In the past, Alicia had frequently postulated on revisions to her processes meant to thwart that costly inconvenience from happening too often, but she eventually categorized that action as the crossing of the proverbial line unscrupulously.

Making even larger sums of money wouldn't have been any more difficult than bringing more people into the fold by lowering her own standards. That had been on the table as an option many times as well, but ultimately it only would have led to the defection of too many of New York City's perpetually and intentionally single, all extremely wealthy and connected, who Alicia had depended on to reach her current success. Those elite stalwarts were the key to attracting great press, great reviews, guest hosting spots on talk shows—they were the epitome of adulthood's popular kids, the very same type of individuals who'd have never given Alicia the time of day back in Kansas. Being able to refer to them as friends was far more precious to her than the visibility that their social status and rolodexes provided her company. Many of them, in particular the males, had been given lifetime memberships, gratis, so long as they'd stay members. Only a handful needed to commit, and in exchange for their loyalty Alicia had covertly promised each of them that she would continue to recruit the most amazing combination of beauty, brains, and, for lack of better combination of words, fun-time-gals for the titans of hidden celebrity to prey upon. Her taste in women was appreciated, if not revered, by this upper echelon of Manhattan's one-percenter playboys. And as long as she had these "gentlemen" in the stable, prominently listed on the company's home page as potential future mates, women—exceptionally attractive women—would continue to join, and in turn, other lesser men would follow the women. It was a fairly simple business model, though turning it into the well-oiled machine it had become, had been anything but easy.

The final piece of the synopsis, delivered with a delicate vocal bounce to each and every lucky single, had always been,

"I'll be back in touch with you within the next forty-eight hours, even if I've decided against having you attend a preliminary function. And regardless of whether or not I decide to extend that invitation, rest assured you will hear from me personally. It was a pleasure to meet you, and I'll be in touch."

To her own surprise, very few people, if any, had ever said much more to her at this point than an emphatically smiley, "Sounds great."

There had been the one time where the interviewee turned out to be a magazine's Lifestyles reporter, working undercover. The mole's disgust with the entirety of Alicia's presentation and organization had caused the reporter to crack under the pressure. She boiled over towards the end and shouted at Alicia, "Go fuck yourself!"

That public dressing-down had left Alicia briefly shaken. She legitimately pondered the moral make-up of her vetting technique, but it was a self-reflection that had only lasted the entirety of the fifteen minutes between dismissing the phony applicant and welcoming the next scheduled and legit appointment.

The journalist's scathing critique hadn't gone unnoticed. It was a page-filling feature released a few weeks later in the city's freebie rag, and if it'd made any impact at all, it might have been responsible for the generous uptick in membership inquires that came shortly after its release. Nonetheless, the very same tweaks that had altered Elite Two Meet's written application, those made in order to keep the rapists and riff-raff out, had also seemingly prevented other magazine's attempts at chicanery. The possibility of anyone making a mockery of Alicia again had also been drastically minimized by her declaration that a repeat performance of this kind would assuredly result in the swift termination of the entire staff.

On this particular morning though, roughly forty minutes after she'd first asked her latest female applicant, "So, why *are* you the way you are?" Alicia had not even begun her synopsis. Nor had she spoken many words other than, "really," "go on," and "you don't say." If it hadn't been for the candidate-in-waiting's bold decision to approach the table in order to ask if she should bother with hanging around, Alicia might have let her current interviewee speak for another hour, maybe more.

The proclamation of her own errant attention to the time was in the right, and it flustered Alicia, jarring her out of the trance the woman across from her had held her in, just long enough to blisteringly condemn the brave nuisance. "I'm sorry," she said, "I think you must be confused. I'm quite certain we'd decided upon the ninth, and I believe I'm correct when I say that today is the second. Am I not?"

Lies, quick and easy, they came with the territory—and Alicia's perfected authoritative delivery of polite condemnation, coupled with the intruding appointment's self-esteem issues, sent the scamp on her way. That left Alicia, at minimum, another half hour to uncharacteristically enjoy actually getting to know the lanky brunette who had seemed hardly one bit fazed by the interruption of their conversation.

Alicia stared into the eyes of the woman who had been a stranger less than an hour ago with an immovable intent. Trying to keep the momentum, she found the façade of civility required to keep their nearly one-sided dialog afloat. Alicia apologized and meant it.

"I'm sorry Lisa, please... tell me more."

SATURDAY
AUGUST
THIRD

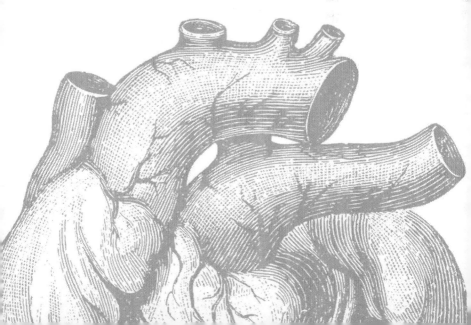

CHAPTER TWO

Sophisticated—God, I'm sophisticated!

—F. Scott Fitzgerald, *The Great Gatsby*

I woke this morning absolutely certain of two things, maybe three: One, that the media's darling mastermind behind the latest craze in Twenty-First Century matchmaking had taken a liking to me and would most likely be ringing me with a formal invitation to join her and her carefully curated flock of wannabe-coupled. Two, that no amount of caffeine and nicotine was going to make me feel the slightest bit better for having ever metaphorically put my name into Alicia's she-she-la-la hat for the selecting. And three, that neither of those revelations was going to help me secure another pack of smokes.

To hate on that blonde quaffed moppet from yesterday morning would be entirely too easy. I'm sure countless other failures have and do—those she has rejected before the courtesy of an in-person meeting, and those who have actually had the "privilege" of sitting across from her scientifically modified, Hollywood idea of what it means to be a winner in this life. Maybe she gave them two minutes or *even* the hour she granted me, and hate on her without having once given any significant thought as to what exactly was or is the driving force behind all her transparent and burning loathing.

Her success, her demeanor, her ownership of what advertising and society would have one believe are not only to be coveted, but obtained at all costs—her celebration and proliferation of the very distractions pushed onto a public desperate to forget the simple fact that it is themselves they hate—pick whatever you like, I'm not caffeinated enough to care what reasons anyone else might decide to use as justification to hate Alicia Lynn Wilde. At least I know why I only feel like I hate her. It isn't rocket science. Bottom line here: I hate *me*.

I surprised myself—not the easiest of tasks—when I decided to go ahead and enter that café and subject my very existence to yet another critical eye, especially a set of peepers that wouldn't ultimately lead to a gig and a paycheck.

Accepting a good poking and prodding style appraisal from a would-be employer is one thing, but opening up this delicate flower and copping to its fragile inner-workings to some decorated stranger, who at best can place me into some situations with the very types of men I shouldn't have a problem meeting already, all under the guise of a casual coffee? Well, it seems suspect of my character—at least my own assessment of my character. I'm not sure what my motivation was, but I done did it.

Devon will be so proud of me—that queer fuck. Why do I get the feeling I'm only subjecting myself to whatever lies ahead here in order to enliven his otherwise miserable existence? "Easiest way to meet your future someone special," my ass.

His skilled performance as some movie-buddy-cupid aside, and any modicum of actual sincerity in his claims of wanting the best for me, I think I can add one last thing, a fourth item, to my list of today's absolute certainties: He only told me what he knew I'd wanted and needed to hear in order to get me to agree to try and insert myself into Alicia's dumb circle so that maybe, just maybe, someday he'd have the opportunity to take a crack at bat in the game of getting some supposedly hetero-celeb to take note of him long enough for a full-on Devon-style de-closeting.

When she calls later I guess I could just say, "Thanks, but no thanks," then hang up the phone before I change my mind. I'm fairly confident that it's a *when* and not an *if* by the way.

Do I want to go through with this? I can't afford it, that's indisputable. What am I trying to achieve? I've got to think a gal can get the break she believes she deserves on talent alone. What's my motivation? At best, I'll meet the man of some other woman's dreams—I haven't had a dream I can remember since before my ninety-day stint across the Hudson—some testosterone fueled gatekeeper to an instantaneous path of bona fide celebrity. At worst, I'll be armed with dozens of new charming anecdotal misadventures to share with Devon on the longer days we spend on set together. I'm sure that's exactly what he wants too.

Maybe it's the nicotine from this fifth cigarette, but if I am being ingenuous with myself, regardless of the outcome, I can honestly say that I'm at least partially relieved to have had someone *approve* of me—even if it is someone that I'd not wish upon anyone, and she hasn't actually phoned or written to say as much. Sue me.

SUNDAY
AUGUST
FOURTH

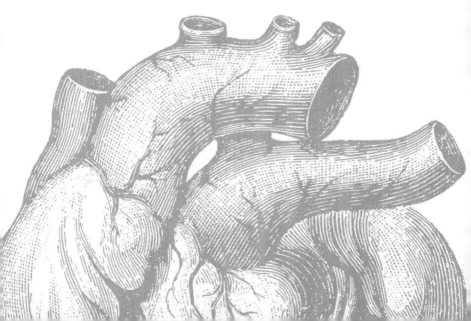

CHAPTER THREE

It's better to be unhappy alone than unhappy with
someone—so far.

—Marilyn Monroe

Routines are as necessary for success as they are essential to ruts.
Alicia had built the world in which she found herself by sticking
to a regimen of her own creation, though that Sunday evening
was slightly less typical than had been the norm of the many
months prior. Earlier in her venture, she'd prided herself on
emphatically trying to practice the very effective habits of other
self-supposedly successful start-up owners, presidents, and
CEOs. She'd gathered their wisdom from the numerous schlocky
laundry-list-help-and-how-tos so many of them had penned, and
she did so by charging them in bulk to a very nearly maxed
corporate card. After reading the lot of them as quickly as
possible in order to return them for the credit, the process was
repeated with a new batch until she'd devoured all but a few
tomes from *Entrepreneurs' Magazine* best-of list. By her own
admission, remembering which—if any—had actually guided
her into the formation of her own empire-building practices
would be difficult.

Alicia sat, as always, in her overstuffed, oversized Cardinal red chair. It was the only piece of furniture within the cavernous modern space she called home that didn't reside there solely for its exceedingly uncomfortable showcase form. The peace of mind that usually accompanied her lolling upon it was suspiciously absent. She tried to enjoy the same rituals she'd fancied almost any other Sunday night during the previous two years. The three to four hour window of that evening had typically been the only time during her chaotic weeks that allowed for a proper and private unwinding. For Alicia unwinding meant pouring over all the press she and Elite Two Meet had garnered since the company's inception. Anything so much as a blurb was given her full attention within that time, and most of the articles, interviews, mentions, and shout-outs had been absorbed by the brain behind her deep brown eyes numerous times.

It was shameful—or at least she thought the near-ceremonial act of egotistically bathing in her own hype *should* feel shameful—but truthfully, until that night she'd been able to blur the indignity of the act. As she saw it, reading about her favorite subject matter while sucking the milk chocolate off of Flipz pretzels, in between deep pulls of the hazy-vapor-like substance that her eCigarette tried to pass off as smoke, was, in fact, her God-given right. The formerly easy cloak of self-assurance had derived from the notion that she'd busted way too much tail to get where she existed before thirty years of age. Compartmentalizing the instinctual twinges innate in all humans that indicate regret, remorse, and a gross display of self-masturbatory ego soothing hadn't ever been any more difficult than switching from vodka cranberries to vodka martinis—the dirtier the better—but never by way of more than three on that most personal of nights. Never more than two martinis if for some reason the previous week's events had led her to a quick decision that saw three Xanax, instead of two, as necessary to cope. On the rare occasion that she found herself on the very back end of a self-declared "bear-of-a-week," four of the popular anti-anxiety remedy was permissible.

It was a four Xanax night, even though Alicia couldn't think of one interaction, detail, or occurrence from the prior week that any rational individual might deem troubling—even one tightly attuned to the various unrelenting minutiae a truly successful business includes. Nearly two full hours into her Sunday night routine, she was equally perplexed that she'd barely made it through the very first article she had selected for consumption. It was an older piece by *The New York Times*, one that she often fell back on when and if she felt slightly uneasy about how her life was progressing. Other pieces had painted her even more fabulous, but *The Times'* interview carried by far the most prestige, and even in her semi-conscious state she knew, as she had always known, that it had less to do with its being a reputable publication and everything to do with its moniker as the only article her father had ever copped to reading.

She looked up from the paper's page, past the perfectly pedicured toes at the end of the brazenly bronzed legs she'd always believed were just a smidge too thick, and squinted to focus on the only other utilitarian item she possessed. In bright oversized digital script, the wall clock proudly declared the time to be eight fifty.

"Just enough time to make a third," she said aloud as she reached for the empty cocktail glass awaiting its reuse beside her.

There was a quickness about the refueling effort, because at nine, and not a moment before or after, Chris would be calling to discuss the upcoming week's event—the guest list, the beverages, the seating arrangements, the activity and theme. Her call and concerns would be made not as an employee of Elite Two Meet, but as some sort of pseudo-volunteer. Alicia had chalked up Chris' desire to be the client who goes above and beyond as likely having something to do with trying to pilfer knowledge about running a successful service for soul-mate finding. Chris would not have been the first if that were true—wouldn't have been the second or third member to deceive Alicia either.

In total, she considered six former female clients her undyingly avowed enemies now. All of them, perhaps even Chris, had come into the fold under the false pretense of wanting to find that perfect someone. In varying lengths of time, each woman's true intentions were revealed: they had joined for no other reason than to learn as much as they could about Alicia's operation, with the hope of taking that knowledge, bettering it, and orchestrating their own climbs to the top. These miscreants had done so in direct violation of the contract they'd each signed, breaching a subsection that stated in the sternest jargon possible that any espionage of that sort would be frowned upon.

Enforcing that little bit of legalese had proven far more difficult than Alicia had been promised by her own attorney, and it was an unholy kind of expensive to go into the lengthy legal battles required to crush the various thieves and their copycat dreams. After the first run at a modest suit against the original offender, she serendipitously learned that it was decidedly easier to vanquish her foes using her connections with various press publications. A few strategic phone calls had expeditiously tarnished the reputation of each of the five other culprits that followed that first, dragging their names through the mud before they'd even inked a name for their second-fiddle operations.

Those previous charlatans shared two distinct peculiarities: First, they had all offered to help Alicia in any way that they could, and yet not a single one of them had professed to wanting anything monetary in return. Second, and only slightly less telling, all six of the women had been Elite Two Meet fixtures— each attending as many events as is allowed per quarter, yet none had ever landed a boyfriend or even a second date. It occurred to Alicia, only in hindsight, that their courting failures had had nothing to do with being sloppy or ignorant in trying to hide their true intent. Instead, her ego assembled a respectful belief in which she estimated that they had been so focused on the task of absorbing the overwhelming amount of information about her own organization, while simultaneously laying the ground work for their sham-versions, that they'd all simply forgotten to act the part or honestly and understandably hadn't had the time to play it.

Like each of those six, Chris had approached Alicia at the tail end of only her second event, wearing a huge smile, to humbly reintroduce herself.

"Hi Alicia, I'm not sure you remember me. My name is Chris."

To be fair to the innocent, this wasn't uncommon amongst those souls legitimately trying to find love, for-real love, with Alicia's tried and true methodology. Those earnest engagement attempts were met with a perfected facial expression that masked her knee jerk thought: *Oh please, you really think I'd let someone I couldn't remember into this parade? Unreal.* She found the repetition of the assumption from so many different members baffling, and on more than one occasion had delivered to herself a heated verbal bashing condemning her naivety and self-subscribed belief that all members should know better than to suppose that she wasn't supremely on top of it all—if not masterminding entire rich destinies for each of them.

Alicia hovered a tad unsteady over her bar as she topped off her third martini with the five most pristine green olives she'd earlier been able to muster from among the swill being offered up at Trader Joe's. She took the first filthy sip as she continued to call to mind Chris' reintroduction attempt like it had been yesterday.

"Hi Chris, believe it or not I do remember you," Alicia said, forcing the same smile she'd baked up for all the other *nitwits* who'd inferred the same.

"Oh great. Well, I just wanted to thank you again for having me—I mean selecting me to be a part of this. I know it's only my second event, but I really have a good feeling about where things are heading."

"Fabulous," Alicia replied at a volume she assumed would end the conversation there.

"I'd love to help out if you ever need it," Chris continued.

Alicia countered quickly, using a retort that had succeeded in immediately terminating any future offers to help made by newbie-go-getters. She'd developed it in the aftermath of the debacles caused by the original six.

"Oh, was something not to your satisfaction this evening? We would certainly appreciate any constructive criticism you'd like to make formally, and don't worry, it won't at all lead to any kind of early dismissal from Elite Two Meet. I'm sorry you felt something wasn't up to your standards, and as you might have guessed, there's an anonymous way to deliver critiques on our website."

Until Chris, this had always been followed by enormously long and overdrawn apologies. And if anyone had ever bothered to investigate that part of the website to make a suggestion, constructive or otherwise, they'd never had the stones to actually send a comment. It might have had something to do with there being absolutely zero language on that page indicating that any comment would, in fact, be anonymous. It would have been too, Alicia made sure of that—just another morality line she wasn't quite willing to cross. She'd had her user experience team build just such a page completely on the up and up, but had also insisted they not say a word about it actually being anonymous in the body copy. And so, until Chris, apologies and future inaction were what had followed all other incidents of benign post-party-small-talk offers to assist.

But Chris didn't apologize, far from it. She stood her ground.

"That's not what I meant, and I think you know it. Have a good night." And then she left.

This hadn't sold Alicia on the idea that Chris was innocent, but it hadn't *not* sold her on the idea of having a little outside help from someone genuinely interested in growing the business for the fair market value of absolutely free.

The phone rang, and true to the atypical form of that evening, Alicia instead let the chime play out without picking it up. She didn't bother checking the screen to make sure it was only Chris she'd be ignoring either. Vodka martini in hand, she made her way straight towards the bedroom.

It was only when the phone had stopped announcing Chris' desire to speak with its incessant ring that Alicia realized she'd broken yet another important part of her routine: it was well past forty-eight hours since her interview Friday morning with Lisa. For the first time in three years she'd not phoned an interviewee to let him or her know, one way or another, about their admission status with Elite Two Meet.

Alicia sat upon her bed, heartily ingested all that remained of the third martini, and with Friday morning's lanky brunette on her mind, the pixie she'd let speak well past the eighteen-minute cutoff, Alicia gave herself an orgasm not once, but twice.

CHAPTER FOUR

Our deepest fear is not that we are inadequate.
Our deepest fear is that we are powerful beyond measure.
It is our light, not our darkness, that most frightens us.

—Marianne Williamson

I'm envious of the shamelessness of the supposedly downtrodden. How any of these people can continue to make a living pretending to be broke, hungry, and sans means, without slitting their wrists in front of the mirrored image of what they've become in their sucker-financed New York City apartments is truly a gift. I want what they have. If I had half the moxie these perfectly-imperfectly quaffed and cloaked *degenerates* had, I'd no doubt be on the cover of *Elle*, *Vogue*, and even *Cat Fancy*. I wonder if any of them have ever considered taking on an apprentice.

This morning the woman shouting, bellowing from the deepest depths of her only imaginary empty belly on my commute into Manhattan, had a bag—a nice fucking bag too— filled with bills that she clearly could no longer be bothered with at least pretending not to have by shoving them under the sandwich or two that a different type of sucker altogether had given her instead of cold hard cash. I held eye contact with her for quite some time, and she knew I knew. Didn't care that I knew, but knew it all the same.

Being able to completely divorce yourself from the consequences of unethical actions must be incredibly powerful. I'm not one to sit around and dwell on the possible results of my accidental and intentional misdeeds, but I do try to give some thought on how they might portray me to the principled minority. To a lesser extent, I also care how my hijinks might make someone feel—maybe more than I allow myself to believe I do.

One morning last year, I was walking down either Third Avenue or Lexington on my way to a temp job I'd taken. The gig was your basic answer the phone, file this and that, shuffle some papers you were sure you'd already shuffled about during the day before, and do it all over and over again to pay for some drugs type of position. Somewhere between twenty-third and thirty-fourth streets, a fairly handsome fella approached me like he'd known me my whole life.

"Hey," he said. "Any chance you want to just head back to your place and fuck?"

If I told you I'd been shocked by what he said, I'd be lying. I suppose his depraved bravado should have rattled me, but there was something about the frank delivery that actually made the invitation seem like a painfully reasonable option for consideration. He seemed neither drunk, nor high, nor insane to me. In that moment—and yes, it was probably I who was a touch high—I would describe my hidden physiological reaction to the question as both flattered and titillated. I didn't go anywhere with him. In fact, if memory serves, I said, "Only if you, good sir, agree to let me use a strap-on on you first."

He smiled pleasantly and delivered a smirk indicating that he knew the jig was up—at least the jig as it pertained to me. After tipping an invisible cap at me, he remarked, "Next time maybe." And continued strolling casually down whichever avenue it'd been in search of a more gung-ho partner I'd bet.

And why not?

What was the worst that could happen to him?

A slap possibly. An empty threat to phone the police perhaps. An aftermath involving a breath-stealing sprint away from a far more offended female; a recap-worthy escape to another part of the city. He was tall, had long legs, I'm sure he could have handled even that type of scramble with incredible aplomb.

On the other hand, the upside, even if his fantasy only materialized for him once in a while, perhaps on the mornings of those nights that'd included full moons, would be sex with a complete stranger. And had it worked with me, it'd have been with what some might call a beautiful stranger. If he'd agreed, in theory, to the strap-on, even though I didn't and don't own and have not ever owned, used, or wanted to brandish one, we might have at least had a cup of coffee before going about our separate ways. And once coffee is involved, who can say for sure that sex isn't an increased likelihood somewhere down the road? The righteously prude is an answer.

Anyway, I was as in awe of his shamelessness then as I am this afternoon of the overweight hungry-shouter's audacity. There is no desire within me for a free or easy ride. I've got legitimate skills and have been ready to bust my ass at whatever opportunities are presented to me, but you still won't find me squawking publicly, offline or online, about it. "I'm great! I have an Ivy League Education! I'm a model! Won't anyone please give me a shot at helping yourself get rich off of my good looks or smarts?" It's a too-bad-for-me predicament.

My Friday morning interview with Alicia might have been the closest thing to a shameless gushing regarding myself that I've ever put together—at least that I can *clearly* remember. Prattling on about me wasn't a comfortable or deliberate affair, but she didn't preclude my incessant ramblings. I love a good silence amongst friends, but am in need of an education on how those long awkward pauses are supposed to work between complete strangers.

Obviously, my soliloquy *really* impressed her too, because she hasn't bothered getting back to me, even after assuring me that she would, regardless of her decision, and would do so no later than forty-eight hours after our initial meeting. I believed her when she'd said it too, and I am pretty certain Devon has said that he'd read of this forty-eight hour notification pledge of hers—one of many published and strictly self-mandated must-dos Alicia employs to keep her company one step ahead of the competition. I wouldn't know. I didn't even fill out my online application, Devon did. Its authenticity is likely spot-on though, because few people on planet earth are as in the know as Devon on the subject of me.

A far from significant percentage of the population are under the impression that they know me. Part of being subconsciously seen all the time in catalogs, direct mail pieces, and other random trash rags is allowing for people to believe that it is possible to be intimately acquainted with you. I'd been quite indifferent with that part of a B-celebrity lifestyle when I was using, I'm a little less enthusiastic about it now. One prong of this whole Elite Two Meet experiment, beyond Devon's real plans for global domination made possible with a quick connection to some of Manhattan's elite, is to grow my comfort level with having the details of my life—dirty or otherwise—

exposed to the masses. Yes, it is time to let the public in on just how fucking fabulous I really am by my own volition, without the benefit of Mother's Little Helpers.

"New money. It's shameless. They shout about every success, every incremental uptick in profit, if they've so much as taken a shiny shit they tweet all about it."

This is my father's view on the whole new way of doing business in a world he increasingly finds repulsive and repugnant.

"Lisa, don't accept our help, that's fine. You can make your own way—I commend it. But do extraordinary things and leave the declarations of just how impressive those accomplishments truly are to the mouthpieces whose job it is to detail what you've done for the rest of them."

And that's pretty much how Dad sees the majority of the population globally. There is *us,* and there is *the rest of them.*

I don't disagree with everything he says, and I *too* heartily oppose the notion that I should have to work overtime to convince anyone that I deserve future kudos. But, this is the world in which we live. Anyone who doesn't religiously talk-up their own bullshit, no matter the validity of its purpose, the enjoyment it provides others, or the sincerity of its intent on the betterment of life or mankind, is left sitting amongst the also-rans.

P.T. Barnum himself couldn't have foreseen the utterly egomaniacal nature and ease of future communications when he said, "Without promotion something terrible happens: nothing."

It is no longer enough to be fantastic. You have to be fantastic at letting people know just how fantastic you are. I hate it just as much as my father, but not because I'm disgusted by "the rest of them." I couldn't care less about what people like Alicia have done to achieve the label of *nouveau riche.* The relentless plugging of oneself, by oneself, and by all means necessary doesn't work for this gal—period.

I won't be calling Alicia or soliciting acceptance from anyone else tonight. Devon has texted me a dozen times, begging me for some news regarding my passage into her club. He will have to make due until tomorrow morning without anything other than the text I just sent him to let him know that I'm alive and well, walking the streets on an unusually mild evening, and blissfully at peace with having talked myself out of ringing Alicia to remind her that she owes me either an invitation or a rejection.

I think he and I can both agree that my father would be tremendously proud of my inaction, even if we also both agree that he'd be proud for mostly the wrong reasons. I won't call Dad to P-R this breakthrough decision myself—and if he knew that, hell, he'd be even prouder still. Therein lies the rub.

MONDAY
AUGUST
FIFTH

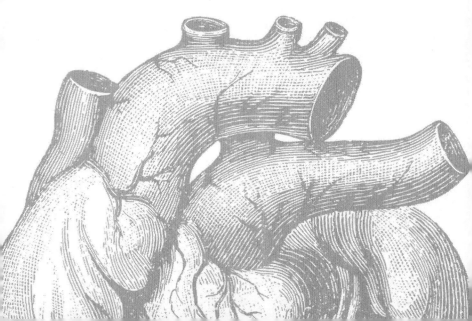

CHAPTER FIVE

Live in such a way that should anyone speak badly about you, no one would believe it.

—Anonymous bastardization of Plato

The repercussions of three martinis and four Xanax aside, Alicia found herself securely back in the familiar confines of her occupational throne first thing Monday morning. The previous evening's oddities hadn't faded from her memory completely, but they weren't top-of-mind. An adolescence spent cramming anything troubling deep into the recesses of her soul had left her with what one might term a "professionally adept" ability at keeping her focus on what she could convince herself mattered in any particular moment.

True to her routine, she arrived at the office exactly one hour before the rest of the Elite Two Meet team. In the second beginning, when her company made the move from home-office to three thousand square foot open office in Tribeca, all of her freshly hired eager little beavers had made attempts at matching the hour of her arrival. Their spirit had been appreciated, but it was the last thing Alicia wanted. The staff of five was beyond ecstatic, though a touch confused, when she called a meeting to inform them that the mandatory time for each of them to show was 10:00 a.m., and not a second before—not one second after either, unless there was a true medical emergency or something of that ilk.

The opening day, with her five new employees huddled around a still chair-less conference room table, Alicia welcomed her hires with a cordial remark about the previous weekend, and then launched straight into the first of many *essential* working relationship edicts.

"I think you'll find me efficient, determined, and unwavering in the belief that my method of operations here will be best for all of us. But, I'm not a monster, and if you've things you'd like to suggest that you sincerely feel will grow this company, by all means, fire away. I've brought you on and am overpaying each of you because you have a unique skill set that mimics my own—and one or two of you might even know a thing or two that I don't."

Her words had thundered about, big booming echoes of masterly pronunciation aided in their amplification by the suspiciously large size of a near-empty office space meant to coral only six soldiers. Alicia didn't believe any of them *actually* possessed knowledge or a skill that she hadn't already cracked, at least as it pertained to running Elite Two Meet. Pointedly, she had wanted to ensure that each of them at least felt like they might be contributing in some more monumental way, and not just doing exactly as they were told.

After firing one of the original five employees, Alicia had not since had to remind the remaining four to do precisely those tasks that she used that first alone hour every morning to outline for them. Despite any of her own notions otherwise, there was a robotic chemistry among her staff. If anyone was having any problems with the way things had been run the previous two years, no one had said as much—which may have been a product of the company's success more than Alicia's management style. She was a firm proponent of the "nothing solves discontent amongst a team like winning" phenomenon, and had accepted the possibility that the effects of two banner years and the bonuses that profitable run had allowed her to pay out might be the more legitimate culprits. In addition, she compensated each individual well above what they'd each indicated was an appropriate salary for their title, position, and function.

Alicia placed her designer juice on to the orchestrated masterpiece of cleanliness that was her desk. A twelve-dollar bottle of some hybrid of fruits and vegetables she truly believed could make up for the breakfasts and dinners she never ate. Lunch was different. Lunch was for wining and dining prospective investors, press, her accountant, lawyer, and anyone else she thought might be able to help her skip a few rungs on her climb to the top.

Her phone pinged, announcing yet another text from Chris. There had been several messages since sunrise. Alicia wasn't visibly put-off by it, but internally she was nursing a growing anger towards Chris. With each new combination of words, she was inadvertently bringing Alicia back mentally into the uneasy feelings from the night before.

When her primary assistant, Deborah, arrived, the very first thing they'd normally do was to immediately discuss which applicants Alicia had deemed worthy; a delectable recounting of the phone calls made over the weekend and the reactions to the good news of their admission, or the pitiable last gasps made by those who were excluded. Chris' constant badgering via mobile device was an unwelcome reminder that she'd broken her forty-eight hour notification rule, and still hadn't bothered to phone Lisa with any news. She had phoned both Friday's successful and unsuccessful interviewees with the good and bad news, but she'd intentionally skipped over Lisa. If she knew why, she'd done a great job of convincing herself that she hadn't any idea.

Deborah arrived, and after five minutes of typical Monday morning chitchat was out of the way, she asked, "So, were the five Fridays we figured to be shoe-ins everything we thought they'd be?"

Alicia looked at her with mild disdain and replied, "They were." She took a deep breath and a long, slow sip of her juice mid-sentence. It afforded her just enough additional time to decide how to cop to not having phoned Lisa. "Sans one," she reluctantly finished.

"Really? Who?" Deborah asked, before she could stop her mouth from serving up the questions she knew she wasn't really authorized to ask.

"The skeletal brunette," Alicia said, feigning disinterest in working any harder to recall a name.

Deborah perceived the nonchalance in her response as an indicative displeasure with her insubordination.

"Lisa," Alicia finally faked recalling.

Deborah went conversationally limp, choosing to stay quiet by design until Alicia led the conversation in the direction of her choosing.

The phone pinged again. Alicia glanced down only to find that it was yet another text from Chris. Her exasperation with Chris' refusal to simply wait for her to get back in touch at her own tempo climbed from her chest, through her throat, and came out as misdirected bile towards Deborah.

"Just because you've picked mostly consistent winners in the past doesn't mean you aren't capable of making a tragic mistake now," she snapped.

Deborah meekly replied, "Of course not. I didn't mean to suggest otherwise." In an effort to move things forward as quickly as possible and leave this unusually tense Monday morning moment behind, she continued, "So, you rang the other four with the great news, and Lisa with the bad?" It was another question she aired with an unintended tone.

"What do you think?" Alicia snapped with considerable disgust.

Deborah found just enough courage to wrap up with a legitimate inquiry.

"Isn't this what I'm supposed to be doing right now? Confirming that Friday's interviews are either in or out, so that I can make the necessary arrangements to include them for this Wednesday's event?"

Alicia quickly evaluated the impact of the mild hangover she was still working. Deborah's question had a rebellious blare, even as the chosen words hadn't served explicitly in the name of insulting insubordination. At that point, Monday wasn't feeling anything like her usual Mondays. The confusion, while entirely self-inflicted, was quietly discomforting. She desired no further reminders of her weekend's peculiarities, didn't want to think about the night before or even the past three days, and the arrival of Chris' umpteenth text did nothing to mollify the seething demon beneath her skin. In a just-less-than-mad panic to quell her irritation, Alicia took a deep breath and manufactured enough composure to agree with Deborah.

"Yes, yes it is. I made some poor choices last night, and I'm not one hundred percent."

Deborah nodded along conspiratorially. A hangover was not only something she understood, but a malady she was secretly relived to see that Alicia was capable of possessing. It was a reassuring revelation: the most dedicated of go-getters make a bad call or two in the wee hours of school-night evenings as well. She smiled and said, "Oh, okay hon. Can I get you something solid to go along with that juice?"

Alicia received the offer with indifference, but still managed to act like she was touched by such a sweet gesture.

"Thank you, but that's entirely unnecessary, Deborah. I'll be fine. Let's just carry on. Please do make arrangements with the four others, and I'll arrange a second interview with Lisa on my own. Sound good?"

It was a rhetorical question. Deborah knew it required no audible answer and nodded with a heavy vertical motion to clearly indicate that she understood completely. She then left Alicia's office to begin the rest of her day's activities.

Alicia thought she'd handled the majority of the situation pretty well, though she didn't understand why she'd let it turn into a situation in the first place.

I should get in touch with Chris I suppose.

Before she could grab her cell, her secondary assistant, Bean—it was a dumb name, but a real name—buzzed her office line. Alicia answered.

"Hi Bean, I'm very busy right now and we aren't meant to discuss next week's theme until eleven. It's not even ten-thirty."

Bean was silent.

"Bean?"

"I'm sorry Alicia, it's just—"

"Spit it out, Bean!"

Alicia's hangover was finally dissipating due to the adrenaline the morning's frustration and its accompanying anger had afforded her.

Bean blurted, "Well, there is an NYPD detective here to see you. Should I send him in?"

Alicia's feverish in-the-moment attempt to uncover a single shred of any idea as to why there would be anyone of the sort coming to her office was for not.

Bean broke her already impaired concentration, "Alicia?"

"Yes Bean. Of course, send him in right away."

Alicia hung up and quickly made minor adjustments to her already nearly spotless desk, as if being tidy was an indication of having never done anything wrong. She knew she hadn't of course—nothing that she could remember—and quickly surmised that her developing pangs of anxiety would be the same for any other normal person meeting a detective at her place of business without fair warning.

After a subtle knock made during the act of simultaneous entry, the detective entered her private office unaccompanied. The first thing Alicia noticed was how much smaller the space felt with the introduction and magnitude of his physical being. Years of instantaneously sizing up men for their possible inclusion into Elite Two Meet had her thinking: athletic for forty-plus, boyishly handsome ten years ago, needs more sleep, a clean shave, plenty of hair left on a body that carries an air of indestructibility. Alicia stood to her feet quickly, extended her hand to shake his and was finally able to force-swallow the stuck-to-the-throat Xanax she'd popped in the milliseconds before, all in time to deliver a cheery greeting.

"Detective, welcome. I'm Alicia Lynn Wilde. Please, won't you sit down?"

CHAPTER SIX

Unless you love someone, nothing else makes sense.

—E.E. Cummings

With her finger hovering just above the call button on her mobile, Chris reconsidered the consequences of trying to get through to Alicia, by her count, a ninth time. Eight attempts, composed of five actual calls and three texts, hadn't succeeded in provoking her to answer. A ninth and subsequent tenth effort would likely do nothing to remedy that. Even in her panicked state, Chris surmised that any additional pestering would do little more than fuel her own growing displeasure towards Alicia—accelerating a loathing that began with the stubborn refusals to pick up or at least respond in earnest with a reciprocally texted promise to reach out very soon. She placed the phone down gently onto her soapstone kitchen counter so that she could focus on the numerous related and unrelated thoughts blistering in her mind.

After a parade of deep breaths, Chris steadied herself in order to begin identifying the most relevant of the clutter collecting in her head. The dozens of only seemingly independent beliefs, assumptions, opinions and foregone conclusions wasn't anything unusual, but the weekend's happenings had done a bang-up job of multiplying the normal assortment by six or more.

Breathe, Chris. Breath. Let's get to the point.

Her commitment to the concentration required to comb through and sort all the hard facts from emotional fictions was unwavering. Separating them meticulously, as she had done most of her life any time situations overwhelmed, she placed each thought to the left and right of some imaginary line inside her head. It was a crude, rudimentary analytical visualization that allowed her to recognize a single common theme in which to anchor any previous bouts of hyper-neurosis. The pertinent information always came relatively quickly, though internally the process could seem dreadfully long. On that morning, within less than two real-world minutes, Chris finally landed on one thought—a lone summation of what was truly working her nerves at that moment.

The world and its inhabitants go about business as usual, all around you, even when you are the victim of a rape.

Chris let the realization sit inside her as she reached for her cigarettes. She was surprised to see that the hand attached to what she believed was currently a calm mind was trembling as it pulled a smoke from its pack. She momentarily drifted away from her previous thought, just long enough to form another related to her inability to keep her hands from shaking.

That's new.

With the cigarette dangling from her lips, she began scanning the room for her lighter, which was nowhere in sight.

No matter.

She bent towards the candle she'd lit earlier with that same lighter.

Sailors are scum anyway.

She took a deep drag and returned her ruminations to the situation at hand.

"What was I expecting to happen?" she asked aloud.

Chris recounted every word she'd either spoken verbally into Alicia's voicemail or had texted to her mobile.

"Not once did I mention rape, assault, the police—not a single word that made any of this seem any more urgent than the usual bullshit we discuss."

Another hit off of her Marlboro Red left her just dizzy enough to decide to seat her weakening frame down upon the pristine hardwood planks of the kitchen floor.

"I hope she's alright. I probably should have spoken to her first," she mused. "Finding out about this from the police won't be pleasant."

After a third drag, Chris heard herself softly and mockingly soothing her psyche. "Oh well. Not everything you want always goes according to the plan, *even* when it's you, Chris."

Without much warning, the previous seventy-two hours, three full days of near sleeplessness, began dictating a full body shut down. Chris' eyes lost focus, her breathing slowed, and her head began to drop. But before the sandman could put her down for a rest she knew was probably needed, she tugged at the bottom of the left side of her underwear, exposing the skin normally hidden by them, and then took the lit end of the cigarette and pushed it deep into her thigh—just above the two throbbing welts from the night before.

No luck. Despite extinguishing the entirety of its cherry into the otherwise flawless pale white skin living next door to the perfectly chemical-crafted tan line just below it, she lost the battle. Chris made the trip from conscious to unconscious accompanied by the docile sounds of a ringtone set roughly six-months ago with the express intent of always letting her know when it was Alicia on the other end. It was the only number on her phone that didn't announce a caller with the factory preset, and the selection of the ditty had been a month in the making.

With her last ditch effort to remain awake foiled, and no hope of standing on her own power to grab another cigarette, the lighter revealed itself. It was lying just below the sink, which made some sense, as she hadn't moved from that spot just over the sink the whole evening before. It'd been easier to deal with the vomit when it came, and it had come, while hovering in and around its stainless steel basin.

Chris' phone delivered one final refrain, and right before it was lights out, her last deep breath escaped as an exhale made in the guise of the phrase, "fuck me."

CHAPTER SEVEN

I am what you made me. I am a reflection of you.

—Charles Manson

Alicia finished leaving a gentle voicemail for Chris, an offering meant to resemble a sincere desire to help, a portrayal of a concerned friend. She hung up. With the thin body of the phone as the only obstacle preventing an even deeper and more painful embedding of her manicure into her own palm, she let out a worded grunt of detest, "Just perfect."

The detective hadn't left, but he was no longer in Alicia's private quarters. She peered through the plate glass windows that divided her workspace from the rest of Elite Two Meet's open-office concept. For the time being, it appeared he'd be busy enough sorting through client files and putting the other members of her team through the same battery of questions he had just finished laying on her.

She hadn't phoned Chris immediately after his mini-interrogation. Instead she'd chosen to wait until after an arbitrary amount of time spent against mentally perfecting the right words and tonality to the delivery of phrases she might have overheard once or twice in a fictional television program in which a counselor comforts the victim of a brutal assault and rape.

I should be upset for Chris. I am upset. But not for the right reasons.

It was an ugly feeling to absorb, but there was no denying its truth. Reaching for the emergency bottles of prescription meds she kept under the pen drawer of her file cabinet while the detective was still lingering about didn't seem prudent. For a moment, she sulked over the now two-years old decision to go with glass dividers instead of brick, or wood, or whatever other types of materials were often used for the creation of walls that actually delivered on their promise of privacy.

Alicia was unsure if the detective was through with her, but was certain she was decidedly done with his accusations. She grabbed her quilted leather handbag, her cell, and a copy of Lisa's Elite Two Meet application. She took three quick breaths, straightened her posture, working hard to align each vertebra in her spine to create the allusion of height, puffed out her chest as she threw on her sunglasses and then grabbed a hold of the door knob. One last deep breath and she exited.

"Detective Jones," she said mistakenly, but intentionally.

"Johnson," the detective corrected her. "It's detective Johnson." His eyes quickly darted from her face to her shoes and then right back. "I take it you're off to something or other? An important meeting perhaps?"

Without hesitation Alicia responded, "Yes, in fact. A great deal of what I call work can't be done from a desk, surely you must appreciate that."

"I do. No doubt, I do."

He made his way from Bean's desk over to the front door, just in time to adequately position himself in front of Alicia—not enough to prevent her from leaving entirely, but enough to make it clear he wasn't the least bit intimidated.

"Besides, we have your home address, your cell, your email. If we thought we needed to find you, I'm sure we could," he said as he took a tiny step back as if to indicate he was allowing Alicia to leave. "Good luck."

"Good luck with what?" she asked.

"The meeting of course."

Flustered, but quite positive she'd hid any indication of having been so, she turned towards Bean's desk and said, "Bean. Please show the detective out when he is finished conducting his wild goose chase."

Alicia headed straight for the door. She turned back to deliver one last thought to the detective.

"I told you, Detective *Johnson*, if Chris was attacked, I can absolutely assure you it wasn't by one of the male members of Elite Two Meet. You are wasting your time, and I don't intend on playing spectator. Good luck to *you*." And with that she left.

On the other side of the door she briefly paused to rummage through her purse, desperate to find anything that would deliver a one-two-punch to the anxiety that was trying to overtake what little common sense remained. But there was nothing, at least nothing to remedy that particular affliction.

She headed straight to the elevator, deliberately pushed the call button twice, and waited with her back to its doors— unintentionally counting the ticks of the cable drum inside that always grew a touch louder as the car approached.

What am I running from?

She kept an eye on the door to the office, simultaneously thinking the situation through, while praying that Johnson wouldn't be joining her for the ride.

I've done nothing wrong here. People get raped in this city all the time, and with a membership as robust as ours, why should anyone be surprised if two members were raped on the same night? I don't control the world outside of the one I've created. This is crazy. It could have been anyone—any millions of someones—and if Chris and the other slut don't even know who the attacker was, why is he here at all? I don't even care if Rohypnol was involved, the two of them should share some of the blame. Being drugged is a sure sign of a sloppy mind—to hell with them.

Alicia's frenzied deliberation left her not knowing whether she was condemning the women or the detective or both. The familiar bell of the elevator announced its arrival and she spun around to climb aboard in order to get as far away from all of it as was possible, at least temporarily. The doors opened, and the preconceived vision of it having been an empty vessel for her escape proved wrong. Startled, she took a quick step back, and her bag slid down her shoulder, though she still managed to catch it just inches before it touched the ground.

"Hi Alicia, do you remember me? Have I caught you at a bad time?"

After a momentary silence, Alicia corrected her posture once more, and replied, "Hi Lisa, funny enough, I was just thinking about you."

CHAPTER EIGHT

Selfishness must always be forgiven you know, because there is no hope of a cure.

—Jane Austen

Sitting only four short blocks removed from the office, in a café she never knew existed, Alicia felt herself floating farther away from work than the mere metrics of accepted distance measurements could ever hope to quantify.

The details of the mess that had been described to her by Detective Johnson were compartmentalized and equally distant, and she now found herself in some strange plane of momentarily living a life where Chris, Chris' friend, and anything they might have endured over the past weekend had fallen far, far off the map that had detailed Alicia's whole world. Instead, she was listening without listening to the no-longer-quite-just-an-attractive-stranger, who remained yet a phenomenon in Alicia's own estimation, currently seated across from her.

The walk from the office to the café with Lisa had been awkward, stilted, but what exactly they spoke about wasn't as memorable as the feeling. She didn't spend nearly the time she might normally have attempting to piece together the roughly five minutes of conversation she knew they must have had on their way over to their destination.

Alicia was begrudgingly smug with herself when she thought, *It doesn't really matter now, does it*?

Surprised by the lack of constant interruptions normally made by her cell, Alicia's muscle memory kicked in and she pawed at the screen of her phone only to discover that she had turned it off somewhere between the uncomfortable elevator ride and the quaint, yet terribly unsteady, table rocking back and forth between her and Lisa as they shifted their weight on it in between sentences.

Lisa continued to speak, as Alicia, getting closer and closer to finding the focus to actually listen, took in their surroundings. All around her there existed a breed of people she certainly knew existed, but couldn't remember having ever seen pass her in all the previous walks she'd routinely made from her home to the office and then back.

The café was packed, and yet there was an unfamiliar stillness among the many souls that were currently residing there. Some were engaged in conversation with a friend or friends, but the majority of them had their heads buried in books, e-readers, papers, and shockingly—at least to Alicia—very few laptops, mobile phones or anything else representing a professional connection to the busy world beyond the heavy wooden door guarding the tranquility inside.

There was nothing uninteresting about the various combinations of words Lisa was using to inform Alicia about herself. This second face-to-face allowed for far more detail than their previous encounter had. Alicia sensed at some point, even as she'd made café-specific observations from the corners of her eyes, that she'd never once taken her direct attention away from Lisa.

In an effort to break whatever spell she was currently under, Alicia put her Chai Latte to her lips and had an intentionally long sip. She pulled it backward, just inches from her mouth, to bring it within her field of vision for inspection. The beverage was infinitely more satisfying than any other she'd had, maybe because of its origin, sourcing, or possibly, though less likely, that the café staff's preparation had rendered it so delectable. However, even she couldn't discount the possibility that this was the first time in a tremendously long time that she was actually able to enjoy a drink that, over time, had become nothing more than one of her presentation-of-self props.

"Alicia?" Lisa asked with a slight increase in volume when she repeated her name a second time. "Alicia?"

A smile, unforced, formed—almost too large to not be considered a fake—on Alicia's face and she apologized, though the expression of regret was only in the tone that she'd used to say, "I'm listening."

There was a brief pause. Lisa wore an expression, intentionally or subconsciously, that one could easily interpret as, "Are you for real?" She sat back, found a familiar slump she often reverted to when she'd decided there was little point in putting more energy than necessary into any seated situation she found herself in.

Alicia sensed her blossoming disinterest, and willed her brain to immediately disregard all the unlocked emotions cluttering it. This wasn't as easy as it sounds, even for someone skilled in the art of keeping a conversation moving forward for the misguided sake of never leaving a single solitary moment silent.

Before she could adequately construct a single piece of dialog that might have achieved an all too familiar goal, she made an admission that left her feeling uncharacteristically vulnerable, "I'm sorry. I'm a little nervous."

"Really," Lisa said cloaked in suspicion. "Nervous about what?"

"I'm not sure. I'm wondering the same."

"Well, if it makes you feel any better, I'm a little anxious too. Though, in my case, I suspect it has mostly to do with not having had a cigarette in the last twenty minutes."

Alicia took another sip of her drink, quicker than the rest, faked looking at her powered down cell as though she was assessing the time and honestly inquired, "Have we been here that long?"

With an absolutely intentionally designed degree of disgust, Lisa shot back, "Yes. You've let me sit here for roughly twenty minutes carrying on about myself, with no indication that you've truly been listening—other than the occasional 'uh-huh' and 'hmmmm.'" She adjusted her slump to indicate an impending departure.

Alicia's face flushed underneath her makeup at the insinuation that she'd not been paying attention. She knew she hadn't really, and uncharacteristically expected to find that if she attempted to parrot back any of what Lisa might have spoken about in the first twenty minutes there, she'd quickly cement her faux pas as fact.

Her fear was quickly dispelled, and despite the prior feeling of certain ignorance, Alicia's memory quickly shoved most of what it had captured subconsciously to the forefront. She immediately found herself armed with an entire recollection of their one-sided conversation. After quickly scanning the surface details of Lisa's twenty-minute monologue, she found the two seemingly most relevant pieces of information she could immediately use as unequivocal proof that she had, in fact, been paying attention the whole time.

"My father, like yours, passes judgment on the world, though unlike your own, he is of meager means," Alicia started. "And congratulations on being determined enough to make a go of life without illegal substances. I'm sure that isn't easy."

Alicia continued searching for ways to relate—things she could say that would not only prove that she had been tuned in to every word, but might also work towards the beginnings of building some topics that she could use to reveal just how much they had in common with one another.

Alicia added, "Do you take any prescription meds?"

Lisa, not easily offended, responded truthfully with a subtle attempt at a zinger tacked on for good measure.

"Nope. Not yet anyway. Why? Is there some sort of Elite Two Meet rule against being a walking zombie?"

Elite Two Meet, Alicia said in her head. She had allowed herself to completely forget that the two of them had only ever met because of it, and that they were seated in the café under the pretense of her desire to further learn about Lisa before making a decision about admitting her into the organization. She forced the next smile and laughed with an audible tremble that exposed just how nervous she was exactly.

"Hardly," she dismissed the question. "It's just…"

Alicia paused to reach deep into her head's vocabulary, trying to find a way to sound less hippy-dippy than she believed she would if the sentence had been finished.

"It's just what?" Lisa pried.

"Well–you have an energy about you."

Alicia paused to see if she'd already lost Lisa completely.

Lisa held a steady gaze, and the same sparkle that served its part as impetus to Alicia's spoken observation, remained.

Lisa didn't verbally respond, but she did return to the posture she'd held previous to looking like she had one foot out the door to flavor country, and Alicia took that peacock like pride as permission enough to continue.

"I'm sure you get that all the time, but, there is simply something about you—around you maybe—that feels like..." Alicia didn't really know the adequate word to describe what it felt like at all, so she bluffed, "like... life."

Other than an uncomfortable smile one might expect from a humble soul trying to take on a compliment they don't entirely believe or possibly understand, Lisa remained silent. In this instance, the awkward expression was accompanied by the nervous fidgeting of fingers dancing around the tips of six Marlboro Reds loosely living within the pack that Lisa had nicked from a friend the day before. Though not her first choice, she held onto them as though the fate of the world was depending on it.

Alicia sought to bring some clarity to what she meant and continued, "My therapists classify me as High-Sensitive. It's probably why, unlike you, I am taking prescription medication, and this might be the first time I've ever admitted to the *defect* as the reason."

Lisa shifted, her smile still disarming, and yet Alicia's determination to make her understand exactly what she meant persisted, though she deviated to familiar excuses almost as quickly as she'd let herself speak the truth.

"What I do for a living exposes me to the best and the worst in people. It's a treat, and a living nightmare. And success, at least as it pertains to my company, carries with it certain pressures that are easier to ride out with a few little modern medical miracles."

Alicia paused long after the additional explanation. Quite sure she'd either said too much or not enough. It was hard to tell because Lisa didn't jump to fill the silence like most New Yorker's might; she sat with a focused scrutiny, behind sky blue eyes with a hint of green, that appeared to be searching past Alicia's exterior and into her soul—at least that's how Alicia interpreted the situation. It put her further off her game, and fed an already exhilarating feeling related to the complete and total loss of control—though she'd not have been able to classify it as such on her own.

Lisa finally spoke, "Sure." She nodded her head in subtle agreement. "I can imagine. You don't have to justify your pill-popping for my benefit. While I've not been at the top of anything, I've seen first hand the rigors it can put a person through. My father for instance."

Alicia adopted Lisa's patience with dead air and uncharacteristically said nothing to fill the few seconds Lisa's pause left between them.

Lisa continued, "In fact—and no offense—it must be dreadfully boring to be so very good at just one thing."

Alicia felt a swell of emotion rise from her gut, into her chest, and she worked hard to contain it before it made the journey through her throat and out her mouth. Was it anger? Was it excitement? She couldn't be sure, but whatever was fighting to be released from deep within her was close to winning and so she excused herself from the table politely.

"I'm sorry. I've got to hit the loo."

She'd never said *loo* before. She'd never gotten up to go to the bathroom in front of a stranger before either. It was a sure sign of weakness as far as she was concerned. Like some women on first to third dates, Alicia had worked overtime in perpetuating the myth that she never pissed, pooped, or farted. And yet, she stood without a moment's indecision and made a beeline to the café's bathroom, where she hoped that she'd be able to regain her composure, address the unknown emotion, in order to return to the table and assert total control over the situation.

Lisa obliged Alicia's journey by sliding her extended lower limb back underneath the table, and even though it wasn't entirely in the way—and easily navigable—the gesture didn't go unnoticed. Alicia ramped-up her normal walking stride, almost perceptibly, and thanks to it, beat the other soul who was headed to the facilities for legit reasons.

Once inside, she locked the door. In her haste, she'd not managed to grab her purse, which given the results of the previous search for prescription helpers would have been fairly moot at this point. There was no medicating her way out of the situation—though as she stared deep within herself she pondered the net result of moving this entire ruse to a nearby bar where vodka could flow freely using any one of the numerous plastic rectangles her pill-less purse, still sitting at their table, held at that moment.

Alicia needed to urinate. Her whole body was tense. After giving it her all and trying hard to force what her bladder held through a seemingly befuddled urethra for what felt like an unreasonably long attempt, she tired of trying and opted to hold it a tad longer. The few minutes she had actually sat on the toilet, in addition to the distraction of not being able to go, had freed her mind just long enough to create three plans for more comfortably continuing her conversation with Lisa, and just barely enough time to finally settle on one strategy.

She stood in front of the mirror, gazing as hard as she could into herself—hoping some other part of her being, locked deep within her brain, body, and soul would eventually explain the what, whys, and hows of what she was currently experiencing emotionally. No luck. Her own confusion about her intentions persisted no matter how hard she peered, and remained obstinately undiscovered in spite of how close Alicia leaned into her reflection. In fact, leaning in had only served in bolstering the notion that, at that moment, she was hideous, frazzled, and in desperate need of salvation by way of the darker room of her favorite bar, the bar she'd already intended on dragging Lisa to immediately.

As Alicia pulled back from the mirror, she momentarily caught herself connecting back to the reality of that day.

Chris. Fuck. I am—or at least I should be—worried about and checking in on Chris.

She reached for her cell on the countertop of the sink without betraying her reflection for even a fraction of a second. *I'll text her, and then deal with it when I'm actually able to pee.*

Her hand, and then hands, found no phone. She'd left it with her bag, and possibly with her humility, she thought, back at the table.

A vicious pounding on the other side of the door assaulted her eardrums, and she jumped inside her skin.

"Are you alright in there?" A male voice asked with equal parts concern and frustration, as the knob on the door began to jiggle violently back and forth.

Alicia flipped the lock back to open, pushed the door forward, and fraught with anxious adrenaline responded in a silent shout, "Fuck you. A polite tap would have sufficed."

The shaggy string-bean of a man standing before her, with one hand still hanging in the air mid-knock, and the other cupping his genitals the way a five year old about to burst from too much Kool-Aid might, replied calmly, "No. Fuck you. I've been knocking on the door forever." He pushed himself through, between Alicia and the door jam, forcing his way into the bathroom, and didn't even bother to close the door before relieving himself and suggesting, "You might want to let management know they don't need to bother with the key now."

Alicia had already begun constructing a retort, something descriptive about his physical appearance, but right before the last required synapse connection that would have pushed the insult out of her mouth, the corner of her eye caught the table she'd been seated at. No Lisa. And as far as she could tell, her bag was also gone, and so was her cell. The shock of it all removed any previous desire to cut deep with words and before scrambling back to the table to double and triple check she said to him, "I'm terribly sorry." The sound of it, the apology in and of itself, was nearly foreign to her ears.

Back at what had been their table, Alicia stopped and peered outside into the street through what the café was trying to pass off as windows. Wherever the sun was sitting was working a real number on what little part of those windows weren't covered in flyers, stickers, or obstructed by the various seated heads between her and the café's door.

Without a single thought in regards to her bag or cell, Alicia could be heard condemning herself under her breath on her way out. "Fuck me. Fuck me. Fuck me."

She reached for the door handle and with a strength usually reserved for the mothers of children stuck under the vehicles of careless motorists, yanked the heavy pine plank barrier with so much force she nearly caused herself to tumble backwards.

The sun, blinding as it can be amongst the skyscrapers of downtown Manhattan, left Alicia unable to make out the four figures standing just outside of the café. The toxic scent of cigarette smoke should have at least clued her into the identity of one of the bodies casually propped against the few feet of brick between the café and the glossy condominium building beside it.

Nonetheless, Alicia let out a panicky and guttural noise that only resembled Lisa's name before pausing outside of the formerly tranquil location in an effort to let her pupils adjust.

"Are you okay, Alicia?" Lisa asked. "I've got your stuff. Wasn't sure how much longer I could go without sucking on a cancer stick." She took another drag before the smoke from her last inhalation had even had the chance to dissipate.

Alicia felt instantly relieved. The sound of Lisa's voice was enough for her to slightly adjust her position so that she was at least facing her. Her eyes found their composure long before her body language could do the same, and they focused immediately upon Lisa, amongst the others, standing before her, with Alicia's bag at the base of the single foot she wasn't using to relax herself in a slick lean against the brick wall.

Feeling the panic emitting from her caffeinated new friend, Lisa threw her free hand up into the air and began swatting the cigarette smoke back and forth as if to clear a path for Alicia to come towards her.

"I'm *so* sorry. I didn't think you'd mind me grabbing it," Lisa said as she reached down for the bag and held it out for Alicia to take back.

On the backside of a huge adrenaline rush, Alicia felt weak in the knees but managed to take the required steps forward necessary to retrieve it. Even more impressive, at least to herself, was what she said with a complete absence of any anger or tone that matched her real frustration with Lisa as she grabbed it.

"No, I'm sorry. It was sweet of you to hold it for me."

Alicia's hand came in contact with Lisa's as she reclaimed the bag, but the momentary thrill of having put her own skin against Lisa's was short lived.

"Not a bad joint for an important meeting," a recently-familiar voice noted aloud. "Though you wouldn't know it by the looks of you."

With those words, the rest of the world surrounding Lisa quickly found its way through Alicia's eyes, and her brain finally registered the identity of the tall man in the ill-fitting suit that was standing beside Lisa, puffing away on the same brand of cigarette.

"Detective. Are you following me?" Alicia struck quickly.

"Nope. But your *appointment*..." He turned back to Lisa, "Lisa right?"

She nodded with a grin that read, "What the fuck have I gotten myself into now?"

"Your friend, Lisa, was kind enough to hit me with a smoke as I passed by," Johnson said. "Been trying to quit, so I don't buy my own anymore. I've become the very type of asshole I used to hate the most—a stranger hitting up strangers for smokes without any regard to their currently outrageous value in New York City."

Lisa threw her butt to the ground, stomped it out, and tried to remove herself from a situation she knew nothing about.

"If you two have something you need to discuss, I'm just gonna be on my way."

"No, no. I've nothing much to say, Pretty," the detective said. "At least nothing new." He turned back to Alicia. "Despite what you might think, nothing going on here besides happenstance. I happened to want a cigarette, and I *happened* to pass a gorgeous woman smoking one. If you're going to beg for a smoke, might as well try to kill two birds with the proverbial one stone, no?"

Johnson's intentions were on full-display, and even if what he was suggesting was a clever ruse to aid in the denial of having followed Alicia to the café, it left her feeling a deep burn from the pit of her very being, that only intensified the moment he shifted his posture just enough to inhabit more or Lisa's personal space.

"Detective Johnson, if there isn't anything new to discuss, might I ask that you leave, so that my friend and I can continue our meeting?" Alicia said as she finally found the firmer footing she needed to make good on coming off as completely disinterested in his games.

Johnson took the last drag off of his cigarette, flicked it twenty feet towards moving traffic without taking his eyes off of Alicia. A slight curl formed on the right edge of his mouth and he spoke.

"Not a problem. Had I realized that Lisa here was a part of something so important—important enough to ignore a double rape involving a friend—I'd have never bothered to bum the smoke in the first place." He turned back to address Lisa directly. "Apologies. Thank you for the smoke. Think I could bum another for my walk home?"

Lisa gave it a quick thought; she'd dealt with guys like Johnson since day one of puberty—maybe even before puberty.

She surmised the quickest, easiest end to what had become a pretty uncomfortable situation might have been to hand him one and to send him on his way. But, even without knowing what Alicia was involved in entirely, she found herself suspicious of the detective's denial of Alicia's accusation—it was far more likely that he'd actually arrived there by following her. That didn't sit well with Lisa; all things related to those with authority never had, and so she denied him what would have been, in all actuality, a third one of her cigarettes. "Nope. Two's my beggar's limit."

"Fair enough," Johnson said, before turning towards Alicia one last time. "I'll be seeing you. Be sure and tell Chris I said 'hello' *if* and *if* you ever get around to connecting with her."

"I was just about to reach out to her, in fact," Alicia said to the back of the Detective's head as he strolled away from them.

Johnson kept his back to them both and replied audibly enough for perfect clarity, "Good. Glad to hear it."

CHAPTER NINE

People only tell lies when the truth is disagreeable to them, or frightens them, or to cover sin.

—Anne Perry

Amid the echoing sound of a gentle knocking on the condominium's front door some twenty feet from where she lay, Chris stirred conscious. While asleep, her body had made little effort in finding a more comfortable posture in which to recuperate. Despite having succumbed to a mandatory slumber in a seated and slumped position against the only kitchen wall that didn't find the floor and baseboard interrupted by cabinets and appliances, she felt surprisingly rested. Her whole being was as effectively alert as it might have been from arising out of a proper night's sleep among the collection of infinite thread counts that cloaked the bedroom's mattress, from a company that had promised exactly this kind of energized result.

She rose to her feet effortlessly, still clinging to what remained of the failed cigarette in her hand, and took in the view from outside her windows in order to try and place the time of day. It was dark enough to be early in the evening, and she rationalized that her current state of near perfect poise, just seconds after awaking, was due in no small part to having been unconscious for the majority of the day's sunlit hours—at least a significant length of time for an internal repair that she'd not known in long enough to question if she'd ever been on the back end of the generally excepted recommendation of an eight-hour rest.

The knocking had stopped, and was replaced by the tinny scraping sound of a key entering with minimal error into its receptacle. In the time it'd taken for the door to go from locked and closed to brazenly open, with a figure just on the other side of it poised for entry, rim lit around the edges of her shape by the harsh hallway lighting that had no business being in what some might term a "ritzy" building, Chris was somehow able to quickly dispose of the butt, pick up the lighter from the floor, and rinse what little vomit was still remaining around the edges of the sink's drain. The visitor wasn't unexpected, but her arrival wasn't playing out in the way Chris had theorized that it might.

"Chris? Jesus, it's dark in here. Is that you?" Alicia asked. "May I come inside?"

Despite the immediate realization that in this moment Alicia would see her as exactly what she was, rather than the perfectly assembled, manicured and made-up version of herself that she presented to the outside world each and every day, Chris nodded and said, "Please do."

Alicia crossed the door's threshold. Before proceeding much further, she used her free hand to conduct a quick search party for the light switch she assumed might be residing just to the right of the entry. When she found it, Chris didn't protest, and with a quick click the numerous former industrial warehouse lamps hanging from the loft's ceiling flickered into submission. All six then flooded the unit with a strategically placed parade of light that presented the near museum quality furnishings, neatly composed amongst the large living space in a way that would force even the titans of *Architectural Digest* to take note.

There among the prescribed perfection of her home, stood Chris, half-naked, uncharacteristically disheveled and worn from all that the previous seventy-hours had put her through. The make-up she wore, the tools of her trade, had found their way onto normally forbidden places on her face, dried flecks of vomit, some large enough to pass as fish food, clung to her snow-white tee. Her hair played the victim of manic hours of endless finger twirling, and the flesh around each of her self-made wounds was still seemingly burning in a deep crimson red.

"Tah-dah," Chris smiled and remarked with what she believed to be an appropriate amount of sarcasm.

Alicia said nothing, put her cell in her bag before gently dropping it to the floor beside her, and gingerly closed the door.

Before Chris could offer any explanation, either for her appearance or the numerous texts and calls made the night before and earlier that morning, Alicia had made her way over to where she stood, had taken Chris' hand in hers, and with little more than a subtle shush formed by the delicate pursing of her lips, cajoled Chris into already feeling immediately relieved. She felt safe, appreciated, and for maybe the first time since taking the Crosby Street Loft, warmly at home within her home.

"Would you like to get cleaned up?" Alicia asked.

Without waiting for an answer, Alicia began to guide Chris towards the bathroom, down what the condominium's designers had tried to pass off as a hallway.

Chris followed obediently, taking in the new and inexplicable glow emitting from nearly every possession within her home. The paintings that clung tightly to ninety-degree angles on either side of the walls were no exception, and like the rest of the décor, each seemed to almost ooze color—appeared to be pulsating with energy and delivering on the forgotten promise they'd made to bring comfort and peace in to Chris' home when she'd purchased them.

Alicia was humming a tune Chris found familiar but couldn't place. She put Chris into the bathroom chair, and without stopping her hymn, began to draw a bath. The song possessed all the tranquility of a child's lullaby but with less formulaic repetition.

"First things first right?" Alicia momentarily paused within the song. "We'll get cleaned up, and then we can talk about all of this."

She then returned to the growingly familiar refrain, in a hushed hum whose tones resonated with far more gravitas in a low rumble that shook the tiles, porcelain, and polished cement floors of the bathroom.

With no break in eye contact, Alicia removed her shoes, hiked up her skirt an extra inch or two, spun her body around, and placed her feet into the water.

"Are you planning on bathing dressed?" she asked Chris.

As is often the case with the first words spoken by a soul only a few minutes removed from a solid slumber, Chris found it difficult to properly annunciate even her simple response to the question.

"No, of course not."

"Good girl."

Alicia continued humming, keeping her eyes busy elsewhere, as Chris disrobed, removing her top and bottom with an anxious haste.

Chris took two steps towards the tub, and when she caught herself in the mirror's reflection, wondered if Alicia would consider abandoning this visit upon the full outing of all of her self-inflicted surface wounds. The cigarette burns, the bruises, and the thin, red, repetitive scars from cutting—a menagerie of intentional pain that existed harmoniously evidential—were all strategically administered to the parts of her otherwise flawless figure, the nifty places that even modern fashions could still completely obscure from an often judgmental world.

Sensing Chris' building unease, Alicia reached to her, grabbed her hand and helped guide her the rest of the way, over the tub's side and directly into a seated position with her back to Alicia and the bathroom door.

The water was delightfully warm, and Chris relaxed, dropped her posture by putting the majority of her figure underneath its bubbled surface. A sudden shift in body temperature left her momentarily nauseous. The past three food-less days weren't serving her well. It'd left her thin—even for her—and the knots in her stomach could have been either excitement of a desperate plea for something more than bile and nicotine.

Chris tilted her head towards Alicia, a subtle gesture accompanied with a unblinking stare, made as an invitation to join.

Understanding. It was in Alicia's eyes, and every minuscule muscle in her face was working to communicate that she did understand—that there would be no judgment, no lectures, no stern cautionary tales about bad girls and the net result of the lifestyles they foolishly lead.

Beyond the bathroom door, down the hall, still lying on the kitchen floor, Chris' cell began to chime, introducing a competing tune to Alicia's hum that echoed off the bathroom walls, slowly overtaking the sweet song.

"Ignore it," Alicia said while steadying herself. She placed her palms at either side of the tub, and without removing her skirt or blouse, gently introduced herself into the water, right behind Chris. With her legs spread just wide enough to hold Chris in between them, she put both hands upon Chris' shoulders, just abut of the base of her neck, and began working into the tired muscle and flesh.

This is love, unconditional, Chris thought to herself.

"It is," Alicia answered.

The phone's ring was relentless, and with each repetition of its default ringtone, it grew louder and louder.

Alicia's hands began to tremble. The energy in the bathroom went instantaneously dark and sinister. Chris could feel the mood shift from within—and as the final painfully audible chimes bounced around the bathroom, Alicia's hands wrapped tightly around her neck. Each finger worked independently to push itself deeper into the skin, and in unison with the others to completely crush Chris' throat.

Chris panicked, but any attempts to fight back were met with the puzzling and painful realization that she was completely unable to move. She was seemingly paralyzed, lacking any ability to speak or shout, and the only movement she registered was the sensation of building tears beginning to cloud her vision. There were no violent kicks, no turbulent splashes made by a body fighting to keep its soul—sure in the belief that her existence was near its end, Chris wondered why she wasn't experiencing flashbacks of the life she'd led. There was nothing to see, nothing to interpret, and only the strengthening volume of the ringtone, the damning sound of a phone gone mad.

Fighting internally with all the strength she had to make something—anything—happen with her limbs or voice as the blackness of a transition towards death began to settle into the room, she finally managed to whisper faintly, "But I love you."

The undeniable truth behind those four words stayed with Chris, amid the repetitive jingle of digitized notes meant to resemble a song that were slicing through the still silence of her condominium, as she stirred conscious. While asleep, her body had made little effort in finding a more comfortable posture in which to recuperate. Having succumbed to a mandatory slumber in a seated and slumped position against the only kitchen wall that didn't find the floor and baseboards interrupted by cabinets and appliances left her on the back end of the routine feeling of unfinished rest. Her body ached, her head was pulsating with a thick thump behind the walls of her eyes, and when her hands found the floor to push herself up, the urine surrounding her was still warm, and the puddle was only on the verge of no longer expanding.

She grabbed her cell from the impending disaster, identified the caller, and answered it with disgust.

"What?"

"Hey."

"Yes. What do you want?" Chris said, with her phone between her ear and shoulder, freeing her hands to open and close drawers haphazardly, the self-humiliating search for a towel she'd not mind soiling.

"Is this a bad time?" the caller posited.

"Fucking Christ, Julie. Answer the Goddamn question. I'm in the middle of something."

With a suitable rag in hand, Chris knelt down with the phone in the other and began sopping up the urine before it found its way deeper into the cracks between the hardwood planks trying desperately through their shiny but worn sealant to soak it all up.

"I was just wondering if you had heard anything?" Julie asked.

"I thought I told you we weren't going to talk about this on the phone."

"I know, but it's been like, three days."

"And?"

"*And*, I guess I just assumed that when I agreed to let your boyfriend fuck and beat the shit out of me that all of this would happen a helluva lot faster."

Chris quickly stood to her feet again, as if to make an unseen point using posture over the phone.

"He's not my boyfriend."

"Sure. I know. But, it was *your* friend, and he was a boy. Either way, like I said, I didn't think it'd take this long for something to happen."

Chris bit her lip, her body instinctually putting the brakes on the conversation.

"Julie," she said with an intentionally redesigned, gentler tone, "I think you set your expectations a little high, at least in terms of the timing of it all, and—"

"Perhaps."

"Let me finish," Chris said, her voice flirting with its initial timbre of condemnation.

"Sorry."

Chris gave herself an extra second to completely regain her phony polite composure.

"Thank you. This is all going to work out exactly as I've already explained to you—several times I might add—if you'd like to discuss it again, let's do that. I just don't want to have the conversation over the phone, okay?"

There was a long silence on the other end.

Chris held the phone away from her ear, directly in front of her line of sight and violently mouthed the words, "FUCK YOU, BITCH!" in the cell's general direction, before putting it back to her ear.

"Fine," Julie eventually said. "But when?"

She hadn't really expected Julie to want to hear about it all over again. It had been a rhetorical offering, made only to get Julie to realize she was being ignorant about the situation. Defeated, by both Julie's insistence, and the urine soaked towel she was clutching too, Chris scrambled to temporarily push off any additional conversation.

"I don't know. Tomorrow I guess."

She put the towel into a plastic bag, tied it, and tossed it into the trashcan.

"Can you at least tell me if you've heard from Alicia?" Julie pressed.

Fuck courtesy, Chris thought. *This stupid cunt doesn't deserve courtesy.*

Before she could unleash a revised verbal assault, there was a deliberately strong series of knocks on her unit's front door. Chris walked over to the peephole, leaned into it from two feet out, and then finished the call abruptly.

"Julie, I'll call you back okay? Detective Johnson is here."

She hung up the phone—even as Julie continued speaking— swallowed the venomous bile and relocated the politeness she had been so eager to discard in favor of the unadulterated loathing she'd readied for Julie mere seconds before.

"Hey. Just give me a sec to throw something on okay?" Chris said through the door.

Without waiting for the detective's answer, she spun around to hurriedly straighten and clean what she could in the amount of time the casual use of the spoken abbreviation *sec* typically bought someone ill-prepared for a guest.

"Sure," Johnson said. "Take all the time you need."

CHAPTER TEN

We are all tied to our destiny and there is no way we can
liberate ourselves.

—Rita Hayworth

"It must be dreadfully boring to be so very, very good at just one
thing."

Devon's eyes lit up in the way they always did when Lisa
shared one of her insightful zingers with him during the
sometimes hours long downtimes between set-ups. Out in the
big-bad-world, her conversations were littered with sentences
like these, delivered to the victims of her possibly unintentional
wit, and were often the very types of well executed insults he'd
only wished he was capable of dispensing to strangers, family,
and friends.

"You did *not* say that," he said, even though he knew full
well she had.

"I'm sure it didn't come off sounding as shitty as your ears
just interpreted it."

"And *I'm* sure it did."

He went back to brushing out Lisa's hair, even though they'd
spent the better part of their third hour together in the location
trailer doing just that.

Lisa pulled out what by her count was only her fifth Camel Light in that last hour. She'd finished off her pack of all-natural smokes on the way to the shoot and had to resort to bumming any available pack off of a production assistant. Lighting it up without counting the actual number up in her head again, Lisa concluded, "Well, regardless of how Alicia Lynn Wilde heard it, I think it's true."

"I didn't say it wasn't. Though, I'm pretty happy and I've got nothing going on outside of being very, very good at this," he said while motioning to the masterpiece that he believed his efforts on her make-up, hair, and general styling had been.

Lisa stared through the smoky haze she'd created, into the trailer's mirror before her, and momentarily lost her train of thought as she took in what Devon had made of her face. Only the iris and pupil of her eyes were recognizable, and despite the numerous transformations she'd undergone via his skilled hands, it was still just as unsettling to see herself as nearly someone else—to see herself as those-in-charge would have the world see her: perfectly unblemished, radiant, with a vibrant, but tasteful exterior crafted around the black tar goo she speculated was growing exponentially inside her chest and slowly creeping its way into any available nook and cranny under her sunless white skin.

In the beginning of Lisa's career, avoiding mirrors during photo shoots had been part of a naive plan she'd outlined for herself in order to keep some degree of humility, if not sanity. This was the same scheme that included: never watching the commercials she starred in, avoiding any magazine that featured her on the cover—though there had only been two—and asking those who worked with and around her to refrain from taking any additional pictures of her that weren't part of the poses and set-ups she was contractually obligated to provide. She didn't want to see the made-up version of herself standing next to Devon on Instagram, Facebook, or any other social media vehicle used by the masses. The final piece of her ultimately unsuccessful attempts to control how she saw herself was to always leave the shoots as she came—same clothes, shoes, her hairstyle deconstructed and redone into the ponytail she'd worn on the way, and all the cosmetics removed and replaced with her own, if any at all.

These little rules had served her well, but right before her rehab stint, even the moderate success she had experienced had left it difficult to avoid the phony-version-Lisa images popping up around the increasingly cultivated real world with far more frequency. A small part of the consumption driven herd had been introduced to yet another nameless and impossible mirage crafted in the American vision of some European perfection, and out in that realm, at times, even Lisa's eyes weren't hers anymore.

"I see you are as impressed with me as I am of myself," Devon pushed.

Lisa tapped the over-an-inch-long ash from her cigarette into the make-shift ashtray she'd crafted from a Dixie cup.

Before drawing what remained from inside the cigarette as deep into her lungs as possible she said, "Even if I did offend her, I've made it to round two." She held her inhale, as if trying to choke herself with the smoke, then let it out and admitted, "I'm *cordially invited* to Wednesday night's event."

She said it as if that news were, in fact, some sort of defeat.

"Duuuuh," Devon said.

"Duh what?"

"Well, based on your version of how things played out this afternoon, it's pretty obvious to me that one Ms. Alicia Lynn wants in your pants."

Lisa let Devon's opinion hang in the air for a moment.

"Don't act the fool," Devon said. "It isn't becoming on the up and coming."

"Fuck you."

"No, she wants to fuck you."

"I get that."

"Thank god, I was beginning to doubt my own opinion of you."

"She has a boyfriend, no?"

"I had a girlfriend once, no?" Devon said, allowing no time for an answer before continuing. "The driven do what they have to do to succeed—I shouldn't have to tell you that. I wouldn't be surprised if those very words live under some hacky black and white photograph framed on your father's desk. And acting like a hetero in order to sell other heteros on the idea that she is the premiere matchmaker for the heterosexually inclined really isn't that mind blowing."

Lisa grabbed for her borrowed cigarette pack, "All in the name of a buck huh?"

"It's *all* in the name of a buck." He motioned his hands in circles towards everything the location around them denoted. "All of it, all in the name of the mighty dollar."

Lisa lit her cigarette, though she had no desire to smoke it. "That's sad."

"People's love of money is always *sad* to the very people who have tons of it."

Lisa took a pull from her cigarette, and ignored the opportunity Devon's last observation had presented to go toe-to-

toe on an issue unrelated to her current situation, but one she relished battling him in to kill time: the pros and cons of being moneyed.

"What about the whole raped friend, Elite Two Meet member thing?" Lisa blurted.

Devon rolled his eyes, "People get raped. It happens."

He said it with an intentional nonchalance that Lisa, rightly or wrongly, chalked up to him simply trying to get her blood boiling in order to make what was turning into a very long and late night go a bit quicker.

"That's true. But normally the friends, even acquaintances of the victims, are outraged, terrified, or at the very least, sympathetic. Alicia seemed annoyed more than anything."

"People deal with tragedy in all sorts of ways—"

"I *mean* she seemed annoyed with her friend," Lisa interrupted.

"Yes. I know perfectly well what you meant."

"Fine then," Lisa said as she disposed of an only half-smoked cigarette, crushing it into the Dixie Cup as if to put a period on the conversation completely. "Christ, it's been over three hours already."

She stood from her chair, lightheaded from having eaten nothing but tobacco since she arrived, stumbled to the door, only to learn upon opening it that the rain outside wasn't showing any signs of letting up.

"This is shit. When are they going to call it?"

"You know they won't," Devon said while patting her chair with his hand.

Three light taps served as a gentle reminder that much more time standing in the door jam and observing a New York City summer night downpour would ultimately mean rebuilding her face from scratch.

Lisa returned to her seat, spun it around in order to sit facing away from the mirror completely, sat down, grabbed her bag, and while tearing through it said, "I think I've got a chocolate something or other in here. We can split it."

Devon had already eaten it. He knew that. She didn't.

"Look, either way, I really don't see how her feelings about a *supposed* rape of a client—a client, not a friend—is relevant to what we are trying to do with you," Devon said as he stood up, removed her hand from her bag, and spun her back around towards the mirror to busy himself with touch-ups that didn't need to happen.

Lisa kept her eyes on his reflection and away from her own.

"Remind me again; what are *we* trying to do with me?" she asked.

"Make you famous," Devon said slightly unsure of himself. "Aren't we?"

"Oh right, *faaaaamous.*"

Lisa pulled the last cigarette from her borrowed pack. Devon frowned as she lit it. He knew it was only a matter of time before she would command him to go running out into the mess outside to find someone else's pack to bum.

"Just go to the event, meet a few people—meet a lot of powerful people—work your magic on them, and try your best not to let them rape you."

Lisa wasn't sure his joke was funny, but anything can *seem* funny after nearly four hours trapped in a five by five foot windowless and now Camel scented tin can, and either way she smiled demurely. Maybe she'd go, maybe she wouldn't—but all she needed to do right now to make it through a fifth hour was to let Devon *believe* she was going.

"I'll go," she said.

"Exciting!" he said with a sudden burst of enthusiasm he must have been saving.

The look of joy on his face—a look that at that moment, Lisa couldn't be bothered with trying to understand—turned sour almost as quickly.

"Wait. Are you just saying that so I'll go and find you another pack?"

Lisa shrugged with no clear indication of a yes or a no in her subtle movements. It didn't matter. Devon knew he'd be going regardless.

"I hope you *do* get raped."

CHAPTER ELEVEN

When our actions do not, our fears do make us traitors.

—William Shakespeare, *Macbeth*

Despite the absence of any decent place to seat oneself for reflective thought on the cobbled SoHo side street that was Chris' block, Alicia was fairly sure she'd been down there, leaning herself hard into a building in an only semi-fruitful attempt to avoid the downpour that evening, for longer than too long. It was just dry enough under the several stories tall ledge of the edifice to eSmoke her way into believing it was absolutely necessary to go ahead with her decision to see Chris. No matter the current time, and despite the counsel of her lawyer, George, who earlier had made it unequivocally clear that going to see Chris, alone, was the worst decision Alicia could make—at least as it pertained to the wellbeing of her company.

George had offered to go with her to Chris' first thing in the morning, and had also suggested he call the victim on Alicia's behalf in order to make sure she was doing as well as could be expected given the circumstances. Option two didn't appeal to Alicia, and she had agreed to meet George the following morning at a coffee shop just a half block from where she was sitting at that moment so they both could execute option one.

After agreeing to meet him first thing the next day, and reassuring him that his suspicions around an impromptu visit that evening were unjustified, she reiterated that she wouldn't reach out to Chris a moment before they were able to do it together. Then she hung up the phone with every intention of leaving her office and going straight home.

Compensating experts with large sums of money for their advice, only to ignore it completely, was a personal pet-peeve, as Alicia had been the victim of that very blunder an infinite number of times with her own clients. Males and females who were paying her big bucks to make a lasting love connection often came to believe they knew better than her about closing the deal. When this happened, she could only stand back and watch as they floundered about, acting too soon or too late, trying too hard or not enough, forcing their fates or ignoring it completely—until whatever initial fire that had been started between a pair had been painfully and clumsily extinguished, with no hopes of reigniting it. In the beginning it pained her to see the repeated failures of those who ignored her best advice, but by year two she took great, but a very secret delight in watching the very same types of failures play out for her and the other clients who might be toying with the idea of running their own show.

So when Alicia deviated from her own assurances that it was straight from work to home that evening, with George's high-dollar advice still freshly ringing around between her ears, it wasn't without a small degree of guilt for betraying herself and ignoring not only him, but the very rules she'd put in place to keep her one step ahead of all the other would-be titans of this or that. But, she hadn't heard anything from Chris—not since the final text she'd sent long before Alicia and Lisa had sat down at the café together that morning.

The drift from her walk home had begun in earnest; she *convinced* herself that an impromptu trip to the liquor store was necessary, under the guise that it was possible she'd consumed most of the supply at home the night before. Even she couldn't lie her way into believing that there wasn't two or three more bottles of vodka handy in the cabinets of her bar, but by the time she had come clean with herself, Alicia was more than half-way to the store and only two blocks removed from Chris' condominium.

The decision to set out for Chris' without any kind of beforehand notification, sent or dialed, was deliberately made, and made before the downpour, when the storm had just edged its way over the city. In that moment, heading over to see Chris made complete sense.

Chris is not just a client, she's a friend. What the fuck is wrong with me? Alicia thought before committing to the final two blocks. *This is the right thing to do.*

Since finding her "dry" spot against the brick building two doors down from Chris', Alicia had mentally bounced between reassuring herself that visiting alone and immediately was appropriate—if not necessary—and then condemning the idea for its defiance of George. Simultaneously, she'd permitted herself to build upon the kernel of hatred she already had for Chris for the monumental inconvenience of whatever mess had only possibly occurred.

The few cab drivers with empty backseats that had made their way down the seldom used street had taken pity on the lone blonde camped out there, each pausing long enough to deliver a sympathetic toot of the horn, offering shelter from the rain and the quickest escape possible back to her apartment and away from the unusual bout of indecision she found herself mired in. She politely declined each one with a gentle wave.

Alone, amongst hundreds of souls above and around her, and after the battling thoughts regarding Chris and how best to address her assault, Alicia also found herself reflecting back on the time she'd spent with Lisa. She replayed the information, true and untrue, that she'd revealed over coffee and then later as they slowly strolled from the cafe to the Spring Street subway station for Lisa to catch her train to the Upper East Side. Alicia had offered to send her that way in a cab, but Lisa had politely declined.

Some of what they discussed had been dressed in the costuming of business as usual. When Alicia offered up the opportunity to join Elite Two Meet's Wednesday night event, Lisa had said, "I'm flattered. And I'll certainly think about it."

To her best recollection, Alicia couldn't remember having ever had someone tell her they'd only *think* about coming. The lack of prescription soothers coursing through her body, as well as Lisa's previous declination of a quick drink on their way to the station, had made it difficult to feign ambivalence to Lisa's nonchalance about the invitation. Right after Lisa had disappeared into the guts of the island, Alicia had bee-lined right to the nearest bar, but the two quick martinis hadn't served her well in their efforts to not let ego take over. However, the third squashed any desire to immediately text Lisa and rescind the invite altogether.

The walk back to her office had been more like a series of stumbles, but any noticeable effect of the cocktails had been significantly reduced by whatever pills it'd been that she'd popped after procuring them from Bean's desk drawer stash.

Hours removed from that quick martini-dash and the pilfering of Bean's private property—if either the booze or pills were still conducting any business in her body, they certainly weren't making it any easier to resolve the feelings Alicia was having for Lisa.

She took another look at her cell, but there were still no new messages from Chris—just a litany of work related emails and texts from her team pertaining to all the minor details that still needed to be sorted before that Wednesday.

"This is a bad idea," she said as she took her first step away from the building, back towards her home. "Just go home."

A sliver of light spilt from the front door of Chris' building, and grew larger as it opened, putting just enough additional illumination onto the sidewalk to make even the downpour an inadequate means for hiding from the souls you'd rather not see. Alicia immediately took back that first step for home and leaned her body even deeper into the wall than before.

It was the detective. He stopped right under the last remaining dry inch of the building's entry, took a quick scan of the flooding street, popped the collar on his sport coat over his neck, and made an immediate right. He headed down the block, seemingly undisturbed by the soaking he was taking, the opposite direction of where Alicia stood motionless and milliseconds away from gasping for new air to fill her hushed lungs. If he *had* seen her, his eerily casual whistling had done nothing to confirm the sighting.

When he was around the corner, she relaxed herself off of the brick wall just a bit, began to breathe easier, and after a longer than necessary coast-is-clear style pause, she removed a real cigarette from the brand new pack within her purse. Then after inhaling as much of the old friend as her lungs could accommodate, while possibly channeling her mother, she thought, *Time to put your big girl britches on Alicia, let's go see her and just get the whole thing over with*. And with that she sprinted through the rain towards Chris' building.

The very same moment, a text arrived from Chris.

Hey. WTF? Are you alive? Call me at home. PLEASE!

CHAPTER TWELVE

True friends stab you in the front.

—Oscar Wilde

Alicia stood outside of Chris' unit's door, her fist in the air and seemingly unable to travel the final half inch necessary to perform even a light knock. Chris' muffled voice was audible, and though Alicia couldn't make out the majority of words being strung together, it was pretty obvious that whomever Chris was talking to was getting an earful—she wasn't yelling at anyone, but she was definitely delivering a lengthy one-sided lecture to the poor soul she was addressing.

Makes sense, Alicia thought. *I'd be upset too.*

She'd only made her way up unannounced by having plied what had become a semi-friendly relationship with the building's doorman over the course of the few other times she'd visited. Even though he knew Alicia, he had reached for the phone to dial Chris in order to inform her of the unscheduled arrival. Before he could press a single digit, Alicia delicately protested.

"John, I'd like to surprise her if possible?"

John smiled awkwardly, caught momentarily in the gray zone between professionalism and courtesy, and with his finger still hovering over the first of three necessary numbers, assessed the situation carefully. This was no stranger, but a fireable offense nonetheless.

"Ms. Wilde, I'm not quite sure a surprise is what Ms. Jones needs right now."

His response suggested to Alicia that Chris' rape was at the very least a certain degree of public knowledge. Though she thought it might be possible he was only being awkwardly polite about the timing of her visit. It was late, so Alicia couldn't be sure of either scenario, nor was she about to mention the crime— *mention it and it will become that much more real.*

"Well, *surprise* might not have been the best choice of words. But, I'd like to go up unannounced none the less."

John did nothing to suggest that he wasn't going to be dialing Chris' unit.

Alicia cautiously continued, "If that isn't a kosher idea with you, I'll be happy to come back tomorrow morning instead. I certainly don't want to put you out."

John glanced down at the security camera feeds unnecessarily—only a place to put his eyes while he considered the implications of a difficult decision.

Since committing to actually visiting Chris just on the other side of the building's front doors, Alicia had been looking for any possible real-world reason to bail on the visit altogether. John's reservations definitely qualified.

"I can see that I have. Don't worry about it John, I'll come back at some more permissible time tomorrow."

She spun around, relieved, but unsure of why the thought of seeing Chris was causing her so much anxiety in the first place. Regardless, it was a welcome sensation, a momentary calm that'd been absent most of a day filled with abnormalities.

Crawling into bed after a hot bath didn't seem like such a bad idea either, and she was on her way.

She reached for the door right as John nervously blurted his full permission from behind her.

"Ms. Wilde, it's no trouble at all. My apologies. Please go right ahead up. I'm sure she'd love to see you."

It wasn't what Alicia wanted to hear, but she was certain enough that if she carried on with the act of leaving, John would tell Chris at some point and the interpretation of her actions might be misconstrued—by Chris, the detective, and anyone else intent on passing judgment.

Alicia slowly turned back around, forced a grateful smile, and said, "Thank you John, I sincerely appreciate it."

Before heading for the elevator, she reached into her bag, grabbed a twenty-dollar bill, and held it out over the counter for John. He waved his hand in the air and said, "Not necessary Ms. Wilde. Thank you."

Alicia felt like that exchange had happened hours ago, but when she looked at her watch with the sole intent of convincing a tired mind that by then it was far too late to disturb Chris, she learned it had only been ten, maybe fifteen, minutes.

Disregarding every impulse she had to slowly creep back towards the lift and head to her own home, she managed to will three light taps to the door—light enough to be heard, and light enough to be unheard too. Alicia didn't intend on performing any more than those three, and hoped the action would result in the latter. It would be easier to put off until tomorrow if she at least *believed* she had tried to reach out.

Nothing came of it. If Chris had heard the "knock," it hadn't stopped her conversation. This was the last sign Alicia needed to finally call it quits on the whole ill-advised plan.

This was a horrible idea to begin with, she thought.

As the mumbled sounds of Chris continued beyond the walls, Alicia walked softly back towards the elevator. With extreme care, she gently pushed the call button. The whir of the elevator suggested it was on its way, and a similar relief she'd felt not long before, downstairs when John's inaction had almost excused her, had returned.

"Come on," she muttered while eyeing the lift's floor indicator.

The quick snapping sound of a deadbolt in motion startled Alicia, and she jolted around to find its origin. Chris' door opened, and she leaned out, just enough to be seen, without committing to opening it completely.

"Alicia," Chris said, almost sternly. "John phoned, he said you've been standing outside my door for nearly fifteen minutes. Do you want to come in?"

Out of the corner of her eye, Alicia caught the black security camera bubble mocking her from its protruding perch in the ceiling above her indecision. She rolled her eyes in the hopes that John would see the displeasure resulting from his having decided to out her after all.

"Hi there," Alicia said, still unsure if she should commit to heading in with Chris. "I'm sorry, I didn't want to disturb you. It sounded like you were on the phone. I can come back tomorrow."

The elevator's doors slid open behind Alicia.

Chris let out a lengthy sigh and then said, "It would mean a lot to me if you stayed, Alicia. I guess you know I've had... let's call it a pretty shit last few days."

"Yes, I heard. Detective Johnson came by the office this morning. I am so so sorry." Alicia was surprised to discover that beyond the tone of her voice, she was genuinely empathetic.

"Don't be sorry, just come and talk to me," Chris said sadly. "Please Alicia."

The elevator doors slid shut behind her and Alicia said, "Of course. I'm so sorry. I don't know what's come over me."

Alicia felt an even truer relief wash over. It was as if a not often used part of her brain had reactivated, allowing for the sense of peace that comes from the humility within copping to one's wrongdoing. The feeling was instantly replaced with an enormous wave of guilt as she stepped further forward, closer to Chris. Alicia's vision finally landed atop of Chris, no longer staring through her, and she registered all the enormous dark purple bruises and swelling still seemingly pulsating on Chris' face. She condemned her own appalling lack of an effort, disgusted with her own intentionally executed plan of not reaching out to her for the majority of the day.

Alicia dropped a heavy head in remorse for her inaction. "Oh my God, Chris."

"It's alright. I'm just glad you are finally here," Chris said as she opened the door completely, welcoming Alicia inside with a half-hearted sweep of her hand. "I was nearly about to give up on you—completely.

TUESDAY
AUGUST
SIXTH

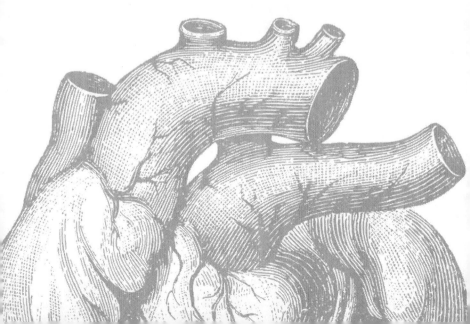

CHAPTER THIRTEEN

Every man has inside himself a parasitic being who is acting not at all to his advantage.

—William S. Burroughs

Charlie Johnson sat behind the wheel of his parked black Ford Crown Victoria with his eyes closed, resting them only. He hoped that he could push off a visit from the sandman for at least another couple of hours. Calling it quits for the day and heading home to put his body to bed made little sense given his current situation.

Two days, even three or four, with very little quality sleep weren't unusual, but when he could help it, he liked to keep any sleepless stretch under forty-eight hours. Being tired usually meant being sloppy, and in his experience, nothing good had ever been born or performed by an exhausted mind—at least not his.

He took a deep breath, and did his best to coerce the minuscule muscles surrounding his eyes into prying open their heavy lids. They parted, but not without a fight.

Johnson reached for what had become a room-temperature cup of formerly hot and now easily day old coffee still sitting in the self-installed drink holder. He swallowed what remained and tossed the empty vessel onto the passenger floorboard. Then, using both hands, gave his cheeks several rapid slaps. He considered leaving his position to duck into a bodega to grab one of the numerous overpriced energy shots prominently featured at a typical cashier's counter, but he'd already put too many of the morning's hours into this tail, and wasn't feeling quite close enough to a pure pass-out to risk going to grab the elixir only to miss seeing Lisa when she finally came around to exiting her building.

There was a whole slew of rational reasons that supported *not* being parked outside of Lisa's pre-war apartment building, and as he sat, baking in the black Ford under an intense city summer sun, he internally reexamined his motives for having looked up her address at all. He damned himself under his breath when he realized he couldn't come up with any better phrasing of a reason for being parked in front of her home than, "She just seems like someone I want to know."

There wasn't much logic behind his decision to case her home—he knew that—at least not as far as it pertained to his involvement with Chris, Alicia and Elite Two Meet. The barely fifteen minutes that he'd spoken to Lisa outside the café the day before had consumed his thinking—had convinced him to put the task at hand aside even as the clock was ticking. Beyond any doubt, Charlie surmised that trying to connect with Lisa under the guise of relevant questioning about her relationship to Alicia, Elite Two Meet, and even Chris wasn't going to make for much of a re-introduction. Even if she obliged and took the time to answer some questions, he wondered, *How would I go about bridging that conversational ruse to something more honest? I'm not going to woo her with questions about a rape.*

As the morning's minutes steamrolled into those of the

afternoon, Charlie doubted he'd get the opportunity to try out any of his flimsy plans for stumbling into Lisa in a seemingly spontaneous fashion. Even so, he clung to the hope that he'd see her come out the building's front door before too long.

Just to see if she was real, he amused himself. *Just to see if she's what I remember her being.*

One o'clock arrived and so had the sandman. Charlie lay slumped over, spittle down his chin, with his hand instinctually resting over the handgun he'd earlier positioned atop his lap. The blaring snarl of increasingly angry city horns hadn't fazed him, nor had the heated argument involving a pedestrian and bicyclist that took place two feet from his rear bumper. Neither incident had caused so much as a tiny shift in his sleeping posture. When Lisa had exited her building, on her way out to grab a lunch item she could refer to as breakfast, Johnson was none the wiser.

He came around about an hour later. Startled by his location, so far from home. He reached for the previously discarded coffee cup on the passenger side floorboard, desperate for a little something to be remaining to remedy a mouth with little or no saliva left. No luck. He opened his driver side door, but the humidity outside did little to reduce the discomfort of the stale air inside. Had he not cracked the passenger window, he speculated he might not have come to ever again.

He took one last long look at Lisa's building, scanning the windows, though he couldn't really be sure which was 3F, with the hope of possibly spotting some sign of her in order to make an educated decision, the slightest carrot to bait him in to sticking around to wait it out further.

With no sign of human life behind any windows and a thirst that could no longer be ignored, he hopped out of the car and headed for the corner bodega half a block behind his Victoria.

I'll be quick, he thought. *I doubt she's still there anyway, and what the fuck was I going to do about it if she had come out?* He answered himself aloud. "Nothing."

From the sidewalk, he craned his head back over his shoulder as he shuffled, attempting one last look before fully committing to the final fifty feet to the corner's store. Observing no new development, Charlie increased his speed with the intent of making his snack break as quick as humanly possible.

Get in, get out, he thought as he hurried through the store's front door and headed directly for the coolers, illuminated glass treasure chests filled with infinite colors of liquid salvation.

Charlie grabbed a Gatorade, chugged most of it before he'd made it to the register, and while paying, peered outside the shop's large plate glass window in front. The timing of it all may have been serendipitous; despite a difficult viewing angle, he caught Lisa heading back towards her building. She appeared taller than he had remembered, but aside from that, his memory had done a sterling job of capturing her natural beauty. She had a restaurant to-go bag in one hand and a cigarette burning in the other. Her pace was speedy; Lisa was covering considerable ground with every step. Despite a bloodstream suspiciously absent of caffeine, Charlie felt his heart rate increase. If he were to succeed in the scheme of *accidentally* bumping into her, or pretending it was necessary to interview her about the case involving Alicia, he'd have to act fast.

Decision time Charlie, he informed himself. *What's it going to be?*

He quickly asked for a pack of Spirit Blues, grabbed and tossed two energy shots onto the counter too, then paid for all four items before practically bursting out the front door.

CHAPTER FOURTEEN

There is no truth. There is only perception.

—Gustave Flaubert

For your average soul, getting only two hours of sleep can mean a death sentence of a next day. That Tuesday morning wasn't the first one she'd ever had after only two hours, but Alicia certainly wasn't a fan of working on less than six, and unlike many New York City women her age, she typically managed to put together no less than seven—and always shot for a total of a legit eight. Like all the other mornings that had come after a night in which sleep hadn't factored heavily into the equation, Alicia still arrived at the office at precisely the mandatory time she had always enforced upon herself.

On her way in, she had given considerable thought to the notion that even if she had decided to stay home, Wednesday's event would likely be as smashingly successful as any of the previous. For a moment she was absolutely positive there was no reason to believe otherwise. It was a new theory, and her crack team would probably prove its validity. But old habits die hard, and the thought was short lived. The effects of a take-away triple espresso had woken the control-freak perfectionist somewhere around midway, and that version of Alicia had quickly squashed and dismissed it. The theory had been foolish, it was a repulsive notion that she ultimately chalked up as the borderline insane ramblings of a tired mind.

"The Devil *is* the details," her father had been fond of saying.

By the time eleven AM had rolled around, Deborah and Bean's own obsessive-compulsive attention to those very same details had reopened the debate on Alicia's needing to go in at all. There wasn't much about the event that hadn't been meticulously considered, and painstakingly orchestrated the week beforehand. Normally, she might have used this small window of downtime to throw the whole thing up in the air with a last minute mandatory all-staff brainstorm.

"Everyone drop everything, and let's figure out how we can prevent this Wednesday from being a complete and total disaster," she might have said. "Your jobs—even my own—depend on it."

A mad scramble, free of groaning, would ensue and for the next few hours—sans lunch—Alicia would lead her team through a series of what-if scenarios. Sometimes these fire drills had actually led to an improved experience, but most of the time the net result of tossing around an infinite number of hypotheticals had been, at best, confirmation that everything already planned was going to be perfectly fine.

Blame the tired mind, but on that morning, Alicia couldn't be bothered with making the office appear frenetically busy. *There just isn't any point*, she thought.

Alicia had left Chris' condo at around 4:00 a.m. that morning, after a few hours of conversation that had included a somewhat repetitive, but deeply disturbing retelling of what Chris and another client, her friend, Julie, had gone through on that previous Saturday night.

She left Chris asleep on the sofa. She had quietly and gently removed herself from underneath Chris' head, replacing her lap with a pillow, and had done so with near surgical precision.

Before heading back to her apartment to put what time she could against her own slumber, Alicia stood over Chris, hovered delicately above and silently delivered a prayer. She looked peaceful, albeit badly damaged on the outside. The whole day prior, even when Alicia had given Chris' rape any thought, she'd never once allowed herself to imagine something like the broken and twisted body that Chris' soul now inhabited.

Alicia knelt beside her, kissed her lightly on the forehead, and whispered, "I'll see you later today." And before she stood back up to leave, she added, "I'm so sorry Chris. Truly."

The assault's details weren't crystals clear, even after numerous retellings. A great deal of the hours they'd spent together were filled with uncontrollable sobbing, in between Chris' best attempts at reconstructing a hazy synopsis of what had happened to her and Julie, sometime in the witching hours of the previous Saturday night.

Alicia knew Julie, she'd interviewed her the same as any other member—but beyond that initial meeting, and the brief conversation they'd had after Julie's preliminary event when Alicia had phoned to offer her full-fledged membership, they'd rarely, possibly never, engaged in another word. There was nothing uncommon about that. Many of the outfit's more successful members never spoke to or approached Alicia after the very same meeting and phone call. Chris and a few others had been the odd exception, and most didn't make a point of trying to cultivate anything more than a standard nod-and-smile client/owner relationship. Alicia was intent on staying out of the way, even as she felt in control of them all.

"Tell me everything, tell me nothing. I just wanted to make

sure you were okay," Alicia had said to Chris after an awkward first fifteen minutes looking to and away from each other, while sipping whiskey from heavy weight tumblers.

In hindsight, Alicia admitted to herself that the visit had been to learn everything she could in order to prepare for anything that might come of it regarding the welfare of her organization. But, within the act of physically sitting and seeing Chis, she had come to also believe that she could, maybe should, just be there to be there—to offer Chris what comfort one can simply by being a present and empathetic soul.

Chris' eyes found Alicia's. Throughout the retelling of her ordeal, they never wandered away from their focus again. She spoke slowly, methodically, and even when pieces of the narrative seemed to make Chris too uncomfortable or upset—including the tears and wails that sometimes forced themselves between her words—there was a subtle poise to it all. The manner in which she delivered what she could remember didn't faze Alicia. In fact, it had been the observation of this very signature calm, coupled with her own successes, that had ultimately made having Chris contribute some time to Elite Two Meet as more than a member condonable by Alicia.

The previous Saturday, Chris had met Julie in the not-quite-evening hours of the afternoon for a meal that many night owl New Yorkers still refer to as brunch. And even though Chris assured her that they hadn't begun drinking until later that evening, Alicia suspected a Bloody Mary or Mimosa had been a part of her and Julie's meal nonetheless. The same New Yorkers who call four o'clock meals *brunches* often don't consider the Bloody Mary that goes with it to be drinking—at least not *real* drinking. And, Chris had indicated that it was six-thirty when she and Julie had finally paid the bill. By Alicia's estimation, that was a considerable length of time to dine without partaking in some manner of libations. Two and a half hours to be exact.

"We'd planned on brunch, and that's it," Chris said. "But Julie told me that she wasn't feeling like being alone."

"Why was that?"

"I suspect it had something to do with her being *in between* jobs."

"I see," Alicia said.

Julie's current bout of unemployment hadn't made it on to Alicia's radar, but Deborah would have only made verbal note of it had the length of time been deemed excessive or if the circumstances surrounding any dismissal had been unbecoming enough to justify the downgrading of a member of Elite Two Meet to probationary status.

Resisting the all-business urge to ask Chris more about Julie's possible ineptitude specifically, Alicia prodded, "And so what did you two get up to after the restaurant?"

"We spent about an hour wandering around NoLita and the East Village, it was too early to go anywhere else really."

"Out you mean?"

"Yes," Chris said. "I asked her if she wanted to kill some time back at my place until we devised a better plan, but—"

Chris paused long enough to suggest that a forthcoming part of the story with actual pertinence was on deck.

"But what?" Alicia almost demanded.

"Well, Julie seemed hell-bent on just getting the night started."

The emphasis made by the long silence following that statement suggested the beginnings of a bout of blame-gaming might be next.

"Okay, so Julie was depressed, you guys decided to get

drunk," Alicia snarled with an inappropriate impatience. "It doesn't matter—let's skip ahead." Her hands were animated, behaving in an almost accusatory fashion, focused in the general direction of Chris. "Where did it happen? Where did all of *this* happen?"

Chris stood up from the sofa abruptly, and Alicia knew she'd erred. She reached her hand out quickly to grab Chris' and tried to usher her back down on to the couch. Holding her hand in hers, she apologized.

"I'm sorry—I am. Please, sit. Stay and finish and take as long as you need."

Chris said nothing.

"I'm a terrible bitch," Alicia said trying to infuse an infinitesimal degree of humor into the situation at her own expense.

It appeared to work, and Chris agreed sheepishly, "You are. We all are."

The tiniest curl of Chris' lips, on just one side of her mouth, left Alicia feeling self-congratulatory, proud that she was handling the discomforting suspense of it all as well as she believed anyone could expect.

As if to make a point of taking advantage of Alicia's hesitant permission to squander the evening hour's remaining ticks, Chris proceeded to methodically outline their entire journey: A booze-crawl that began at the very first East Village bar they'd come across, from there to a new vodka room just below Bowery, on to a failed attempt to get into a velvet-rope VIP situation in the Meat Packing District, and finally a cab to the dive bar that no-one outside of Manhattan would ever refer to as "a dive bar."

Chris went out of her way to tally the drinks they'd consumed at each. And, if her memory of the beverage types and total was at all accurate, Alicia counted roughly a dozen, and that didn't include the two unclaimed brunch cocktails she was certain had served as the impetus to the journey itself. Chris had also detailed the origins of each and every drink as it pertained to who ordered them, bought them, carried them or served them up to her and Julie. Before she'd even begun unfolding the drink-a-log from the scene of the crime, Alicia had counted at least three different men who might have had the opportunity to dose either of their drinks. There was no mention of having put anything solid into their bodies either. If Chris' story was credibly factual, that meant neither she nor Julie had eaten anything other than the Eggs Florentine and a mixed basket of bread sometime around five. By the time the two of them had entered the last bar at around one in the morning, anything those afternoon edibles might have been doing to counter the effects of the vodka in a Bloody Mary, the wine, and then the even more vodka swimming in subsequently smaller amounts of cranberry juice would have been minimal, if not altogether irrelevant.

Chris eventually revealed that part of the night had included the decision to reach out to Jeff Dufour and David Miller, who were also members of Elite Two Meet. To the best of her recollection, Alicia believed Jeff was a criminal defense attorney, and that David was the owner of a dot-com that had something to do with helping people make the oh-so-difficult decisions concerning eateries. Chris hadn't singled out either as having been their attacker yet, and Alicia kept to her promise, letting Chris continue speaking unabated with only the occasional nod and transitional verbal prompts.

"The last undeniable memory I have from before, from before he raped me—raped us—is dancing like maniacs with Jeff and David, and then having excused ourselves to use the bathroom," Chris said with an intense vocal tremor that grew more pronounced with each and every word.

"And Jeff and David had joined you guys when again?"

"There. They were waiting outside for us when we got there."

Alicia gave a great deal of consideration to all the consequences of Chris' answer and said, "And you think Jeff, or David, is the man who raped and beat you?"

She had tried to deliver the question with the least amount of malice possible.

Chris finally removed her hand from what had been Alicia's comforting grip.

"I never said that," she insisted in something resembling snark.

Chris' demeanor instigated an uncontrollable pop of anger in Alicia.

"Why in the hell do I have a detective bothering me about it then?"

Chris rolled her eyes, "Bothering you about it?" she said. "Bothering you about what happened to me?"

Alicia knew what she'd said hadn't been pleasant, but her own inertia wasn't something she could restrain.

"Yes, if you aren't sure that it was either of them—if you didn't name them—why did the NYPD pay me a visit this morning?"

"I didn't ever say it *wasn't* one of them."

"But you don't know who it was," Alicia said. "Am I right?"

Chris shot up off the couch and bolted straight for her liquor cabinet. Without a word she made herself another drink. She put the glass to her lips and stared at Alicia who was still seated with a posture that suggested she would be unrelenting in demanding a firm answer. Chris slammed the drink back down and on the verge of shouting, provided one.

"No, Alicia. I don't. I have no real idea who in the fuck followed us into that bathroom. No idea who it was that beat the shit out of us. And not a single clue who it was that then fucked us—over, and over again—before beating the shit out of us a little bit more just for good measure."

Her hands could barely bring her drink to her mouth. She cupped it with both and finished it quickly.

Alicia stayed seated, silent, and with a renewed and tremendous sense of remorse.

Chris continued only slightly less furiously, "All I have, Alicia, is horrible memories and what you see before you." She poured another drink as she continued. "Living reminders of an intense pain I wouldn't wish on anyone. I can smell his breath. I can taste his stink. I can feel him all over me, and no amount of soap is going to remedy that."

Alicia started to get up from the sofa.

"Don't you fucking do that!" Chris shouted. "You can't leave me! Please!"

She came out from around the bar and sat back down beside a now motionless Alicia. Alicia was frightened; she was deeply ashamed.

"I'm not. I'm sorry."

She reached out again for Chris' hand, and unsteadily removed the tumbler from the other. She pulled her closer, despite a noticeable resistance from Chris.

"I'm sorry, I'm sorry, I'm sorry," Alicia repeated softly.

Eventually Chris' body gave in, and allowed for the embrace. Holding her close to her chest, Alicia squeezed Chris closer, trying to absorb the pain—will it away from her body and into her own—while rocking back and forth with Chris in her arms.

"I'm sorry," Alicia said one last time. "Please Chris, believe me."

"Why should I?"

"All of this—" Alicia replied without any real idea what it was she was about to say in that moment. "I guess all of this scares the shit out of me too."

The not-so-subtle buzz of her vibrating iPhone brought Alicia back into the present.

Hi. Thanks for being there for me. I wish you hadn't left. XO Chris

Alicia let herself feel good about having made the decision to be a friend first, and a nervous CEO second. It was a selfless sensation that had begun in earnest the night before, and wanting to hold onto that kindness for as long as possible is precisely the reason she chose to send the phone call from her lawyer that followed straight to voicemail.

I'm not a bad person, she thought.

Alicia looked out through the floor to ceiling glass walls that denoted where her office within the offices of her company sat— a small empire that she'd built from the ground up, on her own, without the aid of anyone other than those she'd employed once it was rolling. Her team was busy, the very team she'd handpicked to keep the company growing as successfully as it had, all of them, handling everything necessary for Wednesday night while she sat alone in her room, and still crushing on an unobtainable near-stranger like a silly little school girl—despite now being privy to Chris' ordeal.

Her emotions—half a dozen or more—were bouncing their way around inside of her, pounding from within, and looking for her to help them escape. Had she been asked to describe everything she was feeling at that moment, there would have been no short combination of words adequate enough to capture the sensation. It was unpleasant at first, but she sat a long time with them, trying to absorb all of it, before common sense dictated that she reach for the proper prescription in her bag to squash them in order to move forward with the rest of her day's plans.

After she'd swallowed twice the indicated dose, she had a momentary reflection on the action itself.

No. I'm not a bad person. But, I've got to figure out another way to deal besides these. She put the pill bottle deep into the back of her desk's drawer. *Where am I going with all of this? And if it's not with Lisa, then who?*

She rested her head upon her desk. Only seconds after she had drifted into a nap, the iPhone's buzz ripped her right back out of it. She picked the device up to discover Chris' second text of the day.

Maybe you and I could take a trip together, just a thought.

Had her body afforded her physical abilities for just a few more moments, the sting burning in her gut, ignited by the text itself, might have made its way from there, through her arms, and out into the world via tapping fingers. Staying awake was a battle Alicia wasn't going to win. The words she wanted to text back to Chris so badly never made it any farther than the inside of her head.

Chris, for fuck's sake, will you please leave me alone.

And then she was out cold.

CHAPTER FIFTEEN

Acting is a nice childish profession—pretending you're someone else and, at the same time, selling yourself.

—Katharine Hepburn

It's true. I *should* have a lot more money than I do. Even the smaller modeling and acting gigs I've done have paid decent wages. Residual checks, even the smaller ones, add up quick. Explaining my lack of funds to the friends and family who see my face in and around the routines that occupy their own dreary little lives could be simple—drugs cost money. Drugs *had* cost money—lots and lots of money. At some point I'll clue everyone in on that little detail. Until then, anyone who feels so inclined can go about judging me for having pretty much only decided to hang out with Detective Johnson for the free smokes he'd brought along. I'm no fool—a whore for tobacco, maybe, but certainly no fool.

If I said I was surprised to have had him *run into me* I'd be lying, because I wasn't. Startled? A bit, but surprised that he'd maybe taken certain liberties with the credentials that allow him access to databases on public citizens? I probably should be, but the cops I've had the pleasure of knowing over the years have never seemed all that ethical either. Who knows, maybe he really did just happen to be in the neighborhood carrying a pack of unopened American Spirit Blue. You'd think after all New York City has put me through that I'd except that at times amazingly bizarre coincidences are actually redundantly normal. And, maybe the questions he'd asked about me, Alicia, Elite Two Meet, how much I knew about her, about it, and what I thought—even given my limited acquaintance with both—might also have been legit. The cigarettes could have easily been nothing more than his way of establishing some form of camaraderie between us before interrogating me.

Do I really care what reasons he had for finding me? No. I'm happy as the filthy pig-in-shit that I am. After all, I didn't have to spend my own fourteen dollars on twenty new little friends today. Make what you will of it.

His ineptitude at better pick-up strategies might have been the reason he told me all about the dating club's case though. I'm sure his superiors wouldn't approve. In fact, I even asked him twice, "Are you *sure* you should be revealing all of this to me?"

"Sometimes telling fresh ears can be of great help," he said.

It was interesting to hear all of it—at least the all of it that he seemed to know about. Having been on the dosed side of some nitwit's dosing-drinks scam, I count myself among the luckiest of party-time gals that nothing other than a painful night of extreme vomiting had ever come of it.

I'm not sure anything I had to offer was of much help. Scratch that, I *am* sure everything I had to offer was of *no* help.

But, he certainly helped me. No concoction of my own excuses or justifications will be enough to convince Devon that my decision to abstain from joining Elite Two Meet is the right decision. At least now I'm armed with bits and pieces of a truly horrible tragedy that I can use to bolster the defense of my decision against using a dating service to further my career. Why is he so Goddamn certain any of Alicia's higher profile gentleman will be of any assistance in that arena anyway? It seems highly likely and far more probable that in the end I'd be nothing more than another conquest for the chasing. Devon won't say he sees it that way, even though I know full well that *he* knows full well that this scenario carries far better odds.

It's a discussion—possibly an argument—I'm really not looking forward to having with him. It gets old trying to defend yourself to the people who supposedly care about you.

That's a shit thing to have said.

Lumping Devon in with the rest of the clods who've pushed and pulled me in the directions of their choosing—into the deals, contracts, and situations that would ultimately serve them best—is really not fair. It *would* be fair to say that at least Devon believes he is right about this, and while I'd certainly be dragging him along, best I could, into any future fame scenario, I think it's safe to say that, deep inside, he wants me to live the life I want for myself.

The thing is, most of what he bases his beliefs regarding what he thinks I want from life stem from all the conversations we had before I got clean—before *we* got clean. I'm a little ahead of the curve maybe—at least I count me as someone who thinks I am a little ahead of the curve.

Christ, maybe I've never wanted any of exactly what I've worked so hard to achieve. That's a depressing thought. Seems like a whole bunch of time down the drain. Endless hours spent schmoozing, partying, scheming, back-stabbing, and all manner of hoop jumping, while putting a real hurt on my insides, just to achieve a goal I might have only chosen while under the influence of narcotics and the people who peddle and abuse them.

First things first: I don't need this decision or the necessary conversations required to make it hanging over my head all day. I can tackle the rest of these damning observations about myself further down the road.

As for Elite Two Meet, I'm not doing it.

I have no desire to join. I possess zero enthusiasm for playing dress-up and trying to win the hearts of the next mogul of anything, and if I decide to use my supposed and newly formed fear that some of its members might actually be rapists—so be it. Either way, I've got to tell Devon sooner than later.

Since Alicia wants to meet with me, yet again, tonight and for God only knows what, I'll just go ahead and give her my final answer then. No sense in turning down a free dinner, no sir, not for this gal.

CHAPTER SIXTEEN

If you cannot get rid of the family skeleton, you may as well make it dance.

—George Bernard Shaw

The muffled and crude ring tone recreation of Montell Jordan's *This is How We Do It* was a good indication that Lisa hadn't lost her phone after all. The timing of the tune was impeccable, as Lisa had all but given up looking for the device in favor of just emailing Devon her bad news instead. Somewhere in the small barely-one-bedroom, calling to her from amongst the stacked semi-packed and unpacked moving boxes, the phone had decided to prove it still existed.

Lisa had never wholeheartedly committed to a full-on furnishing of the apartment, and what little she did have had been haphazardly thrown into twelve medium size moving boxes by a friend while she was in rehab. Conventional logic had her returning home to live with her mother and father, but when she was done with her ninety-day stint, she had completely disregarded everything the institution's counselors had wanted her early sobriety living conditions to entail. The act and idea of completely unpacking the boxes had been a carrot she dangled in front of herself many of those early sober evenings—a promise she'd make in the spirit of a life filled with forward momentum. But with each new morning's light, the promise was broken in favor of the decision to leave a good deal of her hidden possessions as they were—and was easier to blame on the more universally excepted scapegoat that is laziness, rather than pin it to her very real fear that in truth she believed one or two things might trigger a free fall into relapse.

As she dug through one box and then into another, clamoring for her cell phone, the relapse-oriented excuse she'd used to refrain from unpacking for months seemed more like the lie, and laziness more like the truth.

Lisa found the phone and sensing it was already on its last ring, answered it without bothering to see who was on the other end of the call first.

"Hello!"

"Good afternoon Sweetie." Linda didn't wait for a reciprocal salutation and continued, "Or should I be saying good *morning* instead?"

"I've been up for quite some time Linda."

"Oh honey, I'm just making a bad joke. You mentioned you were probably going to have to work late last night. I just figured you might have slept in."

"Well, I guess next time I tell Dad something, in what I thought was an unspoken and understood kind of confidence, I'll just assume he's going to tell you regardless."

"I really don't see what's so secret about it."

"True. But, if he's telling you about my life, I've got to believe it doesn't end with a simple regurgitation of my evening calendar."

"Nope," Linda said, with a tone intent on offending. "He tells me everything—wouldn't have to if you would."

"I'll see what can be done about that," Lisa condescended.

"Honey, at some point—not necessarily today—but, at some point do you think you might clue me in on what all this hostility is about?"

Lisa said nothing, and neither did her mother.

"I've got nothing to say about it today. I know that," Lisa finally broke.

"Okay, okay."

"So, is this just a general check-in kind of thing? Or, was there actually something you needed to talk to me about?" Lisa asked.

"I just thought I'd phone to see how things were going."

"What things are we talking about here?"

"Do we *need* to play games?" her mother asked.

Lisa didn't budge, and plopped herself down on the beaten love seat she'd found down the street in order to settle in for what could sometimes be a long-haul conversation.

"I'm not playing any games, what is it—what thing would you like to know about?"

"Should I pick just one?"

"Yes, pick just one, and maybe, just maybe, I'll tell you about it."

Her mother let out a huge sigh as Lisa held the phone away from her ear.

"Fine then. Are you still clean?"

"I just got out of the shower, so yes."

"Jesus. You know damn well what I mean."

"I do. And while I can understand why you think you have a right to know, what I said before is still the way this goes."

"And that was?"

"If I'm using, not using, using a lot, or nothing at all—it's none of your damn business."

"I'm quite sure I could find dozens of qualified professionals who'd disagree."

"You should then."

She could hear her father shouting an unintelligible question in the background.

"What did Dad just say?"

"He wants to know when you are coming home."

"I'm not coming home."

"He didn't mean for good," her mother snapped back. "Will you be coming to visit anytime soon?"

"I doubt it. I'm barely making enough right now to feed myself."

She could hear her mother cup the receiving end of her phone and parrot back what she'd just said for her father to know. Then she could distinctly make out what he said in response to Linda's retelling. "Tell her that we will pay for it."

Before Linda had the chance to pass the offer along, Lisa replied, "Tell Dad I appreciate the offer, but if I come back—I mean for a visit—it's got to be because I've earned it."

"But you *will* earn it, we all have faith that the acting thing is going to work out. Then you can pay us back."

"I don't believe that."

"Believe what?" her mom asked.

"I don't believe that you believe 'the acting thing' is going to work out."

"We'll don't *you*?"

Lisa hadn't been asked about her opinion on success' odds that bluntly since her group psychotherapy leader had grilled her with the very same inquiry. Caught between the truth as she was coming to understand it and the mythology of who she had only thought she wanted to be, she finished the phone call with two all-out lies.

"Yes. I think it will."

"Great. Think about coming home then, please honey."

"I certainly will. Good bye, Linda," Lisa said and then hung up the phone while additional spoken words emitted from it.

She pulled her knees under her chin, and then surveyed what little she had that was symbolic of an American dream gone well—including the remaining boxed items. Realistically, very few classically normal human beings would ever describe her situation as one "working out." It was an observation that even the strongest detractors of modern consumerism might make as well.

She selected Devon from her phone's contacts list, wanting to text him, but with no earthly idea of exactly what she felt like saying at that moment. She watched the blinking cursor as it begged for the entry of a message, hypnotic in its silence, until her phone's screen dimmed completely. Then she unlocked it once more, and repeated the same as she tried to convince herself that Elite Two Meet might actually lead to the career *boost* Devon relentlessly insisted would materialize because of it.

CHAPTER SEVENTEEN

Listen, smile, agree, and then do whatever the fuck you were gonna do anyway.

—Robert Downy Jr.

"I don't really care that you think it's a bad idea," Julie informed Chris. "I've got zero interest in letting this whole thing drag on, and I think going tomorrow night will definitely turn the screws."

Sensing that Julie wasn't quite finished, and having already made up her mind that whatever Julie said she was going to do next wouldn't be what Julie ended up doing at all, Chris didn't respond.

"I mean, seriously, I look like shit," Julie continued. "And if memory serves, you do too."

Chris found her reflection in the floor to ceiling windows of the living room, and assessed the validity of what Julie had just said.

"Mm-Hmm," she noted.

"I've spoken to a few people, and the rumor mill is already buzzing—the last thing Alicia is going to want everyone else to see tomorrow night is our fucked-up faces."

"Maybe," Chris said simply to aid Julie in wrapping up the conversation.

"Are you even paying attention?"

"Of course Julie. I get it."

"So you agree?"

"I'm certain I've already made it clear that I don't," Chris answered. "But, you seem pretty hell-bent on making a spectacle—and maybe it *will* work—but, I'd prefer we wait and see if Alicia and her legal counsel come around on their own."

Chris had said as much earlier in the call, and was pretty sure she'd outlined *laying low* as part of the plan when she finalized it with Julie multiple times in the weeks before. She'd already made peace with the fact that she'd misjudged Julie's intelligence, and accepted the certainty that controlling her with mere words wasn't going to happen. At that point, she'd only been keeping Julie on the phone to prevent her from doing anything dumb sooner than she indicated she was planning.

"So are you saying you aren't going to go then?" Julie asked.

Chris sat down on her couch. Curled up in the same position she'd fallen asleep so peacefully the night before. The scent of Alicia's perfume, the molecules carrying it, still trapped in the cushions, released from the fabric as she pressed her body and head deeper into the cushions.

"That's what I'm saying," Chris said.

She couldn't see Julie, but the silence over the line indicated she was likely fuming.

"Are you also saying that I can't go?"

"Would it matter?" Chris calmly asked.

"Well, I just think if we were both there—if we both showed up—it'd be a lot more uncomfortable for Alicia than if it were just me."

"Probably."

"Will you at least think about it?"

"I *am* thinking about it."

Julie continued putting new words against the same argument in favor of both she and Chris attending, and Chris allowed it. It was easy enough to keep Julie engaged with benign interjections while she considered what options existed to deal with Julie's poor judgment and insubordination.

She rested the phone horizontally atop of her ear, freeing up her hands in order to address the growing desire that the microscopic remnants of Alicia had instigated—invisible to the eye, yet so powerfully present, floating all around her, embracing her body, and caressing her skin.

She managed to fumble what little she was wearing to the floor, without losing the phone from her ear.

The aroma, coupled with the mind-made memories of their night before, orchestrated an aggressive symphony for an audience of one—explosive brass, thundering tympani, accompanied by the methodical repetition of melodic woodwinds and strings. The composition built upon itself steadily, layering additional instrumentation throughout and racing towards a crescendo and resolution, both physical and mental—all the while serving the secondary effect of pushing Julie's incessant droning about how much more sense her plan to blackmail Alicia made further and further into the distance.

In addition to the feigning of consideration of her plan, all for Julie's benefit, and getting herself off, Chris' began visualizing solutions for dealing with her not-so-savvy partner-in-crime's disobedience. She worked simultaneously at honing in on both her climax and the necessary sequence of events she'd have to put into effect in order to make sure that Julie would never make it to Wednesday night's Elite Two Meet event.

With the passing measures of the soundtrack driving her

future handiwork, each next step revealed itself clearly and chronologically:

First things first, I've got to end this phone call with Julie.

"Julie, do what you will. I'm not going to condone it, but I'm not going to pretend I can stop you or talk you out of it. Let's talk again later today, and who knows? Maybe I'll have changed my mind by then. Toodles."

Next up, call Randy. I hadn't planned on bringing that dumb fuck back into this, but so be it—but even this might be too much for that horny little fucker. I suppose I could pay him if absolutely necessary.

"Randy, it's me. I'm still so fucking hot from the other night—Julie too. In fact, she'd like to take the games up a notch. Hear me out. How familiar are you with abduction or kidnapping role play? Great. Here's the scenario: Julie would like for you to go to her apartment tonight, rough her up, kidnap her—the whole thing, tie her up, bound and gagged, and then have you take her someplace else. Somewhere she doesn't know about. Just take her back to your place; she'll be blindfolded so it won't matter. Keep in mind, that since she is playing the victim here, she'll most likely be acting that part out too—screaming, kicking, and whatever else she has to do to try and stop you. Don't fuck it up by pulling punches; she wants as real the thrill as possible. You think you can handle that? I thought so. Then, she wants you to keep her there until I tell you it's time to let her go. I know, it's fucked up—but I figured you might be into it, and she's comfortable with you—actually, she won't shut up about how much she enjoyed the fuck you gave her Saturday night. Ah, honey that's sweet, but I don't mind—I'm not the jealous type, you ought to know that by now. Bottom line here: Are you game for slapping her around a bit, kidnapping her, and holding her

tied-up and bound at your place until I tell you it's time to let her go? You do this right for her though—do this right for me—and I guarantee she and I will fuck you six-ways to Sunday. Good boy."

He'll say yes. He'll do whatever the hell I tell him to do, and if he doesn't I guess I could always start spinning it the other way. Tell him that Saturday night had gone too far, and she was considering pressing charges against him—how's saying that going to work out? I don't know, but if he isn't as into this bullshit as I think he'll be, I'll deal with it then.

Stupid little bitch, Chris thought as her body released all of its growing anticipation into a dozen consecutive spasms, so violent she almost lost her footing and the phone from its perch.

"Chris, what can I say to change your mind?" Julie asked desperately.

"Julie, do what you will. I'm not going to condone it, but I'm not going to pretend I can stop you or talk you out of it."

Julie tried to interject one last time, "Dammit, Chris—"

"Let's talk again later today, and who knows? Maybe I'll have changed my mind by then. Toodles."

Julie continued, but Chris hung up.

She reached for the laptop sitting on the coffee table in front of her, figuring a few search results related to the type of role-playing *favor* she was about to ask Randy to execute that night might help put his mind at ease. He hadn't been at all sheepish about using both she and Julie as punching bags three nights ago, but since she'd not be there to bark out orders to him this time, finding a few articles that legitimized the scenario before ringing him seemed prudent.

As she scanned over the results of her foraging, some of what Julie had said on the phone began to provoke minor hysterics of her own. *Alicia could have stayed longer*, Chris thought. *Should have stayed longer.*

She copied a few link addresses from her browser into a pink company issued notebook to share with Randy if necessary. She tried to assure herself that the growing doubt regarding her rape's effectiveness on Alicia was only the byproduct of having had to listen to that spoiled imbecile go on and on about how inefficient their plan had been thus far—though Chris felt it wasn't truly off schedule to begin with.

Chris recalled Julie having whined, "Alicia hasn't even reached out to me. All I got was a lame-ass just-checking-to-make-sure-you-are-okay email from Bean."

Julie is going to fuck this up, Chris speculated. *But she's right. Why isn't Alicia doing more?*

It was almost four, and Alicia hadn't responded to a single text that Chris had sent that day. She hadn't phoned, hadn't come back around, hadn't scrawled a note on her way out indicating she was somehow complicit, or penned a later offering suggesting she'd do whatever it might take to help Chris get through it all. She hadn't done anything more than pop-by, and Chris realized even Alicia's visit wouldn't have occurred had her nosy doorman not spotted her hovering beyond her front door.

Alicia's lack of genuine concern over the matter was evident, and while Chris would never admit to Julie having been the voice of reason that exposed Alicia's less than stellar effort to connect and correct the situation, she did decide that perhaps a little additional prodding wasn't uncalled for.

Before phoning Randy in order to detail for him the future activities of his Tuesday night, she scrolled through her contacts until she found the recently added Detective Johnson. Without pause she opened a dialog box and furiously typed.

Have you even bothered to question Jeff and David? The two dudes from ETM who were out with us that night? LMK.

She dialed Randy. With her phone in hand, moved to her bedroom to begin assessing what she'd be wearing later that night. Randy didn't pick up, and it went straight to voicemail. She disconnected the call and rang him again only to hear the computerized regurgitation of his digits a second time—and then a third.

Pacing from bedroom to bathroom, from bathroom to kitchen, from kitchen to deck, she redialed Randy's number over and over, cursing him aloud as she looked for yet-to-come texts from Alicia in between dialing him. She thought about heading straight over to his apartment across town. She considered what Julie's fate might be if she wasn't able to get a hold of Randy. She moved rapidly among the furniture of her home, trying desperately to reach him until she stumbled back into her bedroom—dizzy, angry, and unable to force her lungs to draw in oxygen at a steadier rate.

After a final attempt to connect with Randy proved unsuccessful, she hurled her cell towards the wall. It met the pristine peach coat of paint with a great thud, before falling onto the floor below unscathed. Chris began dry heaving and backed her way into a corner until she was able to perform a controlled collapse of her body to the ground.

From across the room the phone's jingle grew steadily more audible, until its tune finally registered to Chris, right before it stopped ringing. She slowly crawled over to retrieve it. When the rings began to sound again, she quickly snatched it up and answered.

"Hey Sweetie, what's shakin'?" Randy asked.

"Where the fuck have you been?" Chris demanded.

"Napping. Sorry, I missed your call—"

"Calls," Chris emphasized.

"Yeah, calls. Whatever. What's up baby?"

Chris took a deep breath, if she was going to get Randy on board with this, a seductive civility would be key.

"I'm sorry baby, it's just that I'm still so fucking hot from the other night—Julie too," she whispered.

She paused to assess his interest level. Silence accompanied by increased breathing.

"In fact, Julie would like to take the games up a notch."

"Like what do you mean?" Randy asked.

"Hear me out. How familiar are you with abduction or kidnapping role play?"

It took a couple of ticks of the clock, but Randy finally uttered, "I've heard of it."

Chris let out a slight sigh of relief, "Perfect."

CHAPTER EIGHTEEN

It's a great huge game of chess that's being played—all over the world—if this is the world at all, you know.
                          —Lewis Carroll, *Through the Looking Glass*

A muffled pounding created by the flesh of a fist against paned glass echoed around the insides of Alicia's skull. She woke and through the haze of tired eyes saw the culprit behind the impromptu alarm was Bean.

"Alicia. I'm not positive, but I think you mentioned meeting a client for an early dinner, no?"

"What time is it?" Alicia asked aloud while answering her own question with a quick glance at her phone.

Five o'clock. She'd been out for nearly three hours.

The feeling of a comfy confusion the conclusion of any nap affords in the first few minutes thereafter immediately gave way to a ferocious anger. And Bean didn't flinch when Alicia unleashed a cuss-filled tirade on her—irrationally demanding to know who thought it'd be a good idea to let her cruise through a whole afternoon asleep at the wheel.

"Tomorrow's event is critical, Bean," Alicia concluded.

"They all are," Bean responded with an unfamiliar edge to her tone.

It reeked of the beginnings of future insubordination, but in that moment Alicia was silently willing to chalk it up to her own tired mind's short circuiting connections. The nap had left time decidedly not in her favor—and the few pre-party decisions she had used as the impetus for even being in the office were quickly abandoned in favor of putting herself together quickly enough to meet Lisa on time.

She snagged her bag and stormed past Bean on her way to the company's unisex bathroom down the hall.

The feeling of being beyond tired, even after the impromptu nap, left Alicia's train of thought unusually scattered. As she locked the door to the bathroom behind her she made note of just how many seemingly unrelated themes introduced themselves on the short walk from her office to the facilities. Muscle memory had her already reaching into her purse to grab something pharmaceutical to get her back on track. As her fingers fumbled around deep inside her bag, she caught a glimpse of herself in the mirror.

One of the more deliberate decisions made during the planning of the Elite Two Meet offices had been a bathroom design that through the use of lighting, paint selection and even its proportions had been built to give the occupant their best possible look at themselves. It hadn't been a decision made exclusively for potential clientele visiting there. Its purpose was rooted in the idea that anyone who worked there should and would get to see the best representation of his or her outward appearance throughout the workday.

The decision to spend extra capital on how the bathroom could best elevate a person's confidence had accompanied several other design and operational ideas intended to have the very same effect. Everything from the gratis beverages in the fingerprintless stainless steel refrigerator to the custom built desks tailored for each individual employee was part of her feel-good work-good scheme. Over the years, Alicia had often internally debated if any of it was actually delivering the intended effect. But she had never questioned the way the bathroom had turned out, or the way it seemingly gave a lift to anyone who had entered upon his or her triumphant exit.

Before she allowed herself to believe that what she was seeing in the mirror was an honest representation, she scanned the room for a failed bulb. Nothing appeared faulty, and when her eyes found themselves again, staring deep into herself, a nervous giggle escaped.

There is no running from myself today I guess.

As she analyzed all the very things that any professional retoucher would have had immediately removed from a photo of her face, she felt a brief and oddly foreign, but comfortable moment of relief. It was short lived.

From her bag, she began to retrieve the necessary solutions for what her own brain had almost immediately branded "hideous" just seconds after an attempt at genuine acceptance. Maybe it was the familiar ritual of readying herself or simply the elapsed time between being zonked on her desk and that moment, but she found her focus. And with each stroke, application and reinvention of the reflected self-portrait before her, a last ditch plan to ensure Lisa's participation in Elite Two Meet formed completely. By the time she'd exited the bathroom, her arrival at that same vanity location just moments earlier felt like a distant memory from a lifetime ago.

CHAPTER NINETEEN

Man does not control his own fate. The women in his life do that for him.

—Groucho Marx

Randy hadn't given much thought to the clothing he was wearing when he raced out to "kidnap" Julie. Kneeling over her seemingly lifeless body crumpled below him on her floor, he caught a glimpse of himself in a full length mirror she had leaning against the bedroom wall of her Lower East Side railroad.

Doesn't a kidnapper wear all black? he asked himself.

Chris' earlier, near hysterical demand that he not waste any time in "getting on with it" meant Julie's *fantasy* had begun with several loud pounding jabs of a meaty clenched fist on her door, delivered by a guy in track pants, cross-trainers, and an oversized t-shirt emblazoned with the words "Just Do It." Holding two fingers clumsily to Julie's neck as if he knew anything about finding a pulse, he surmised that the stink still about him from the workout earlier that morning was playing in favor of a believable performance. A storyline he was basing on years of films that featured slicker fellas clad head to toe in slim fitting black attire, who would eventually throw a limp body like Julie's into the backseat of some sinister sport utility vehicle or the trunk of an exotic sports car they'd then use to transport her to their hide-outs or lairs.

The intent had been to coax Julie back to his apartment using the illusion of a gun made by a pointy finger through the pockets of his pants, but she'd really acted up the part and her stubborn refusal to come with him after he *broke-in* escalated to a point where Randy felt a solid open-handed southpaw to her jaw was what the script called for. He'd done his best to throw it at fifty percent, and the last thing he'd expected to happen was for the delivery of the swipe to knock her off her feet, causing her to smash the back of her head against a dresser.

Best he could tell there was no cut, gash, or open wound—he hadn't found any blood by running his hand through her hair, but a large knot seemed to be forming just beyond the crown of her skull. He thought he felt a pulse, and by eyeing her exposed abdomen carefully, it was evident to him that she was clearly breathing—or that he was at the very least imagining that her lungs were filling and exhaling to some extent before his eyes.

As he stood up Randy speculated aloud, "As a kidnapping scenario goes, I suppose you being knocked out cold is a fairly accurate portrayal."

Even so, he knew Chris would be disappointed if he didn't follow her specific directions—and while there were few, she seemed fairly adamant about making sure he and Julie ended up at his place. She hadn't said anything concrete about joining them at his apartment, but it seemed like a real possibility given the sexual nature of the stunt.

"You two are nuts," Randy whispered as he peered through Julie's window to the street below. "Too many folks buzzing about for me to just haul you out of here passed out."

Even as he said it, he didn't quite believe it. New York was a funny place—filled with unusual people used to seeing unusual sights. The city was filthy with stories of ignored broad daylight muggings in which passing citizens offered no help, heads buried in phones and selfish minds focused on staying out of harm's way. It'd take no longer than a few minutes to get her into a cab; he could pretend she'd had too much to drink or carefully weave a tale about a friend in need of a rehab—anything of that ilk would be easily passable with the right commitment.

Continuing his conversation with himself, Randy used the mirror to gauge the conviction of a possible future performance, "My friend here digs kinky shit, I'm fake-kidnapping her to 'rape' her back at my place. You know, just another Wednesday in the city."

An answer as absurd as the truth might likely be chuckled off by a curious cab driver, and while Randy hadn't committed to removing her from her apartment just yet, he decided it was a good idea to dress his "victim" for the possibility of light travel.

She was still pretty banged-up from their previous Saturday tryst, and while Randy rummaged around her closets for some clothing he found himself replaying how the first ten minutes of this second encounter had played out. On his way over to her apartment he'd speculated that her role as an unsuspecting abductee would mean having to force his way in under false pretenses. It had been quite the opposite.

His best effort at beginning the charade found him covering the peephole to her unit's door and banging on it lightly—the way a neighbor might—with the hopes that she'd unlock the door and he'd be able to "barge" his way in. And that'd likely only happen because she was in on it and certainly couldn't be expecting him to scale a fire escape. Chris' detailed instructions hadn't included much on how to get the charade started.

When that knock led to the almost immediate click of an unlocked door with no accompanying inquiry, Randy just assumed Julie was making it easy for him. And so he grabbed the door's knob and put all of his weight into it, expecting to find at least some resistance from Julie. There was none though, and he nearly lost his balance as he clung to the door, flailing his way into her apartment.

It was pretty obvious she'd been expecting him. *I'm the casual acquaintance gone wrong*, *maybe*, Randy had thought.

"Shut the fucking door!" Julie barked before he had even found his balance.

Confused, Randy heard himself say, "Sorry, I wasn't really sure how you wanted to begin this thing."

Julie rolled her eyes—a clear indication that she was already disappointed with his acting skills. Flush with the adrenaline that accompanies embarrassment, Randy made a conscious decision to ignore any other words that came out of her mouth. She turned away from him and he decided to go for it.

"Chris' idea of how this is all going to play out is beyond fucked," he remembered hearing Julie say as he grabbed her from behind with the intent of forcing her face first into the overstuffed couch floating in the center of what limited space the apartment afforded an item with no business being there.

Randy had expected a bit of a struggle, but he'd definitely underestimated Julie's five-foot-four-inch, maybe one hundred and five pounds strength. While fighting and freeing herself from him, Julie's every other spoken word was met by the deaf ears that his momentary rage had created.

Even now a lot of what his memory was suggesting that might have been uttered by Julie during the melee was seemingly nonsensical.

If it was all a performance—the surprise, the fear in her eyes, the pitch and quiver in her voice that accompanied the rampant denial that she'd done anything wrong—she deserves a friggin' Oscar, Randy thought.

Regardless, knocking her unconscious hadn't been the plan, but it was certainly making dealing with her a lot easier than he'd expected.

Amidst the silence of her slumber and his internal indecision on what to dress her with in order to move the body to his place, blood began to build up between the tough outer membrane of her central nervous system known as the dura mater and her skull. An epidural hematoma collecting beyond the serene but still bruised porcelain skin, back behind closed eyes and her cropped blonde locks.

When Julie started to come to—regaining consciousness just as Randy was attempting to slide on a pair of extremely tight jeans over her thighs, tugging them with little success in a desperate effort to reach her waist—neither she nor Randy had even the slightest inkling that she'd be dead by the following morning. Had either entertained the possibility, it certainly wouldn't have been the conclusion of a narrative related to an increasing pressure in her intracranial space—a compression of delicate brain tissue that would eventually cause her brain to shift.

Julie propped herself up, dazed from the fall, and waited for her eyes to focus in on the cause of the current discomfort below her waist.

"Randy. What the fuck are you doing?"

He'd been so preoccupied with trying to work the denim onto her—his mind still racing with possible next steps to ensure a successful charade—that he hadn't even registered that she'd awoken. Startled, he tilted his eyes to hers and put the dressing on pause. His hands were trembling due to a combination of adrenaline and the usual amount of delirium tremens he'd grown accustomed to at around four every afternoon.

Julie found focus just long enough to make note of the pair of pants the clod had selected. The jeans were a relic she'd left in the closet as a reminder of the shape and frame she'd been able to flaunt several years prior.

The thought, "Dozens, if not one hundred options in my closet and this clown picks the only offensive item left," rattled around in her head.

"Randy—"

"Bitch, shut up. Just shut up and this will all go fine," Randy forced out the line the very way he had scripted it on the subway ride over.

When Julie rolled her eyes, his embarrassment rose up from the gut and manifested itself in the form of a second, far more intentionally violent punch to her face.

Her arms buckled from the velocity and Julie found herself horizontal yet again. The sting registered, filling her eyes with tears that made it difficult to see. Her brain worked towards constructing a sentence that might end the scenario, but before she could deliver the phrase, the hard pull of duct tape across one cheek to the other sealed her mouth shut.

Randy grabbed her arms, squeezing her wrists together, he rolled the tape around over and over again while pinning down what little squirm she was able to manufacture with the whole of his body resting right above her still not-quite-dressed thighs.

None of what was transpiring was going at all like he'd envisioned. As he spun around while trying to keep his weight atop of her struggling frame, in order to execute the same tape job to her ankles, he mused towards Julie, "I suppose no kidnapping, even a fake one, goes according to plan."

CHAPTER TWENTY

There is always some madness in love. But there is also always some reason in madness.

—Friedrich Nietzsche

With all the self-discipline she could muster, Chris decided to abstain from texting Randy to see if he was on schedule with Julie. She'd given him fairly explicit instructions and wasn't due to rendezvous with him back at his place for another two hours.

"Whatever you do to her before I get there is up to you, pervert." She'd concluded their earlier call with her best effort at sounding light about the whole thing.

Texting him to check in on how this trumped up pho-fantasy abduction was going could only lead to two possible outcomes: One, he was doing just fine with it. Two, he was bumbling through it, running into problems, and would likely ask her to come meet him far earlier that had been planned. Chris was resolved to the reality that the second scenario was the most likely one.

Can't be everywhere at once. And even if Julie immediately saw through it—or didn't believe me when I told her Randy was only coming over to grab her on his way over to meet me, the dumb fuck has still probably figured something out.

Her final decision regarding the matter had been to believe that if anything was wrong, if indeed it wasn't at least playing out close to how she'd envisioned it, she would have heard from one or the other. Randy or Julie would have phoned, texted, or both—neither had, and at that moment it was all Chris needed to stay the course. It was too close to six, and if she didn't hustle, there was a good chance she'd not arrive at the Elite Two Meet offices before Alicia bailed.

Seeing Alicia immediately was the only option. Repeated attempts to reach her had gone unrequited and had left Chris with no other choice but to put herself physically in front of her.

Point A to Point B travel at that early evening hour in the city was tricky. There was no real rhyme or reason to what mode might actually be fastest. A cab might, the train—but ultimately the only absolutely certain methodology to an unobstructed journey was to walk. It might take longer, but at least one could be sure she was the sole decision maker. Short of cataclysmic catastrophic events—the kind that shut down city blocks—the only delay on city travels made by foot is the mass of humanity who is privy to the same guiding logic on destination arrival best practices.

As luck would have it, there was a steady drizzle falling, just enough damp inconvenience to keep the sheepish within their offices for a while longer, waiting out the "storm." The herd was thinner than the norm. Still, Chris found herself rooting for the skies to open up—few things kept the sidewalks more passable than a solid rain bomb.

As she maneuvered her way through the limited hustle and bustle, her conviction to believing Alicia would be pleased to see her was bolstered by their previous evening's interactions—that night was replaying in Chris' head on a loop, over and over again. The occasional cat call, the horns, the general murmur and hum of dozens upon dozens of people speaking to one another as they walked together or shouted over the city's own buzz into their phones to the friends and family awaiting their arrival—all of it fell to a hush behind the memories of that one recent evening. The first time Alicia had seemingly let her guard down. In Chris' mind it was the night that in some distant number of years from now could and would be marked as the true beginning, a new beginning, for her and Alicia both.

The only interference interrupting the repetition of her evening by Alicia's side was the occasional bout of speculation as to how this next night would play out. No stranger to sleep deprivation, Chris chalked up her inability to completely foresee exactly how Alicia would react to this unscheduled pop-in as nothing more than a tired mind. A mind exhausted and flush with all the pent-up emotions it'd carried concealed for the last two years.

Tonight could be special. Tonight could be the night. Tonight will be the night it all comes together. The decision is mine to make, no one else's.

With an increasing speed, Chris continued her way down Houston Street. The larger width of the avenue's sidewalks fed her momentum. And while the drizzle had hardly grown into anything more substantially drenching, its duration had surely left many Manhattanites still clutching their bags and staring at the skies from out of their office windows.

The minor vibration made from Chris' phone went undetected. A second and third pulsation, each accompanied by a sharp *PING*, did little in breaking her concentration.

As she made her way across the intersection of one of the smaller cobble stoned streets of SoHo, the blare of a Mercedes' car horn startled only the souls who had witnessed the sudden almost-pulverization of Chris' petite frame. The shouts from the driver went unheard and the jeers from other pedestrians made in the name of her audacity did not register.

Turning south onto the last street east of Sixth Avenue, Chris' imagination had finally come around, constructing a perfect tale centered on her and Alicia. A story that started with them walking hand in hand the following day, late in that afternoon—work be damned—it could wait, and they'd make their way to the restaurant of Alicia's choosing to feast on a midweek brunch, the type of meal experienced by those lucky few who had never let the rigors of success or corporate society's absurd scheduling stereotypes get in the way of denoting a special occasion. These were the people who lived on their terms, and a strong, unbreakable bond between these couples had always been the secret to their devil-may-care attitudes. That life, one in which the end of any day would include seeing and being with the only other human she'd ever loved, was hers to have—it was waiting for her right around the next corner.

A fourth and fifth pair of back to back vibrations accompanied by pings emanated from the back pocket of Chris' jeans. And while that'd likely have not been enough to disrupt her trance, their arrival coincided with perhaps the only thing capable of putting the brakes on a fantasy yarn moving at the speed of a runaway train—the corner of the eye recognition of the very object of her desires, Alicia.

Chris stopped, stood frozen, and reached for her phone out of habit as her eyes—even from a distance—took in every detail of Alicia's peaceful face. Her gaze hovered just above the sightline of the device's screen that she held in both hands in front of her, and had the cell not demanded her attention once more with its incessant buzzing, it's unlikely she'd have bothered to give the culprit behind the inconvenience any attention at all.

Randy (6). The phone's display read.

She unlocked the interface, prepared herself for the string of text messages that would likely depict the failure that would detain her from the new life—a delectable future she could begin with just a few short steps across the street at a café that she'd previously never bothered to acknowledge.

The dainty speech bubbles wrapped around each little line of copy only increased the hilarity of Randy's words themselves.

You there? 4:33

I've got her. 4:34

She's a good crier. 5:10

Yello? 5:25

Getting naked over here. 5:25

You on your way? 5:35

A swell of warm relief washed over Chris. Somehow, someway, Randy had come through. He'd delivered in a way she'd not truly believed he'd been capable, and yet, if the words she read through the increasing condensation on the device's screen were to be believed, the one person who might have stood the best shot at derailing Chris' perfect plan was now an "abductee."

Ego's sweet endorphin rush had Chris feeling particularly tickled when she typed and then sent her replies.

Just fuck her until she passes out.

I'll be by soon, and then you can fuck me.

The smiley emoticon that popped up right after was exactly the response she'd hoped to see from Randy.

She placed her phone snuggly back into her pocket and

before even looking up began to cross the street. A grand entrance was called for—a shout from the crosswalk might have been audible had the café's owners chosen to leave the large, swinging plate glass windows open in spite of what was now hardly even classifiable as a spit from the sky.

As Chris arrived onto the other side of the street, she was certain Alicia would sense it. But, in fact, her own gaze had never deviated from its dead-ahead stare into the direction of some brunette seated across from her.

Chris presumed it was one of the many typical last minute meetings Alicia was fond of having even when all of her parties' loose ends had been tied, retied, and tied up again.

She opened the door to the café, wiped her feet with extra effort onto the joint's tired and abused doormat, then chided herself for performing such a ridiculously passive spectacle to make Alicia realize that she was there.

A member of the wait staff waved to Chris, gesturing towards an empty table far across the room from Alicia and her companion. Chris politely declined as she surveyed the occupied tables in the pair's proximity. Every two top was accounted for, save one with an empty chair across from a single diner whose head was buried deep into the latest electronic gadget meant to pass as a meaningful way to spend some time.

"Alicia."

Chris headed towards the extra seat to grab it, but before her first step forward had a chance to land, the look on Alicia's face—a panicked expression, laced with condemnation of Chris' actions and communicated almost exclusively by only the heated thoughts behind her eyes—left Chris nearly stumbling. Alicia's brow furrowed with the silent but painfully loud formation of the words, "Not now."

Chris' phone made yet another attempt at grabbing her attention. Meanwhile, Alicia, without so much as a second thought, returned her attention to the woman seated across from her.

CHAPTER TWENTY-ONE

Without obsession, life is nothing.

—John Waters

Charlie Johnson had done what he considered a bang-up job of sitting in the same café as Alicia and Lisa while going unnoticed. It had been no easy task—following Lisa from her apartment and then managing to sneak into the establishment while she and Alicia engaged in conversation just two tables removed from its entrance. Lisa had used three forms of transportation on her journey downtown, and Johnson had left his car to the fate of meter maids, and then managed to sprint underground barely in time to climb aboard the same downtown express train. When he and Lisa surfaced from the Spring Street station twenty minutes later, he was caught off guard when she'd successfully been able to hail a cab during the evening rush. And had she used the cab to travel much further than the ten or so blocks she did, he'd likely have lost her completely. The glut of vehicles attempting to make their way east to west across lower Manhattan in order to escape via the Holland Tunnel had made tailing Lisa's ride on foot relatively easy. Choked intersections are rarely a friend to man, but they had played heavily in Charlie's favor.

If either Lisa or Alicia had seen him arrive and enter, then take a spot on the opposite side, they'd made no indication of it. He hadn't planned on entering at all. Then again, he hadn't planned on playing the role of stalker when he'd bid Lisa farewell after their brief conversation earlier that afternoon. He'd left her there, on her stoop, the fresh pack of smokes he'd given her in her hand, and with what he believed would be the memory or impression of the best version of himself. He'd edited his own thoughts on the matter on the heels of making that assessment to include, "best version of myself made under false pretenses."

Charlie found the why behind his tag-a-long to be reprehensible, and he'd mentally beaten himself up about it throughout the entire journey down. He had absolutely zero in the way of solid logic as it pertained to shadowing Lisa—he was working a job, and any effort to convince himself that trailing behind her made sense with his own brand of mental gymnastics had failed miserably.

When he finally sat down, he'd made one last gasp at a justification that didn't have anything to do with simply being smitten: *Alicia is here. If she sees me, that might turn up the heat.* He didn't bother with trying to make himself believe in that reason had validity directly after he'd thought it.

When Chris walked into the café just thirty minutes later, she'd also made no indication that she'd seen him—even after the waitress tried to flag her into taking a table not three feet from where he sat.

People see what they want to see I guess.

He was momentarily relieved. Chris wouldn't have been at all pleased to find him sitting there, nursing an overpriced latte. She'd made it beyond evident that the *only* thing she thought he should be doing that day was interrogating the two unlucky clowns she was trying to implicate in this whole charade.

"Get under their skin," she'd said, "Make them believe it, but for the love of Christ don't pressure them so hard that they lawyer up. Remember, they know they didn't do anything and the minute lawyers get involved with this—things get a lot trickier."

He'd had every intention of making the two necessary treks to the separate office locations of each "suspect" that day. Even though he had disagreed with Chris' suggested methodology—the timing and pace of the conspiracy mostly—he'd still planned on going ahead with it. It was her money after all, and he had reminded himself of their hierarchy repeatedly ever since agreeing to help shake Alicia down.

She's the gal with the cash. And I'm the guy who needs the cash.

It was that simple.

Still, this wasn't his first rodeo. And earlier on in the fabricating and scheming of it all, he'd made his case to Chris for a slow burn.

"You put all this out there too fast, you'll spook the whole lot. You need her panicky enough that she considers settling with you discreetly, and not so panicky that she holes up, guns a-blazing, as the ship goes down."

Metaphorically speaking anyway.

Johnson had put a bit of effort into profiling Alicia before agreeing to take part. Based on a solid supply of interviews with her made available for public consumption by various magazines and papers, he'd assessed that bilking her out of hundreds of thousands of dollars wasn't going to occur without some fight from her.

"The folks who earn it—truly earned it, not these blue bloods who grew up already chin deep in it—they aren't as quick to part with large sums," he'd warned Chris. "I'd advise you to find another mark, one who doesn't have an appreciation for money—someone who didn't throw their whole existence into building that fortune. Some Richie Rich who wouldn't miss five-hundred thousand dollars any more than we miss a nickel."

Over the course of the first couple of weeks, all of his attempts at trying to convince Chris of a far easier con had been met with zilch in the spirit of collaboration.

"Playing out a straight-up rape claim, a she-said-he-said type of deal—one in which you are pointing the finger at some high profile douchebag, the likes of which you surround yourself with every time you go to one of these Elite Two Meet shindigs, would be much easier. Go after the 'John,' why add the extra layer by trying to use the very same claim to bilk Alicia of her wad?"

Chris would nod, feign interest in hearing him out, and for a while Johnson had naively became convinced he'd eventually get her to deviate from going after Alicia.

"It's no harder than a few drinks too many, forcing the issue back at his place—sans protection—and then me showing up a few days later with a picture or two of you with a black-eye, some bruises and a vague indication that things aren't going to go his way."

Chris always responded in the same eerily civil fashion, "That isn't the plan I hired you for, Charlie."

"This personal?" he had asked Chris.

She never answered the question directly, and it didn't matter. He knew in his bones that for Chris this had little, if anything, to do with Alicia's money. It was pretty apparent that Chris had plenty of it. And while he'd have preferred to wait to play a game with someone who understood the benefits of keeping a con all business, his own situation demanded a quick fix—he needed the cash, and he needed it yesterday.

He'd accepted the possibility that at some point whatever real motivation was behind Chris' hell-bent dedication to scamming Alicia would likely present problems that he'd have to clean up. He wasn't looking forward to it, but like so many other partnerships before theirs, he pressed forward secure in the knowledge that he'd dealt with plenty of unforeseen messes in the past. This was clearly some sort of revenge job, the kind he'd sworn off of, but two hundred and fifty thousand was the payday. A sum just fifty thousand shy of what was required in order to save his own skin.

He'd only ever envisioned having to play janitor at some point much further down the road. When Chris entered and didn't spot him, he'd no intention of interfering—whatever came of her "impromptu" pop-in would likely be an uncomfortable spectacle to watch, but he made the quick decision to sit still and let it unfold in front of him. For better or worse.

You are playing this all wrong, lady. But then again, what the fuck am I doing here?

His last second commitment to snag Chris by the arm before she had any chance to turn the situation ugly came on the heels of watching Alicia mouth the words "not now" and then registering the intense disappointment and hate those two words ignited behind Chris' eyes.

Grabbing Chris had left them both exposed. Alicia's failed attempt to pretend she hadn't noticed had tipped Lisa off to the impending commotion about to unfold a few feet behind them as well.

In addition to Alicia and Lisa, the whole joint had to have heard the venom in Chris' from behind the teeth shout as she spun to address her captor.

"What the fuck do you think you are doing?"

"Sit with me, won't you?" Johnson said as he intensified his grip on her upper arm.

Before a rebuttal could work its way from her brain to the six inches of air that separated their faces, he squeezed her even harder and repeated, "Sit with me, won't you?"

The short-lived hush that had fallen upon the café and the prying eyes that accompanied it vanished as Chris agreed to follow Charlie back to his table.

He pulled the seat opposite his out for her—not as a courtesy so much as assurance that she'd take it and refrain from heading back towards making a huge mistake. Somewhat surprisingly, she sat down without any resistance, but the fire behind her eyes betrayed any other outward attempts she might have been forcing in order to appear at ease with the situation.

"Let's play this out proper, shall we?" Charlie asked as he sat back down across from her.

No response.

Charlie decided to wait her out. He took his mug into his hands, sipped what had become a less than lukewarm pick-me-up, and held it above the table as he tried to maintain unwavering eye contact with Chris.

A young wannabe New Yorker, fresh from the farm, dressed in Gap's very best black and whites and trying so desperately to play the role of an experienced waitress, popped over and blurted, "Can I start something for you?"

"Fuck off," Chris mumbled while never removing her eyes from Johnson's.

Before the waitress could spit out an undecided reply—a decision between calm levelheaded compliance or instead an equally curt delivery of something similarly crass—Charlie defused the situation by making an order for Chris.

"She meant Mocha Latte with whipped. Thanks."

Their server spun around and headed back to the bar where Charlie could just barely hear her deliver that order to the barista with some colorful adjectives for added effect.

A quick observation of Alicia's body language left him relatively comfortable with the idea that she'd decided to chalk this near interruption up as nothing more than an unfortunate coincidence. He speculated that at the very worst, Chris' arrival there might have appeared to be the desperate actions of a recently raped friend seeking counsel and comfort from someone who was supposed to care. If that was the case, there was zero indication from Alicia, who best he could tell, seemed to be making some sort of pitch to Lisa as she picked at the large salad in front of her.

The best consequences of Chris' arrival coupled with his own *outing* there would hopefully be an even more paranoid and panicked mark. And even if she'd managed to find the focus to finish whatever it was she'd brought Lisa there to explain, Johnson decided to believe that somewhere underneath Alicia's calm exterior demeanor was a festering worry that would play into his and Chris' hands soon enough.

He turned his full attention back to Chris.

"You are probably wondering why I am here."

The rage in Chris' face almost immediately turned into a faked indifference. Like a machine, the transformation was as quick as flipping an on/off switch.

"It isn't where I told you to be. I'm *sure* you have a reason."

Charlie knew she didn't mean it.

"If I told you I just happened to be here when they both

came in, would you buy that?"

"Does it really matter?"

"I suppose it doesn't."

Chris leaned back in her chair, never once letting her eyes wander away from Charlie, forcing her body to hide any residual anger coursing inside.

"I'm beginning to think maybe you aren't the guy to get this done for me, Charlie."

"Is that why *you* are here?"

"Does it really matter?" Chris repeated.

Their server broke the tension temporarily with the stinging clink of porcelain butting against porcelain as she set Charlie's order down on the table in front of Chris.

She asked, "Anything else?"

When neither bothered to reply she rolled her eyes hard enough to nearly hear it.

"I guess all that really matters, Chris, is where we decide to go from here."

"Play it out, you said."

"I'm suggesting that, yes."

Chris pulled herself out of the intentional slump and leaned into the table on both elbows, pushing her body against it as far as she could so that nothing she said to Charlie next could be lost amidst the growing noise of the now almost full café.

"Are you ready to listen to me?" she asked him.

Charlie didn't bother with a response, but he noted that the same burning hate from earlier had returned behind those crystal blue eyes.

"Brother, I don't know what it is you did. I don't know why you need the money you say you need, and I don't really care. But if you fuck this up for me—and right now I can't say you are

doing a whole hell of a lot that doesn't seem amateur at best—
and I swear to Christ, if you fuck this up for me, I'll cut you out
of this world. You'll get nothing. So why don't you do us both a
favor and get back to doing *exactly* what I tell *you* to do—no
fuck that—exactly what I *told* you to do."

"Are you threatening me?"

"Come on, Charlie, don't play dumb." She leaned back
shaking her head in disgust. "Be dumb, but don't play it."

CHAPTER TWENTY-TWO

I'd rather be hated for who I am, than loved for who I am not.

—Kurt Cobain

Alicia finished her spiel to me. It seemed like at least a solid twenty minutes of uninterrupted, unrelated flattery, shooting with a battery of misguided and disjointed butter-ups, insults, and insinuations.

"I need more women like you Lisa, the future success of this little social experiment I've cooked up absolutely demands it."

"To the best of my own recollection, no one I've ever offered membership has turned it down without at least attending their first function—don't be so holier than thou about the whole thing."

"This could be the beginning of something bigger than the both of us. You've opened my eyes to the possibilities, and I just know that if you'll come tomorrow night, you'll see, it'll all work out—you are simply a different breed."

Everything that had preceded her pitch's conclusion revolved around one basic premise: She'd decided to let me into her VIP harem for free.

She hadn't used the word "free" once though. And had clearly gone to great lengths prior to meeting me there to construct a grand rationale as to why I'd be the first ever admission gratis. I'm as susceptible as most to the sweet siren song of compliments laid on thick. There were many, but despite her grand command of the English language and her ability to verbalize such a simple notion as though it were the impetus and architecture to some improved future version of the scheduled co-mingling of the city's power players—I remained suspicious of her true motives.

The length of her presentation had made devouring my salad a relatively easy task, and had she invited me out to hear the same exact monologue the following night I'd have agreed to hear it, so long as it too included a meal that didn't require my money.

When I was quite certain she was done speaking—I'd been wrong twice before during her idea of a conversation—I offered an observation rather than a reply.

"I wonder, do the moneyed all think the rest of us are simply sitting around hoping to be gifted the opportunity to join their ranks?"

Alicia looked flustered—not because I'd insulted her, but because she believed I'd not heard a word she'd just said.

"It's not like that Lisa. I'd say having you come on is more a favor to me than me doing you any."

"I see."

"I don't think you do."

"Alicia, come on now—don't undo the last half-hour of buttering me up with a proposal seeped in just how wonderful I am by insulting my intelligence in a single quip."

At that point, I wasn't exactly sure where I was trying to direct the dialogue. The old habit of pushing buttons just for the sport of it reared its ugly head. I had been working on that character defect fastidiously with my sponsor, but it was delicious to have the upper hand and the old me really didn't see the point in playing nice. I'd not bothered to go outside to burn one since arriving there, and that wasn't working in Alicia's favor either.

"No, no," she said. "I don't think I did an adequate job of explaining why I think having you come aboard makes so much sense. I'm saying it was my fault."

"You are digging yourself deeper," I suggested.

The calm Alicia had possessed during her entire presentation gave way to the fidgety indecision of a child. The eye contact she'd held with me so firmly for the majority of our rendezvous was no more, and she grabbed for her bag below the table in order to retrieve her phone. I wasn't about to allow her to remove herself from the moment under the guise of checking in on work or whatever other cockamamie excuse she was about to cook up.

"Okay," I said.

That grabbed her attention. A small grin returned to her face as she put the device back onto the table and turned her full attention back on me. Of course, I was hardly finished.

"So, let's say I come to you in a few weeks…"

She nodded along, naïvely excited about the future I was describing.

"…and tell you've I've been raped by one—no two, maybe three—of some of those hand-picked gentleman of yours… gang raped possibly… would what happened here just moments ago play out virtually the same?"

The newer little voice in my head, born only recently as a byproduct of my sobriety, was trying desperately to tell me to take my foot off the gas. It lost out to the demon. Alicia sat still with her head down and her eyes up, like a scolded puppy.

"You mouthing a not-now-warning to *me* as you sit across from the next shiny object, trying to convince her of the very same line of bullshit you just shoveled my way? Ambivalent—or at least feigning ambivalence—about the situation one of your members finds themselves in because of the very same—and clearly deeply flawed—creation you are trying to hock?"

Alicia's expression had turned. Some part of my soapboxing had ignited the fuse, and whatever self-pity she might have temporarily indulged in had given way to a building rage. I could see it, and it was exactly what I needed to keep going. I wanted her to fight back, as there's no sport in picking on the silent and defenseless.

"Attractive as your offer is, if I were to accept it, wouldn't that make me complicit in your disturbing showing here of seemingly zero empathy?"

Alicia took advantage of the small pause I'd left her between that last barb and the new one that was forming in my head.

"Grow up, Lisa," she flatly delivered with a trace of a mother's scorn. "The world doesn't stop and start on the whims of criminal activity."

She used her eyes to gesture towards Johnson and the blonde. "Perhaps I didn't handle that appropriately. Maybe I'm overwhelmed by the situations I find myself navigating this week, I'll concede on that."

The anger I'd hoped for and needed in order to fuel my own hadn't shown up. Unless Alicia was setting me up with some temporary dip into rational thinking before unleashing a more hostile form of verbal lashing, the very kind I required to feel okay about what I'd just said, my own growing feeling of remorse was certain to continue. She didn't and so it did.

"I came here tonight to see you, Lisa."

"Obviously," I spat weakly in one last attempt to escalate things.

"No. Listen to me," Alicia directed with just the slightest crack in her voice. "I came here tonight to see *you*."

I'd be lying if I told you that any of what she was driving at had sunk in the very moments after she said it. I'm probably not as bright as others make me out to be, or, at the very least, have issues with subtleties and absorbing what some folks more easily infer when reading between the lines.

As such, my response of "I get it" was hardly accurate. Those had been three words thrown into the mix only as a bridge meant to help foster additional dialogue. And if Alicia had any inclinations or intentions to further explain herself, some grand clarification wasn't granted the opportunity to materialize.

The blonde had returned, hovering over our table unannounced. If she'd been standing there very long, it was only because she'd managed to blend in with the commotion of the café's bustle. The energy emitting from her being was uncomfortable, and I sat uncharacteristically motionless as I watched an absolutely silent exchange occur between her and Alicia. No words were spoken for what seemed like an eternity, and by the time either had come around to trying to put any audible exchange out into the world, Detective Johnson had reappeared.

He came up from behind Alicia's acquaintance, and like I'd just barely witnessed him do earlier, placed his oversized mitt of a hand onto her shoulder, delivering a squeeze that seemed intent on preventing any sudden movement.

"Let's go, Chris," he said.

She didn't respond. He left his hand heavy atop her shoulder but it had no effect on the impenetrable stare directed at Alicia.

He repeated the suggestion as the muscles and tendons in his hand twitched, digging deeper into Chris' blouse to gain a firmer hold, betraying the calm in his voice.

"Let's go, Chris."

It was subtle, but I could swear that the woman, Chris, just ever so slightly shook her head from the left to the right directly at Alicia with a shallow sigh of disdainful disapproval before she acquiesced. Johnson made a bumbling attempt at some sort of an apology on behalf of them both as they left.

Alicia and I sat amidst the discomfort the scene had created. I was waiting for her to either continue from where we'd left off, or begin a new conversation based on what had just transpired. She said nothing though as her eyes darted back and forth between yours truly and the exit of the café and then out through the window as she tried to watch Chris and the detective vanish among the city's sheep.

"I'm going to smoke," I announced.

"Okay. I'll get this. Meet me outside?"

"Sure," I lied.

I'd had enough, and I'd already made the decision that my own wellbeing dictated that I remove myself from all the negative energy that I'd helped birth there.

She'd text me later with a message letting me know that she'd been disappointed not to find me waiting outside, but that she completely understood given what had occurred. I wouldn't bother with a response.

Shortly thereafter, on a very long and wet walk home, my mind provided a more adequate interpretation of some of what had revealed itself prior to our meeting's unexpected and awkward conclusion. Combining the additional conversation between Alicia and I with the fading representations of the physical expressions made lockstep with the words themselves, I began to contemplate a deeper motive behind our interlude. I've always considered myself a worldly sort, but in truth, there are still so many things my naivety prevents me from seeing for what they are.

A text from Devon bubbled up on my phone.

Details please.

I quickly tapped back, *It's tremendously difficult to chain smoke during a downpour.*

Hardee har har. Details please.

There are those moments in life where, not for the sake of trying at all, your existence and the world's meaning and your place in it is scarily easy to grasp. They are very brief poofs of clarity in which I feel like I have a complete and total understanding of all the facts that lay before me. I suspect they are nothing more than the misfiring of synapses and some accidental introduction of dopamine into the brain that mimics the illusion of inner peace. For me, they often occur in the microseconds after I'm ripped from some pattern of what I'd describe as deep thought.

I wrote Devon back, far more confident in the message's meaning than in the actual words I'd chosen to convey it.

She's sweet on me.

And I wasn't the slightest bit surprised when he insisted on meeting me at my place even after my repeated attempts to text him off and out of it. His promise to delay his arrival so that I might have me an hour of alone time to take care of a few things wasn't nearly as effective as his proclamation that he would be bringing snacks and smokes.

CHAPTER TWENTY-THREE

It is a man's own mind, not his enemy or foe, that lures him to his evil ways.

—Buddha

The age of forty-six is hardly a tally of years that anyone might deem an impressive run at life without the proper context. If that four and a half decades belongs to a twenty-five-year veteran of the New York Police Department, as a police and detective, those with any inkling about the daily filth operating beneath the advertised polished tourist destination would disagree vehemently with that erroneous assessment of the subject's lifespan.

By his own estimation, Charlie Johnson had only made it that long because of three things: dumb luck and timing had him partnering early on with one of the NYPD's smartest old hands, he'd never married, and he had an uncanny gift with gut feelings that got him in and then out of all kinds of unimaginable situations. Even if he hadn't let his own personal circumstances go haywire, he was pretty sure he'd still be working—and likely wouldn't have ever made the turn to what some might refer to as crooked.

He hated that word, crooked.

Many nights found him alone arguing with himself about the nature of his various indiscretions over the past two years, and usually giving in to the half of him that presented the flawed thinking that deemed all of them as justifiable to win the debate. A head hit the pillow a lot easier that way, and there isn't much time for sleep when you are chasing the Big City's loonies to begin with. Besides, he'd no intention of continuing to abuse his power once he got his situation sorted. Charlie hoped when that day arrived, he'd be strong enough to commit to going back on the straight.

Not long after having nearly dragged Chris out of her own way back at the café, he'd agreed to let her head back home on her own. Now, that miraculous intuition of his—that gut feeling—had him wondering if he'd ever make it to that future date to see if he would have what it takes to be the upstanding police he had been.

Around the corner from the café, under the cover of shoddy scaffolding, he and Chris had "talked" it out. He'd let her leave, but he suspected she'd seen it the other way around.

"I don't expect to see you near either of them again until I give you permission," Chris said.

"Whatever it is you think you know about shaking this woman down doesn't mean squat to me. It's pretty evident this thing is personal, and that's just poor form."

"You want out, fucking say so."

There wasn't time to bail on the payday he'd been promised, and in addition to that, he was becoming increasingly concerned that what he'd always envisioned as a relatively simple extortion scheme might balloon into something far more tragic. Turning his back on the money wasn't an option, and theoretically it'd be far easier to affect the situation to a manageable conclusion working it from the inside.

This bitch is certifiable.

"I'm not going anywhere. I'm in so long as you chill the fuck out too."

"Do I look like anything *but* the picture perfect representation of calm to you?"

Charlie knew there wasn't much point in saying otherwise, in fact, on the surface anyone looking from the outside in would probably say as much about Chris. To say he could smell the fury oozing through her veneer of complacency might have been a bit of an exaggeration, but only just a bit.

The rain hadn't showed any signs of slowing, but Chris put her hand out, palm up, from underneath the construction's canopy and said, "Detective, I think we are through here. Not that it's any of your business, but I'm thinking it's time for me to dawdle on home."

"I don't believe you."

"I don't really care, Charlie. We could stand out here all night and you'd still fail to completely realize that you've got no cards to play right now."

He felt his fist clench, nails digging into the fat of his palm, and thought hard about the consequences of delivering a quick crack to her face—just a solid pop to try and reestablish some footing in it all by sheer force. The indecision left him alone there as Chris turned and walked away.

Some ten feet down the sidewalk she nearly sung her words, "After all detective, that's why I bothered to drag you *specifically* into this caper in the first place."

He watched as she disappeared among the few dozen drenched souls braving their way home for the evening. The use of the word *caper* was a nice touch—a jab at his age Charlie figured. He'd have to hope she was truly heading home, following her made a lot of sense, but not nearly as much as trying to catch Lisa before she left the café.

I'll play this out. But there's no reason she needs to come along for the ride.

By the time Charlie got back to the restaurant, Lisa and Alicia were no longer seated at the table by the window. He couldn't be sure, but as he looked up the street he thought he might have spotted Alicia walking a full city block due east. If it was, it appeared as if she was alone.

He stood there assessing the facts: None of the buildings had bodegas on their bottom floors. If they had, he might have been able to find Lisa picking up a new pack of cigarettes for the journey back home—if she had even decided to walk. The rain was coming down stronger than it had been even a few minutes before, and though nights like that made for city streets filled with occupied and unavailable cabs, he speculated it wasn't out of the question she'd snagged one. If he'd been a driver, he'd have stopped.

Miserable night like tonight, only a fool wouldn't go out of his way to pick up an angel.

He had her cell number now. She'd been hesitant to share it with him during the intentional bump-in earlier that day, and had only spoken the numbers aloud once for him to try and memorize it. In an effort to do exactly that, he'd pretty much intentionally ignored the five minutes of conversation they'd had right after she'd recited the digits. As soon as he had made it back into his car, he'd entered the numerals into his own phone. Ringing her and texting her with a warning to remove herself from all things Elite Two Meet wasn't the first magical correspondence he'd envisioned for the two of them. Nor did he believe she'd bother to listen, and if he kept his business brains about him he'd have to admit to himself that Lisa might make a good pawn.

Alicia isn't going to want newbies flaking out on her because of this thing. The angle here just might be playing up the rape allegations with Lisa even more—get her spooked about joining this ass-backwards dating ring. I do that, pair it with two unhappy male clientele being unfairly accused—Alicia will have to clean this thing up, she's no dummy—she'd see the benefit in settling this debacle quick and clean. I gotta believe that.

Quick and clean, that was the new plan. The adrenaline from the last few hours' circus had helped camouflage the reality of a body operating on far too little sleep, but it was beginning to wane. Charlie decided against heading back north to retrieve his car in favor of tracking down the accused, Jeff Dufour and David Miller. As he wandered from the café in search of a cheaper caffeine fix from a bodega, he beat himself up over not having already gone to "interrogate" them.

Chasing a girl in the midst of all you got going on here Charlie? What are you thinking? One last hoorah I guess. When this is over, I'll still be short fifty. I can't worry about that—pull your shit together, go see the fellas, and at the very least you'll buy yourself some time with the two-fifty. Short of fucking over someone else in all this, that's the only play I've got left.

The salvation he was looking for laid behind the bright blinding lights of one too many neon window signs. Through the downpour the tiny market that doubled as a liquor store seemed like some future oasis. The rush of the passing traffic prevented him from crossing right away, and Johnson leaned against a street lamp to steady weakening knees as he waited for the easygoing blink of the little white walking man's permission.

There were few audible sounds other than rain's steady beat down on the city's pavement and the slick swoosh of the traffic's tires plowing their way through the street's growing puddles. In its own way, it was hypnotic—peaceful to the point of soothing Charlie back into his reality, where he was and what was around him at that very moment. He felt a familiar twinge and the hair on the back of his neck stood erect despite the deluge's best effort to keep it down. He was being followed, and Charlie knew it.

CHAPTER TWENTY-FOUR

A good plan violently executed now is better than a perfect plan executed next week.

—George S. Patton

Randy's hovel wasn't terribly far from the café, and any additional rain that evening had little chance of rendering anyone any more soaked than they already were. Chris had made it an only slightly difficult journey by walking the opposite direction for a while. Drenched, she stopped momentarily to make an attempt at assuring herself that the schmuck Johnson hadn't decided to tail her. If he wasn't already on his way to either Jeff or David's, there was little she could do about it, but she wasn't about to indulge him by allowing him to come along with her for the night.

He didn't appear to be anywhere in the vicinity, but who could be sure—he wasn't an idiot and she knew that, in fact, she'd banked on his expertise playing in her favor when she'd gone through the trouble of seeking him out in the first place. Contrary to what movies portray, getting in touch with a cop on the take isn't as easy as just phoning a few friends in the know. And even after their introduction had been made, plenty of awkward conversations revolving around insignificant small talk had to occur before she'd felt comfortable enough to lay out the real reason she'd bothered to dine with him a handful of times.

Drug dealers were a good place to start. In New York City those were easy—toss a stone into the East Village and you'd likely hit a handful. Any successful executive had her own connection, and while she was no stranger to partaking in party favors, her dealer had always been more of a business expense than personal. Clients from all over the country came to New York City—buyers, marketers, advertising agency and distribution specialists—all in the name of strategizing a healthier bottom line with her and the company. But few expected to leave having only spent their two to four days there in hours upon hours of presentations, sitting in quiet rooms and discussing their various charts and graphs. A great time wasn't a perk of the cosmetics business, it was the business.

Her dealer might have had the information and contact she needed, but for her the prudent path involved using him in order to meet another of his own kind. Then, just to be absolutely sure there were an advantageous number of implicating layers removed, Chris had sought out a fourth dealer from the mental Rolodex of the third who'd she had met via the second. Each new introduction had her traveling further and further away from her neighborhood, parting with large sums of cash over the course of multiple meetings, in exchange for bits of information that accompanied the drugs. Finally, one night she found herself maneuvering alone deep into the parts of Brooklyn that most white Manhattan dwellers don't ever see unless they've had their car towed and hauled to the large storage lot situated there.

Swoopes was the name she'd been given along with an address the previous dealer assured her housed a different kind of smack.

"Go see my boy Swoopes if you are looking for something far beyond that recreational shit you've been buying from me," he'd said.

Heroin would hardly prove useful as an indulgence for her clientele—few ever wanted to try anything harder than Ecstasy, but she was operating with the conviction to the belief that the information she needed could only be legitimate coming from the men who toil and thrive in the worst of human debauchery.

Getting in to the backroom of the bar hadn't been any harder than saying, "I'm here to see Swoopes." But the actual meeting of the man himself had proved much more difficult. On her first visit, she'd been given no other option but to buy and leave immediately. Chris had mentally prepared herself to have to try the product right then and there, but no one seemed to care about that apparently fictional protocol. All attempts to meet with Swoopes himself were met with a curt refusal.

"Take your shit and go."

And so that first time, she did exactly that.

A second and third trip to the backroom of The White Elephant, hurriedly made over the next ten days directly after the first, had convinced the man she'd yet to meet that Chris was either dealing his supply herself or was working narcotics undercover, possibly DEA. The cronies there had not bothered letting her know of the opinions forming about who she might be, and so the fourth and final time she visited, she unknowingly obliged when they told her they needed her to head further back, toward another door at the very rear of the joint.

"Hey-hey, good to see you. We movin' business to the way, way back now," one of the usual faces said as he motioned towards what Chris believed to be the building's alley exit. "Can't be too safe. Watch your head on the way through though—not sure why, but that door musta been built by some midget muthafuckers."

She'd sensed that the ask wasn't negotiable, and then prepared herself to deal with the worst possible scenario waiting for her on the other side. Just like the previous visits, she'd come armed with a substantial amount of cash. As she crossed the threshold into what was indeed the alley behind the building, she felt confident that the sum would be enough to buy her way out of whatever sequence of events awaited.

The alley was illuminated by a high noon sun, with glints popping off the various metal alley accouterments, it was bright and an adjustment for the eyes. The door shut firmly behind Chris as she made her best effort into the glare to survey for any immediate danger. No one had bothered to follow her out, and as best as she could tell there wasn't anything human waiting among the thick scent of a couple day's not-yet-serviced garbage. For a brief moment she felt insulted, the dizzying nausea of embarrassment began to form while she contemplated whether or not this was simply their way of having a laugh at her expense. It was short lived.

A black, eighties Monte Carlo with purple trim silently made its debut around the north corner. Running south through the alley, away from the approaching vehicle, was an option, but Chris decided against it. Instead, she stood firm and focused her line of sight towards the vehicle, trying to peer into the interior through an illegally dark windshield tint. She held the stare as the car steadily crawled closer.

Leonard Swoopes was seated comfortably in the passenger seat. His driver, Bones, kept a steady eye on the skinny blonde who didn't seem much, certain he'd be accelerating shortly to prevent her from trying to scramble the opposite direction.

"Whoizdis crazy bitch?" Swoopes said aloud with no expectations of an answer.

Despite the audible hum of another vehicle that had joined them from the south end behind her, Chris kept her composure. She resisted the urge to turn and assess this new addition to the party, and stood motionless with her eyes only on the Monte Carlo.

"Fat Man, you gonna grab her and ask her to join you— politely muthafucka," Swoopes rumbled into his cell.

Both cars came to a stop about five feet from Chris, one in front and the other from the rear. Neither bothered to kill their engines. The unsettling click of a door opening behind her was enough to break her concentration on the sinewy shadow she could now make out seated in the front of the Monte Carlo. Survival impulse demanded an override of any further physical attempts at playing the part of cool customer, and she shifted her vision to the enormous blob of a man that had exited the front passenger side of the black Land Rover to her left.

In between shallow wheezing, Fat Man said, "Skinny, Mr. Swoopes would appreciate it if you'd join us in the back of this ride for a how-dee-doo. Should I escort you, or you wanna join us proper?"

Chris' shoulders dropped as the tension left her neck. She hadn't been shot to death, and while things weren't exactly what she'd call peachy, the request had felt like a small victory. Without a word she approached the truck, and moved toward the rear passenger door that Fat Man had so courteously opened.

There was no one else in the back of the car, and the driver never bothered to turn around as she climbed aboard. She swung her feet into the vehicle as Fat Man closed the door gently behind her.

"Watch them dawgs."

The interior reeked. A bizarre combination of marijuana with just a hint of the scent of new car able to fight and find its way through the smoky haze, just present enough to semi-register with the olfactory lobe of any passenger that wasn't partaking themselves.

The door to her left opened and a slender dark man, skinny but made of muscle, sat himself next to her. His oversized shades and knit cap hid any indication of age. Fat Man closed the door behind the new passenger, who then turned to address Chris.

"I appreciates the cooperation, chee-ka," Swoopes said aloud, adding just a hint of bourbon to the mix of odors mingling about the car as Fat Man's anxiety sweat joined them from upfront. "Let's hit the road Dee. I'm sure the lady and we ain't all got da time for much else."

The Monte Carlo in front of them took its time executing an awkward three-point turn in order to lead the way out of the alley. The driver, Dee, was quick to flip the turn signal on to let all the rodents know they'd be making a left upon exiting. The social conformity of that action struck Chris as just a little amusing, and she felt a smirk form before she could do anything to self-correct it.

"Somethin' funny chee-ka?" Swoopes asked as they turned onto the thoroughfare.

There wasn't anything amusing about the situation, but Chris couldn't contain the smirk and it grew to a smile. There was an odd feeling occurring, along the lines of an out-of-body experience, the predicament she found herself living through had a predictable quality and the entirety of the situation moved in slow-motion. An uncontrollable laughter was pressing up against her throat, desperate to be unleashed. Stifling it in the name of self-preservation, she managed to respond by clenching her lips together while shaking her head in the negative toward him.

Swoopes reached for an ebony box of Djarum Black clove cigarettes sitting on the console between the driver and front passenger seats. Had he not asked Fat Man a question directly after lighting it up, Chris was certain she'd have lost containment on what they'd likely have deemed an inappropriate display of disrespect.

"Fat Man, doz fools assure you dis bitch ain't packing nor wearin' a wire?"

Fat Man did his best to turn the tiny head attached to his body by umpteen rolls of fat in the direction of the question, and within the repetitive wheezing he'd been emitting since they'd met responded with a weakly affirmative, "That's what they say, Boss."

Dee had snaked through a few blocks, zigzagging his way in a general direction that Chris felt was moving them farther and farther away from any convenient mode for her to use for the trip back home. When she saw the Belt Parkway appear before them, and sensed that the driver was seeking out an entrance onto the damn thing, she decided that waiting for Swoopes to get down to business wasn't in her best interest. Chris had little concern for her safety, but she was incredibly put off by the potential inconvenience of whatever destination they'd decided was necessary to start an actual discussion.

"Is there some particular protocol I need to be aware of here? Or can we just start discussing the reason I've bothered trekking out here to see you. This is the fourth time I might add."

Swoopes coughed on his own laughter. "Shit lady, I wish you would. Ain't no effin' pro-toe-kall."

"Bitch got balls, you must admit," Fat Man contributed from upfront.

Dee was still headed towards the Belt Parkway's next entrance, and though she'd made peace with the idea that she'd likely not make it back into the city in time to keep her dinner reservation, Chris threw out a question with no hope for an appealing answer.

"Any chance we can have the conversation somewhere that isn't going to take me fucking hours to get home?"

"Chee-ka, I like what you have to say and I'll have Dee here drive yo petite little ass any ol' place you like," Swoopes responded. "Quit wastin' my time, and I'll quit wastin' yours."

"Fine then. I'm not here for more drugs."

"No shit."

"I figure a man like you, who deals in what you deal in, must know a few people."

"I got friends if that's what you mean."

"Right. Well, I'm looking for some help."

"We ain't the fuckin' A-Team chee-kah."

Dee and Fat Man were substantially moved by the quip, and Chris decided to wait out their laughter.

When they'd dropped the level on the cacophony, she continued. "Simplest way I can put it—"

Swoopes interrupted, "Please, break it down like we third graders."

Chris fought the urge to roll eyes and took a quick, deep breath before repeating her last six words in order to finish.

"Simplest way I can put it is I'm looking for a bad cop. A real cop—a member of the NYPD who maybe you know, or someone you know knows, that can help me with a situation."

"I'm a pretty adroit problem solva, why not lay it on me?" Swoopes upped.

"I've got an acquaintance who needs a little motivation, and while I'm sure you and yours are excellent at all kinds of things, I really need a cop. Not someone pretending to be one—that won't work. I need the real thing."

The Land Rover was cruising at a quick clip up the Belt Parkway now, past JFK and deep into some part of the borough Chris was loathe to explore.

Swoopes baited, "The *real* thing, huh?"

"I'm not dealing with a moron, and I'm not looking to achieve a solution through brute force. The situation requires a dirty cop—for lack of a better way to say it—and if you know one, a damn good bad one, I promise I'll make it worth your time."

"Ohhhhh," Swoopes breathed out. "So there is sumthin' in this for me?"

"There certainly can be, yes."

"Like I said before, I got friends. But you best be hittin' me with some specifics though chee-kah. This ain't no pro-bono operation and if I don't like what you've got to say, well, we all just as likely to end this ugly as we is tie it up pretty."

"Quarter of a million specific enough for you?"

"That's exactly the type of detail you might want to start with the next time you go slummin' wit us," Swoopes said with a wink. "Dee, turn this bitch around—ain't no point no more."

Dee didn't answer with any spoken words, but he had been quick to flip on that turn signal again in order to indicate his intentions to pop off the Belt Parkway almost immediately in order to head back to The White Elephant. On their way, Chris answered a few pointed questions from Swoopes. By the time they'd returned to the very backdoor in the alley they'd left a half-hour before, she had a name: Detective Charlie Johnson.

"I'll put *him* in touch with you, chee-kah."

"When?" Chris asked.

"When it happens is when," Swoopes said as Fat Man opened her door.

Chris swung her legs out the door to exit, ignoring Fat Man's extended mitt and assistance and said, "I'm in a bit of a hurry to get this going is all."

Before her feet could hit the ground, Swoopes grabbed a handful of her hair and violently yanked her from behind and onto her back, facing up at his own mug now hovering above her. Fat Man grabbed her by the feet just to cement the gesture's impact, and Swoopes was quick to snag her free hand before it could successfully land a crack to his face.

"Bitch, you need da remember three things right now: One, just forty minutes ago you wuz due to have a date with my boys before I gutted you and tossed yo skinny ass in a ditch. Two, I don't *do* favors and I don't give a fuck if this shit you've cooked up works or doesn't—the introduction alone means I get paid. The second you and Johnson connect is the second I ring the register. Let dat sink in chee-kah."

Fat Man released his hold on Chris and Swoopes let go. Chris calmly did her best to exit the vehicle gracefully despite the rush of adrenaline the warning had given her. This time she accepted Fat Man's hand, and he helped her stand up outside before shutting the car's door behind her. Chris slowly spun back around to confront Swoopes through the open window.

"Fair enough. What was that third thing?"

Swoopes smiled, a big toothy grin that he hoped she'd read as a subtle appreciation for her own brand of bravado.

He dropped the smile, and stared through her from above his shades.

"Three, if you thinkin' that two don't sound fair, just remember number one," he concluded before telling Dee he was ready to head out.

Chris had managed to cover quite a bit of ground between the café and Randy's while lost in the mental reconstruction of how she'd ended up working with Johnson in the first place. That final warning, Swoopes' number three, and the way he'd tried so hard to vocalize it like he'd meant *business* was meandering about her brain. To Chris it was as tragically comical right then as it had been mere moments after he, Fat Man and Dee had left her to find her own way back home from East New York. The humor she found within Swoopes' threat was bolstered by Johnson's own assurance after they'd met that he'd personally never known Swoopes to kill anyone that hadn't actually crossed him, and that'd he known him for a long, long time.

"He has his own code," Charlie had said. "Fuck him over, become a loose end, sure, you're as good as dead. But he's not in the business of killing people for sport."

She allowed for a momentary relishing in the act of scheming some future maneuver that'd leave her off the hook and Swoopes and his friends rotting at Rikers.

Amid the literal walk down memory lane, she'd managed to make two phone calls. The first was to Randy. She'd kept it incredibly brief despite his efforts to lengthen a conversation that hadn't needed to go beyond, "I'm on my way over."

He hadn't sounded particularly enthusiastic about her impending arrival. Without going into much detail he'd assured her that Julie was enjoying herself and all was proceeding according to plan.

Chris wasn't of the opinion that his definition of success was even remotely close to hers, and after she'd hung up with him, dialed her go-to dealer. She placed a relatively benign order—a handful of various benzodiazepines and a teener for herself—and asked that it be delivered to Randy's address. The prescription Xanax and Valium were going to be necessary to ensure their predicament with Julie remained an easier, manageable situation. Cocaine wasn't really her thing, but the last few days hadn't passed with a lot of quality sleep and Chris didn't foresee a good deal more coming anytime soon.

Unable to shake the image of the woman that had been sitting across from Alicia, she'd committed to a first order of business upon her arrival to Randy's place. Digging up a bio on the mystery brunette wouldn't be difficult. Accessing Elite Two Meet's intranet and taking a quick trip through the New Applicants Folder would be the quickest way to gather the information Chris required, so long as Randy had a computer— or the Internet for that matter. While Chris had spent a few odd evening hours indulging him there from time to time, she'd never inhabited the place long enough to consciously or subconsciously inventory his worldly possessions, or lack thereof.

When she'd spoken to him earlier, she had instructed Randy to cover the cost of the narcotics if she didn't arrive by the time her dealer's associate showed. She came upon his street; it was glistening. The lamps dotting the block every twenty-or-so-feet were illuminating the storm's handy work. It was still relatively quiet out given the early evening hour, few pedestrians had dared to give it a go outside yet, and she easily spotted Randy outside of his building paying for the drugs just like she'd asked. She felt a momentary surge of warmth from within despite having arrived there a shivering and drenched heap of flesh and cloth.

She paused, still some distance from the transaction, and decided it'd be best to allow Randy to conclude it without any hindrance. The sudden halt on her momentum exposed the reality of her physical wellbeing, and for the first time since the weekend her brain registered all of her body's various stings, swellings, and the throb of muscles that were in desperate need of legitimate rest. Silently, she mentally applauded her decision to have included the blow in her order.

It's going to be a long night, guess I'll sleep when I'm dead.

CHAPTER TWENTY-FIVE

Everyone thinks of changing the world, but no one thinks of changing himself.

—Leo Tolstoy

Alicia had opted for the familiar. Almost immediately after what she'd deemed "a best effort" with Lisa, she decided to return to the office to indulge in the habitual Tuesday night task of re-reviewing all of the extensive details for the following evening's event.

Upon her return, she was pleased but not surprised to find Bean still there. Over the previous two years, she'd kept Bean and the others there deep into the wee hours of any evening prior to an event. On this night, thinking back she could only recall a handful of instances where those additional evening hours had really been at all necessary.

Resisting the urge to mimic some self-inflicted protocol, and keep Bean at the office any later, if only as a living, breathing distraction, Alicia said, "Bean. You and I both know that there's nothing left to review. Tomorrow night's mixer is just another rehash of the several prior to it. I'm certain it'll be effortless."

Bean heard the words, but hadn't stopped pinning each individual page of the planning deck to the wall outside of

Alicia's office. It was the same collection of information she'd always prepared for the team to stand in front of and endlessly comb over, rearrange, debate and then repeat again. Facts and details outlined, all apparently deserving of their own page: the guest list, each member's mini-biography, each member's standing with Elite Two Meet as determined by their previous connection successes, seating arrangements, the order of introductions, the best potential matches, the activities, the evening's song selections, and the rationale behind each of the menu's carefully selected courses and beverage options.

"Bean," Alicia repeated as she stared at the overabundance of information. "Go home."

Bean snapped to, turned towards Alicia, rubbed her eyes with the palms of her hands, and meekly grilled her about the validity of the directive.

"Is this some sort of test Alicia?"

"Don't be stupid. I mean it. Go home," Alicia said as she removed herself from any potential additional exchange between them by entering her office and closing the glass door behind herself.

Alicia did her best to not engage in any further eye contact with Bean through the glass partitions. If Bean didn't leave soon, she suspected it wouldn't be long before she changed her mind about having dismissed her, and reversed the course of that polite action by insisting she stay put out of some unexpected and sudden fear of being all alone. She sat behind her desk, and played the part of a busy person, shuffling through the duplicate deck of the exact same papers Bean had hung outside her office until she was certain that her loyal employee had left the building.

When the elevator announced its departure to the ground

floor with the muffled whump of its doors and the hissing whirr
of a motor most likely in need of an inspection, the empty
feeling of solitude that had started as a nag just mere minutes
after she'd left the café swarmed over Alicia's whole being.

In a futile attempt to shove the emotion back into some dark
recess of her body and brain, she opened her laptop with the
intent of scribing work related responses to that day's flagged
emails. She found the folder compiled habitually by a member of
her staff, though she'd long since forgotten exactly whom she'd
put in charge of it. There was no shortage of correspondence
from the various vendors eager to be a part of the profitable
machine she commanded. Their messages were carefully crafted
with the express intent to woo her into believing their bar,
restaurant, event space or the like would be a mutually beneficial
partnership, if not one that'd supposedly favor Alicia in the long
run for a "reasonable" booking fee. Woven in between those
solicitations she could always find a handful from larger
organizations wishing to make her acquaintance immediately to
discuss any possible desire to fold Elite Two Meet into their
versions of similar singles connection services—grand schemes
that promised to make her wealthy and usually included some
token title within the organization that hoped to swallow her own
whole. Tucked throughout the pageant of well-dressed beggars
and wannabe associations, Alicia could typically find one or two
from media outlets. She garnered the most pleasure from reading
these invitations from the editors, reporters, broadcasters and
producers who were all hoping to feature her and Elite Two
Meet in some capacity. Full blown interviews, minor blurbs,
pictorials showcasing the latest event, or opportunities to dress
the part for a national broadcast—these attempts to gain
audience eyeballs on the coattails of her successes masqueraded

themselves as tiny personal victories, a public record of all her efforts that would long outlive the memory of the the woman herself, some distant date in the future.

If any of the usual requests, invitations, and potential partnership plans were there that evening, Alicia's brain had done a poor job of acknowledging they existed even as her eyes combed over them. She read each, but read none. Hundreds and hundreds of words strung together, shouting as loud as they could for her to respond, all of which were met with the silence of a blinking cursor.

I am living a highly lucrative lie.

When conscious thought resurfaced, these were the words Alicia saw staring back at her from the digital box created to help her craft a status she could unleash upon each and every one of her social networks all at once. She'd typed it almost unwittingly, and read it repetitively to herself while her pinky finger hung precariously over the return key of her laptop.

I am living a highly lucrative lie.

The sadness that had enveloped her for the past two hours was met with a quick sting of adrenaline—just the slightest indication of hope, a small sliver of light at the end of the darkest of self-constructed tunnels hung in the balance of an anticipation born from the possibility of simply letting her tiniest finger drop and descend deep upon that little square button labeled ENTER.

She sat with the status some more, and then added a semi-colon followed by a close parenthesis. A winky-emoticon meant to add some insincere levity to the previous seven words. She reached up to delete the new addition, and then typed it back a second time before immediately removing it again.

Enough time had passed that she'd managed to construct every conceivable outcome of putting her declaration out into the world. She wasn't delusional about the impact her revelation might have, given the delivery method. She didn't expect that it'd rattle much—it wouldn't be the undoing of her or the company, it wouldn't instigate any significant change, and its fate most likely would come in the form of a comments section littered with sardonic quips. "Aren't we all? LOL." "Preaching to the choir, Sister!"

Still, she allowed herself to momentarily believe that it'd at least be an admission she'd have to face having made the following day. If nothing else, it might serve as a morning reminder that for a brief moment on the evening before, she had decided to pursue a new path towards a different life—a chance to exist in the world as who she truly was instead of the carefully caricatured persona she'd always believed she needed to be.

I am living a highly lucrative lie.

She contemplated hitting ENTER, letting it out into the world just long enough to gauge the interest level it might generate. There was some comfort in knowing that it could be extracted from the digital memory of a sleepless world almost as quickly as she'd unveiled it. Likely no one was sitting around waiting to snap a picture of the very next Tweet from the Chief Executive Officer of what, in the grand scheme of things, actually amounted to a small-potatoes singles' dating service.

The idea of *not* hitting the ENTER button—not forcing the message out into the ether—almost instantaneously weakened the small but growing excitement within her.

Deleting it and keeping it a private notion will absolutely feel like a monumental defeat. So just hit send and be done with it you imbecile. You are over-thinking the hell out of this.

She hit ENTER and watched as the little digital wheel spun just long enough to suggest it was taking her information public.

It appeared on her wall and within thirty seconds the post had numerous fans in the way of multiple thumbs up. Alicia felt ashamed for sticking around long enough to see how her small part of the world's attention might respond.

When the first comment appeared, Alicia couldn't help but laugh as tears formed beneath her increasingly heavy and swollen eyelids—she'd been just about right.

That's why God invented martinis! ;)

WEDNESDAY
AUGUST
SEVENTH

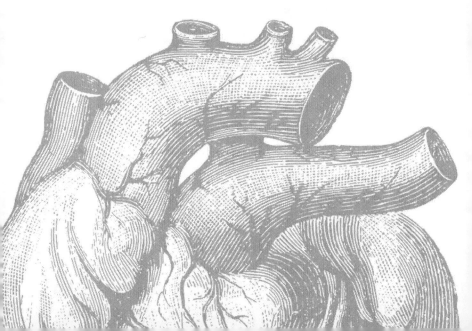

CHAPTER TWENTY-SIX

Don't let me die with that silly look in my eyes.

—Mike Patton

Randy sat on a familiar stool at his go-to coffee shop. It was his regular morning-hang because it doubled as a bar by the afternoon, and the booze there was always on the ready, no matter the time. On this drizzly Wednesday, hours before the rat race would start buzzing outside the bar's door, he was there a touch earlier than was the usual. The alcoholic's beanery was empty, and he sat alone and feeling every bit his given name, Randolph, that he had shed on his eighteenth birthday long ago—the very moment he had decided his hometown of Reading, Pennsylvania no longer held a decent future for him. That was eight years ago, but this morning that hypothesis about his quiet origins—the kind made daily by teens born between the coasts—felt as fresh as if the decision to move to New York City had happened in the past week.

This wasn't his routine morning-after-morning. Ten or ten-thirty had always been what he had deemed an acceptable time to start drinking on any average day; even if he hadn't seated himself in his usual spot at seven-forty-five that morning, he was pretty confident that this day and all the others that followed for the rest of what remained of his life, wouldn't be classifiable as normal ever again.

Hunched over the bar, his meaty forearms already working overtime to keep his suddenly exhausted upper body balanced, he could still feel the sting of the wounds he'd acquired in the waning hours of the early morning darkness before. Two shots of Jameson and the three Bud chasers had worked their special magic on the gash Chris had created above his left eye, but those same five drinks hadn't quite gotten around to completely dulling the pain pulsating from underneath the blood soaked dishrag he had wrapped around his right first. The barista-bartender, Jimmy, had provided the make-shift bandage without so much as a nod suggesting a question to the wound's origin.

Fear—a legitimate fear for his life, like none he'd encountered in his previous twenty-six years of living—coursed through his body. As he motioned for another round to Jimmy, he caught a glimpse of himself in the mirrors just inches beyond the fantastically colored bottles displayed so neatly on the multiple tiers of the bar. The gaping wound on his forehead appeared much larger and much deeper than the frequent blind inspections made with his fingers had indicated while stumbling around other neighborhoods looking for another watering hole to finally open. None did—at least not soon enough for him. Despite his own best advice to leave town, get away from the crime scene, he found himself drinking not nearly far enough removed from where he'd bared witness to the desecration of a human body. He sat quivering in the company of the memory: an indescribable punishment that even modern day horror films hadn't prepared him for.

"What did I do?" she had asked after the primary blow to the back of her skull, in a voice that had reverted back to a child's pentameter and tone. And now, her final four words—at least the final four Randy could actually understand—were on automatic repeat inside his head, along with the image of her outstretched arm, her trembling hand, and her eyes—still filled with life, but hidden behind a wall of tears on the verge of bursting.

The night's plan hadn't unfolded the way Chris had suggested it would. Nothing she had said to him in the final moments before fleeing the scene—her almost upbeat assurances that the apartment would eventually be flawlessly devoid of evidence—had left him feeling confident they'd not eventually get caught. More accurately, he'd left believing she'd ensure he'd take the blame if she didn't first kill him too.

When Chris had noticed his unsteady hands, she'd said, "Just go home, Randy. I'll fucking handle the rest of it."

So he left, and now naturally wondered if *he* was the "rest of it" she planned on handling.

Played. Drifting from present to past the way a mind soaked in booze permits, *played* was the word Randolph fixated upon.

Four months ago, a late night introduction to Chris had temporarily changed his life dramatically for the better—no more scrapping for his piece of the dream, no more *only* believing he was just around the corner from the type of break that would lead to big and wonderful things. Chris was the ticket to it all. She'd made no concrete promises of delivering the objects of his ambitions, but had renewed his confidence by filling his head with what had seemed like genuine enthusiasm for his efforts. She said she knew people. Randolph knew people too, but not the type of people he knew that she knew—and it was those upper-echelon types that made or broke star-struck hacks like him every day.

It now seemed certain, that those big and wonderful things

would most likely be big fucked-up things. The nature of their first meeting should have planted a seed of concern to begin with, should have provided some insight into his current predicament at the very least.

"I'm actually a really *nice* girl," Randy sarcastically mimicked to himself in the mirror before drowning the notion with the remaining whiskey in front of him. "Bullshit."

Those were the first six words Chris had spoken just moments after he'd finished ejaculating as deep as possible into her throat. Prior to that declaration, they'd only conversed online, using the hidden identity email addresses provided to clients of the website he'd used to post a drunken solicitation he never even remotely believed would receive an answer.

Looking for young woman to help me fulfill choking on cock fantasy. Small dick, so some acting required. LOL. Hit me up.

The request had sat unanswered on his Backdoor.com profile page for a very long time. He'd forgotten that he'd ever posted it in the first place. And then, one afternoon, Chris reached out.

"No one here to blame, but *you*, Randolph," he said half aloud and half internally, before his mind returned to the current predicament.

In between the horrifying and increasingly blurred mental recreations of all that had transpired in such a short period of time, he had just enough working brain cells to formulate the words, "I'm a loose end now. I'm next." And when what his head was telling him finally sunk in, he doubled down on his order, demanding that Jimmy hook him up even as he'd just placed a fresh round before him moments before. True to form, Jimmy stayed mum. New York City bartenders, even the ones doubling as baristas in the morning, don't ask a lot of questions.

An older gentleman entered the café and without giving

much thought to the bloodied hulk slumped next to him, bellied up to the bar and ordered an iced coffee to go. Randy fixed his attention on the well-dressed stranger, as best as his inebriation would permit, and held it there in hopes that maybe this morning commuter might make some remark about his current state of being. But despite meeting Randy's stare with his own, the stranger said nothing. Before he turned back to pay Jimmy for his iced coffee, Randy could swear the guy was reading his mind, and simultaneously communicating a deep understanding of the situation before him. The stranger delivered a sincere sounding "Have a great day" directly to Jimmy, and to Jimmy only, then practically sauntered out of the bar—at least as far as Randy was concerned.

Habit took over, and Randy stood up from his barstool, threw back the remainder of a shot, and chased that with the nearly full pint glass of Budweiser before him. Impulse control wasn't his forte, and it seemed to him that the stranger had it coming—it didn't matter why he had it coming. The combination of remaining ego and liquid courage trying so desperately to camouflage the underlying fear, married to the insulting casually dismissive stare of that stranger, had boosted Randy's adrenaline just enough for him to find his footing and beeline for the door in order to catch up to the suit, punish him for his courtesy if nothing else.

Jimmy said nothing. And Jimmy did nothing. As far as he was concerned this was *typical*. A word he'd only recently picked up during his English as a Second Language classes. In his mind, this was just that: the type of thing that happened when the man named Randy came to the bar, albeit a touch earlier than had been the norm in the previous months they'd spent together.

Randy made it as far as it took to grab the door, but let it go immediately, and like a puppy sure of an impending beating, cowered back to his seat at the bar. He asked Jimmy for another, and Jimmy turned around to do the job he held.

"He won't be needing that round, Jimmy," Chris' voice echoed with an authority amplified by the cavernous and empty dwelling around them.

She closed the door behind her, effectively removing what little natural light the city's skyscrapers hadn't prevented from following her inside. "Randy, you piece of shit. Let's go home. This isn't going to help anything."

Jimmy stood back and under his breath practiced the new word at a just barely audible level, "This is typical."

CHAPTER TWENTY-SEVEN

True, I am in love with suffering, but I do not know if I deserve the honor.

—Saint Ignatius

Had there been anyone else perusing the isles of the New Canaan, Connecticut Food Emporium, they'd have likely assumed that Linda Denton was hosting a teen's slumber party that coming weekend. Her grocery cart was practically bursting with colorful packaging, the kind specifically designed to communicate, even from afar, the fun one can have eating and drinking chemically rich concoctions. Popsicles, squeezable liquids, sugary sodas, easily-nuked finger foods, oversized bags of chips next to pre-made mini-vats of various "authentic" dips, riding along with cookies and other hermetically sealed confectionary delights like a proud parade of America's most nourishing innovations.

Eight AM treks to the grocery store were certainly not her norm, and Linda marveled at the ease and efficiency of it all when shopping at that early morning hour. She wasn't the only body there, but the few others she'd seen while darting about the two-dozen aisles wore the bright blue vests that branded them worker bees. Twenty-five minutes had barely passed and there was sparse room available in her cart for much else. As she rounded the final aisle cap on her way back towards the front of the store, she could hardly contain the excitement that'd been building since reading Lisa's email just before sunup. If digital communications were to be believed, her baby-girl was finally coming home.

Though Lisa hadn't responded to either of the texts Linda had sent mere moments after absorbing the wonderful news, she'd wasted no time in fantasizing about what her daughter's arrival and stay could be like. The first order of business, after forcing two cups of black coffee and a piece of Melba toast down her throat, was ensuring their home was stocked with the foods Linda still thought might be Lisa's favorites. She hadn't given herself time to consider whether the grown woman coming home still had the same cravings as the knobby-kneed teen that'd left with no return some ten years prior.

As Linda looked up from the cart's contents to the aisle ahead, she found herself among the market's shelves loaded with dozens upon dozens of wines, liquors, and spirits. It'd been an aisle she'd dutifully avoided ever since Lisa copped to being in rehab. Linda's action of abstinence was a decision made as a silent tribute to her daughter—a nod to Lisa's plight that Linda had made even as she was certain she had no substance abuse issues of her own. The sight of it gave her pause, and she stopped to reevaluate the myriad of packaged goods she'd selected with such haste, lying in the cart attached to her by the firming grip of her hands.

She reached for her phone with the intention of reaching out to Lisa in order to shed some light on what types of foods she might actually want to eat during her upcoming stay. The previous pesterings for the exact details of Lisa's arrival later that evening had remained unanswered thus far. Nonetheless,

Linda penned another quickie while speculating that her daughter was likely still asleep. She hit send after momentarily debating whether or not this additional text would brand her as "too pushy."

Let me know what you'd like to snack on while you are here sweetie.

Though that internal debate's result had green-lit the text for sending, Linda felt certain she'd made the wrong decision the instant her phone indicated that it'd been delivered. The majority of the optimism that had buoyed her all morning vanished almost instantly, and she spun the cart around to travel back the direction from which she'd arrived. The speed she'd possessed in obtaining the comfort foods was replaced by a slow stroll as she sought out the now empty nooks and crannies left where she'd grabbed each and every item.

When an employee caught wind of her task, he'd offered to take the cart from her and replace all the items himself.

"Are you alright ma'am? If you forgot your purse, I'm sure we could work something out as to not inconvenience you."

Linda assured him that she'd be fine to do it on her own and offered no explanation. The young man was insistent, but Linda politely refused.

"I appreciate your concern, but if it's not too much trouble, I'd like to handle it myself."

Confused, the clerk replied, "There's no law against it, if that's what you mean."

She attempted a grin, and left him unnerved by the smile's betrayal—a deep sadness ruminating behind her eyes.

You stubborn old broad, is it any wonder Lisa's so obstinate?

The slower stride Linda resorted to in making it halfway

back through the store had fostered far too much time for dwelling on the past. And the replacement of each and every item unlocked a painful memory, even if the snack itself had at one time been integral to happier occasions. Countless attempts at refocusing on what might be a positive new beginning failed in the face of all the blame Linda had put on herself. The mom she'd tried to be clearly wasn't the mom Lisa had needed her to be, and thousands upon thousands of dollars blown on psychiatric fees hadn't swayed her opinion on that.

She decided that if her baby-girl were still to come home, she'd have to be vigilant in her attempts to give Lisa the space she needed—even if all Linda wanted to do was smother her with a mother's love.

Admiration. It was a word Linda had tried using with Lisa to no successful end. But, its failure to resonate with her daughter didn't make it any less true. Even if Linda couldn't always completely understand Lisa's all-out shunning of the family and its material wealth, she'd respected her daughter's desire to carve out her own future–untethered from a bloodline's inferred expectations that often accompany any significant hand-out.

Shivering among the frozen goods that shone brightly from behind their glass prison walls, Linda reached for her phone yet again, this time to reread Lisa's email—the culprit that had sent her scurrying about town that morning like a chicken with its head cut off.

Dad and Linda,

I've given it a lot of thought, and without getting into the nitty or gritty about it, I need a break from this city. If it's cool with you guys, I'd like to come home for the weekend. Tomorrow, in fact. If either of you can pick me up from the station I'd greatly appreciate it. I'll write in the morning

when I decide what train I'm taking. Please don't go out of your way though. I can figure out how to let myself in if you guys aren't going to be around. Talk to you tomorrow.
Sincerely, Lisa

Linda tapped out of email and back to her phone's texting screen, hopeful that her wandering mind had caused her to miss the subtle vibration that would have alerted her to some kind of response from Lisa—good or disappointing, either would have been welcome.

"Some of what that shrink is preaching is sinking in," Linda remarked aloud, cognizant of the fact that in years past the combination of Lisa's email and disregard for pertinent details, coupled with no immediate responses to her search for those details, would have left her bitterly enraged—the ugliest version of herself, and the mother she'd been far too often in the early going after Lisa had all but bailed completely on anything related to family.

The store's activity was picking up. Linda was no longer the lone shopper, though she had to smile at the idea of being its only reverse-shopper.

"It's in God's hands," she said as she resumed forward momentum, pushing the cart and removing herself from the chill of the frozen goods' aisle. "I've got to believe she's on her way, and I've got to lose any expectations I have about what her return here might mean for any of us."

She believed in what she'd said to coax her way onward, and yet wasn't terribly surprised when two aisles later she deviated from the plan by penning a text to Devon. To her knowledge, he was a good friend. She only had his number because some time ago he'd taken it upon himself to ring Linda to let her know that Lisa had entered rehab. In the three months prior to his call, Lisa had dropped off their radar completely. Before then, they'd only even known she was alive because of the occasional calls she made from city payphones to their home phone, but only if they'd let the answering machine pick-up. Anytime either of them attempted to answer they were met with a heavy click. But if they were agreeable to letting the machine get it, Lisa would leave a short message assuring them she was "alive and just fine."

Lisa's family was beyond grateful that Devon had decided to phone, though he'd been rigidly adamant about two things: One, under no circumstances was any member of the family to contact the rehab or attempt to visit Lisa while she was there. Two, he suggested that Linda and Stephen never tell Lisa that he'd reached out to them. To date, Linda had kept her possession of Devon's number a covert affair.

While she was certain she was simply suffering from a typical mother's bout of need-to-know panic, she couldn't help but wonder if the chill she was still carrying had more to do with something tragic than having just been surrounded by enough gallons of ice-cream to feed a small country. She hit send and agreed with herself that this would be the first and last time she'd ever use Devon's number to pry.

Hello Devon, it's Mrs. Denton. Sorry to disturb you, but do you know if Lisa is already on her way home?

CHAPTER TWENTY-EIGHT

The world is a dangerous place to live; not because of the people who are evil, but because of the people who don't do anything about it.

—Albert Einstein

"Lisa, *you* have to be as fabulous as you are—do it for us, the plain-as-Jane people. For fuck's sake, be happy God granted you the assets to *be* big time. Then ride that wave—and the money—into whatever lifestyle you deem normal when your physical gifts don't work anymore. It's not rocket science. Now then, I have to pee."

These were the last words Devon had said to Lisa before his cowardice permitted two strangers, one female and one male, to beat her beyond recognition, into some delirious state of submission, and then finally to death. If the violent destruction of her physical being hadn't been enough, perhaps it had been what he lived through shortly thereafter that found him high, uncontrollably shivering, and wandering aimlessly in search of a subway station somewhere in the Bronx early Wednesday morning.

"Now then, I have to pee," and some of the rest of his final soapboxing to Lisa were replaying on a permanent loop over the vivid visual memories from the night before. It hadn't been his life that had been extinguished, and while some of what had occurred seemed to play out with an unbelievable and ferocious momentum, most of what he'd witnessed was recapitulating itself in his head in an unbearable slow-motion haze.

"Why am I still alive?" he wondered aloud, audibly enough for some early commuters to dismiss him as just another addict trying to find its way home.

"Why am I still alive?" he shouted.

No one gave any indication that they had an answer, or that they cared.

Wednesday mornings in nearly any part of New York City— any weekday morning for that matter—aren't without their share of stumbling shouters with bloodshot eyes.

"Fuck all of you!" he screamed at everyone, and no one. "Fuck every last one of you!"

Before he turned north, he stopped to search his pants pockets for a cigarette. His blood stained fingers trembled along the hem of the back pocket of his designer jeans, fumbling around deep into the left rear pocket, before performing the same task in the right. He leaned against the wall to steady himself, pulling at his coat's lapel in order to investigate the interior pocket just at his chest. Success.

He held up the pack of American Spirit Blue smokes, the smudged letters L and D were still legible on Lisa's pack. She occasionally took to marking her packs when she had been on set. He grinned, but it was short-lived.

Devon managed to use his teeth to draw a single cigarette from the box when using his fingers proved too difficult. Next, he began patting against the outside of all his clothing's pockets in search of the lighter he was certain that he still had. No luck, at least as far as he could tell through the thick denim and tweed he adorned.

For no particular reason, it was only then that he realized he'd lost one boot.

A young woman in a terrible rush witnessed the lighter-finding-failure and stopped just long enough to ignite it for him and say, "Not your best day, friend."

Before he could respond, she had travelled a considerable distance down the street in what had felt like nothing more than mere seconds to Devon.

He inhaled and held onto everything deep inside his lungs, as if his own life depended on keeping the smoke within him forever.

When he exhaled, he released the smoke through his nose. The smell of it was an instantaneous reminder of Lisa, from before last night, and then immediately from last night.

Before Devon had gone to the bathroom, before his final plea for Lisa to do what everyone—except Lisa—thought was best for Lisa, she had informed him, "I don't think going to tomorrow's Elite Two Meet mixer is in the cards for me."

This was exactly why Devon had gone over to Lisa's in the first place. He had speculated all along that ultimately she would talk herself out of using the opportunity. None of the reasons her naïve mind had listed the night before had been anything he hadn't already heard.

"I'm not going to play the games. Why can't I just be what I am and do a damn good job of it? Isn't that enough? Shouldn't that be enough for me to be successful in the parts of the business that I do enjoy?" she'd rhetorically asked.

Lisa simply didn't get it, and Devon wasn't about to let her blow what he perceived to be a shortcut to fame, the chance to conduct some behind the scenes career advancement. Before heading over to her apartment, a lengthy trek from the West Village that he absolutely loathed, he'd already decided, *If I have to escort Lisa to tomorrow night's event myself, so be it.*

"Now then, I have to pee." It just wouldn't leave his head.

After hearing her out for the umpteenth time, letting her drone on about an existence above the circus, that because of his considerably longer time in the business, he *knew* was required to really make the next leap, he had made that last overture to her: "Do it for us, the plain-as-Jane people."

The memory of the play on words—one of so very many he'd adopted into his everyday vernacular—caused a small amount of what little he'd eaten the day before to thrust itself from his gut, through his esophagus, and onto the sidewalk below.

Excusing himself to pee hadn't been part of his performance. He *did* have to go, but even then he thought it had been a clever and dramatic punctuation to his insistence.

Another drag and he was back on his way. The cigarette had steadied his hands just long enough to rescue two recently obtained Vicodin from the filthy fifth pocket home of his jeans. He popped them and then swallowed the two pills using what little saliva his mouth could generate.

"Why didn't he kill me?" he shouted.

An anonymous voice echoed an answer from above, "Shut the fuck up!"

Two blocks ahead, Devon finally spotted the Metro Transit Authority's familiar green globe sitting atop its pole. He picked up his pace for the train's station though it is doubtful anyone would have detected a difference.

"Now then, I have to pee," rang louder and louder within his skull and the recollections of what had happened firmed their grip on his mind. The evening, his actions and theirs, and each additional segment of what had transpired were increasingly unambiguous. It was becoming more and more obvious to Devon that no amount of drugs, prescription or illicit, were going to obscure last night's horrors anytime soon.

The haunting playback began with the memory of the very moment he had headed to the bathroom. Walking backwards, he'd placed one finger to his lips, indicating "shush" to Lisa in an effort to make it there without having to hear her retort to his demands. That's when he heard a soft knock on Lisa's apartment door.

"Saved by the not-quite-bell," he'd thought as he watched Lisa get up to answer it while sealing himself inside her bathroom for the privacy his pee-fright required irrespective of the number of guests and his familiarity with them.

It was deep into the evening, and neither of them had expected anyone, but the volume of the voice announcing its owner on the other side of Lisa's front door seemed to indicate the visitor wasn't a stranger. Nonetheless, Devon had lost concentration on the task of relieving his bladder as he semi-condemned himself for having not been the gentlemanly type who took to the other side of a door's peephole at such a late hour. He contemplated drawing the zipper back up on his pants in order to head back out to the living room and play the proper roll of manly friend, but when he heard Lisa's muffled greeting and the accompanying click of a lock swung to open, he'd decided to at least try to finish what he'd entered the bathroom for in the first place.

"Hi. Yeah, just a sec. Are you okay?" Lisa had inquired. "Come on in."

Overwhelmed by a mind searching for audible clues as to the identity of these *apparently* welcomed late night trespassers, Devon's sphincter muscles refused to cooperate. The mystery of it all had his full attention, and so he resigned himself to the idea that urination might be achievable only after popping out to be a part of a welcome greeting. He zipped up and spun around to exit with a big hello in mind.

Until that moment, Devon had never heard the indescribable crack of a baseball bat connecting with brute force, crushing against the back of human skull. The ground-shaking thud that followed it, quick on the heels of a woman's screaming demand made in unison with Lisa's horrifying moan registered deep within him though—some prehistoric survival instinct that refused to let Devon operate the bathroom door's handle.

"Sit the fuck down, Bitch!"

"Chris," Devon heard a man's voice intensely inquire, "what the hell are you doing?"

The same female voice that'd been so brutal in its previous command turned eerily calm, delivering instructions made simple, as though they were being read to a first grader.

"Randy honey, this is what we came here to do. Now let's lock the door behind ourselves, okay baby?" Chris said before swinging the bat from high overhead, landing it squarely on Lisa's back as she attempted to claw her way up a cheap chair she'd always intended on reupholstering.

The sound that accompanied that second hit had been made more gruesome than the first when married to the ridiculous almost baby-talk style of its perpetrator. Devon felt an uncontrollable scream gaining momentum on the stomach end of his esophagus. He put a shaky hand to his mouth, and reached into his back pocket for his phone to dial 911—even as he knew from previous experience that the very act would be impossible from inside Lisa's zero-signal bathroom. He looked to the ridiculously undersized window that lived just over the toilet; its view to the open-air alley behind Lisa's building suggested that reaching through it with the phone might be successful in acquiring the single bar or two of signal necessary to make that emergency call.

As silently as was possible in knee-high heeled boots, Devon attempted to shuffle lightly over to the window. The unusual banter between the intruders continued beyond the paper-thin door that had been hiding his minimal participation. Straddling over the commode, Devon was able to tilt the awning window outward with only a tiny clicking noise attempting to unveil him. The design of the window allowed for ventilation, even on a rainy day, and not much else through the two or so inches of its opening. Before committing to shoving his arm through that space with his phone in hand, he held the device up in various locations around the pane of glass hoping to see the service indicator grow from zero to at least one bar.

As he floundered about unsuccessfully, the sound of duct tape being ripped from its roll over and over again penetrated sharply through the closed door. Devon stretched forward to slip his arm through the window, hovering his index finger over the dial button in the hopes that he might blindly connect to emergency services. His balance was further compromised when Lisa let out a painful cry for help that was quickly answered by the repeated thuds of a boot to the gut.

"I'm trying to help you, so stop being such a cunt about it," Chris cooed the way a mother might try and soothe a child after a skinned knee.

With his arm as far through the window as possible, and the

phone out of his direct vision, Devon tapped the dial button a few times. If it was working at all he wouldn't be able to see it, but he hoped that he'd be able to at least hear it ring. If it did, when the dispatcher answered he'd have to decide between holding it there and letting them figure it out or possibly trying to whisper his location through the window's opening at an undetectable volume.

"What did I do?" he heard Lisa ask her assailants in the other room. Her voice was hers and yet not her own, meek like a child's, and she delivered the words weakly between shallow, quivering breaths.

Her question went unanswered. Devon wondered if any of his personal effects would betray him. Had Lisa been a better housekeeper the two mugs of coffee sitting amongst their previously used brethren atop her tiny diner style two-top would have most certainly been evidence of his existence. Other than an indescribable whimper emanating from an obstructed throat, only hushed whispers could be heard—an exchange of directives and next steps echoing among an otherwise black silence. Devon leaned closer to the wall and window to try and detect the possible ringing of his phone and was nearly startled into dropping it when music began blaring from the speaker dock Lisa kept on the mantle above a uselessly bricked-up fireplace. The volume and near release of his fragile grip on the cellphone caused him to involuntarily pull his arm back through the window. He looked at the screen, heartbroken to find it'd been unsuccessful in making a connection to the world outside.

Devon backed his way off of the toilet as The Ting Ting's *That's Not My Name* reverberated through the walls. It's volume slightly adjusted from just before, spinning at a level perfect for obscuring any audible clues of what was actually transpiring within unit 3F. At best, Devon could hope that one of Lisa's more elderly neighbors might phone in a complaint. The very same song being employed to hide the deeds playing out in the living room bolstered Devon's nearly nonexistent courage and he began rummaging under the sink for something sharp—anything that he might be able to wield as a weapon.

He sorted through the contents hidden behind the poorly hung cabinets—most of which was dirty laundry shoved haphazardly between the flimsy boxes that held tampons and pads, stray Q-Tips, an old shoe-box stuffed with a collection of used and unused nail polish, a few rolls of cheap bodega-grade toilet paper, and two scrubbing devices that'd seen very little action in their day. He tried both of the cleaning devices out as potential weapons, holding them in his right hand as though each were a knife and thrusting them individually forward to try out their validity as a means of protection.

The next song to play was a ballad. By its very nature, the tune wasn't nearly as effective as its predecessor in protecting Devon's ears from the butchery and its resulting pain unfolding mere feet from where he was kneeling.

"It's funny you know? No matter how thorough the plan, can you ever truly account for all those who'd like to fuck it up for you along the way?" he heard Chris ask rhetorically. "Randy, hit her again—but try not to break that perfect little nose."

The meaty sound of a heavy fist connecting and crushing flesh and bone accelerated Devon's pulse beyond its already deliriously unstable tempo. The swell of the second song's chorus accompanying the violence outside was loud enough to hide one last ditch sorting effort. Devon pulled all of the dirty clothing out of the cabinets and set it beside himself, pushed the boxes aside and scanned the cupboard's remaining contents yet again. At the very back, lying on its side and obscured by the bend of the rusting metal pipe rising above it, was a familiar transparent orange cylinder wearing a white cap. He reached for it, pulled it out from underneath and held it up in the light to read as he backed himself up to lean against the porcelain of the three-quarters size tub behind him.

OXYCONTIN (OXYCODONE HCI EXTENDED-RELEASE) Tablets, 20 mg.

As Devon climbed down the stairs to the subway train, unsure of a destination, he tried to rationalize the decision he'd made to swallow each of those remaining pills his higher power had "gifted" him as he cowered in Lisa's bathroom. His mind attempted to rewrite the situation, altering the intent behind the consumption of the prescription in ways that might leave him feeling vindicated about the action. Among the clutter of varying storylines, the most palatable revolved around a justification theory that portrayed him as a tragic hero: A history that had him gobbling down the painkillers for the express purpose of both prepping himself to get hurt when he stormed out to stop the assault, and absorbing the beating he'd likely receive if he failed to end it.

He'd made no such effort though. Devon tried to convince himself that if he'd only not underestimated the immediate impact the dosage had had on him, given his lengthy abstinence from narcotics, that he would have done more. More than just await his fate behind the cheap bathroom door that had done little to shield his ears from the repeating physical abuses taking place mere feet from his motionless ineptitude.

Devon hopped over the station's turnstile with little in the way of resistance or condemnation from the other early morning commuters. The city was increasingly relying on the good will of its citizens, and few train stops had live-in-the-flesh agents anymore—automation of the underground world below the skyscrapers had likely made sense relative to efficiency, but it'd done nothing to help the mode of transportation feel any more friendly.

"Why didn't he kill me?" Devon asked aloud once more, shuffled his way through all the appropriately suited worker bees, searching for a less congested space on the platform.

Randy's face flashed before Devon's eyes—the surprised expression that the brute had worn upon discovering Devon cowering on the floor of Lisa's bathroom. The awkward and sudden entrance of one of Lisa's attackers was etched tightly to the backs of his eyelids—the strongest of the memories Devon's brain had chosen for him to vividly replay from the night before.

"Christ Randy, I didn't mean to kill her," Chris scoffed. "I'll come back to deal with it on my own you pussy. Go clean the vomit off your face—you look like shit."

Even if Devon's brain had registered the implications of the words he'd just barely heard, it had done little in the way of animating his body. He thought about trying to lift himself up in preparation to go on the defensive, and the thought of cowering even further back, climbing into the tub and behind its curtain, came and passed.

The knob spun, the door opened, and fate introduced Devon to Randy most unexpectedly. Randy hesitated in the threshold, momentarily startled by the discovery, with his eyes looking Devon up and down. Devon recalled possibly having smiled at him, but he couldn't quite visualize how truly engaged his reaction to their meeting had been.

Randy entered the bathroom and closed the door lightly. He stepped over Devon's body, and while hovering above and keeping his gaze trained directly on him, Randy managed to fumble with the sink's faucet, turn it on, and then rinse the bits and pieces of barf that were clinging to the stubble around his mouth.

A new tune took its place behind the last—a track with a blistering tempo and thunderous bass that made any indication of Chris' activity and exact whereabouts on the other side undetectable.

When Randy reached for the towel to the left of the vanity, his movement triggered an automatic response within Devon. He reached for Randy's leg with some vague intention of trying to pull it out from underneath him, causing him to fall backwards and down to the floor. Devon might as well have been trying to use his bare hands to uncork a tree trunk from the earth—Randy didn't budge nor flinch. He took his eyes off of Devon directly, though he could still see him in the bottom of the mirror as he momentarily evaluated the reflection confronting them both. There was no life behind the sunken eyes that were now living among a pale and ghastly complexion. Randy closed them tight and then used his lumbering mitts in a vain attempt at rubbing away the reality he was helping foster.

The already feeble grip of the stranger clinging to his leg had weakened to the point of almost not existing. Randy surmised that ending the life of the unfortunate occupant wouldn't be any harder than wrapping his hands around the man's thin neck and crushing his windpipe. A quick snap of the hyoid bone and he'd be done with it. Chris might applaud the effort, would likely be surprised that he'd taken the initiative to handle the deviation to what was unfolding around them. Once she realized there was another party privy to their transgressions, she'd certainly demand that he resolve it anyway—at least that's how it was playing out in Randy's mind.

It wouldn't be long before she started to wonder why washing up was taking so much time. Randy put the towel back on its rack. He grabbed the faucet's handle to end its rush of now scalding hot water, and was hit by a brief but powerful moment of clarity—had Chris only sent him into the bathroom to clean up in order to ensure trace evidence of his having been there? He turned the knob to off and leaned forward over the sink, using the bottom of his t-shirt to rapidly scrub the metal to try and polish off the fingerprints.

"What's the use?" he wondered aloud before spinning around to address the huddled mass lying below him. With his legs straddling Devon's body on either side, Randy knelt down to hover just above him.

Tears were streaking down Devon's face, flooding behind the lids of his eyes. Initially, he found it difficult to read the assailant's expression and intent.

A frozen memory of that last awkward image of the hulking beast stayed with Devon as he pushed himself further down the station's platform. Like a silent film, he saw Randy, crouched over him, holding up a single finger to his own mouth as he blew an inaudible hush noise past the digit and towards Devon's face.

"Why didn't he kill me?" Devon uttered to himself one last time as he finished the memory, watching Randy standing up, backing up, and then turning out the bathroom's light before shutting the door gently behind him.

The train entered the station at its north end with an enormous racket, kicking up debris with a thrust of putrid air that blew through the other passengers and quickly washed over Devon's skin. At the same moment, his phone found an untimely and rare signal underground, bars had appeared just long enough to feed the device information and it alerted him to the presence of a text via its vibration. Devon hadn't even realized he'd been carrying it around in his hand. His curiosity insisted and so he glanced down to read it, though he didn't recognize the number.

Hello Devon, it's Mrs. Denton. Sorry to disturb you, but do you know if Lisa is already on her way home?

The words, black on white, encased in their inappropriate speech bubble design, demanded recognition among the rapid succession of images Devon's guilt fed him in his final moments—Lisa's lifeless body clumsily splayed face down, haphazardly placed gashes, some deep and some shallow, dark blue and black bruises populating her pristine porcelain skin, her body ghostly white, a disfigured angel seemingly floating in her own blood while it soaked into the living room's worn down wood floors.

An eyewitness would later inform detectives that she was certain that she'd heard the young man say, "Why didn't he kill me too?" before jumping headfirst from the platform and into the oncoming train.

CHAPTER TWENTY-NINE

I don't mind if you're evil, just be smart evil.

—Anonymous

Federal law prohibits the sale or purchase of counterfeit police badges, and yet hundreds, if not thousands, of New York City law enforcement carry the replicas. Like many, Charlie's dupe shield was a precaution against accidentally misplacing the genuine article. Carrying the fake violated department policy, but losing that few ounces of nickel alloy can mean paperwork and a substantial penalty, as much as ten days' pay. His was nearly authentic and just a touch smaller than the original, and no less effective at performing its function of commanding submission. He'd had it made roughly ten years in to his slog with the NYPD after a Sunday bender found him waking sans department issue the following morning. When he returned to the dive he'd called home most of that previous day, he was surprised to see a half-dozen others kicking around with his own in the barkeep's lost and found box.

Armed with a tip from the precinct's own MacGyver, he'd been able to easily acquire the phony in Chinatown from an old Hollywood prop master just a few days thereafter. The impetus of the illegal purchase had been to safeguard against the inconvenience of keeping tabs on the original. At any time in his career he certainly wouldn't have been able to afford the penalty. With the fake in hand, he walked home to put the original under lock and key, rationalizing that his possession of the dupe was a smart way to keep the real one from possible misuse, an assurance that it'd never fall into the eager hands of a criminal.

The irony of his alibi, made so very long ago, always bubbled up whenever he flashed the faux badge to shakedown the next unsuspecting dupe. He'd used it to enter joints, homes, bypass rent-a-cops, and had relied on it to speak to and threaten numerous souls who'd had zero business being interrogated by him at all. Not one of them, innocent or otherwise, had ever questioned the authenticity of his badge or even his own legitimacy. When he paid a visit to David Miller at the offices of Sterling, Miller and Holmes early Wednesday morning, he'd been uncharacteristically nervous about representing an illusion of authority, but the rouse hadn't played out any differently than all of the successful instances accumulated over the previous years.

He was pleased when building security sent him straight to the tenth floor, no questions asked. After the firm's receptionist, a bombshell with an MBA's linguistics that sat small behind an enormous front desk designed to impose, indicated that a quick chat with David wouldn't be a problem, Charlie delighted in the idea that maybe this phase of the plan would play out quick. His gut had him believing he needed it to—he felt himself racing against the clock though he wasn't sure which of the bastards had set the timer or exactly what awaited him once it went ding.

A gross lack of sleep had Charlie itchy. He had spent the majority of the prior evening bouncing in between nodding off in his car and aimlessly walking about, trying to stay awake with repeated visits to the caffeinated swill machines at various bodegas around town. In the last two days he'd only visited home to use the shower, and on that morning he decided to throw on a tie to really play the part of qualified professional. The effect of the energy drink he'd killed on the elevator ride up was already waning and the low level hum of intelligent minds rambling behind the glass of their corporate cages was almost enough to lull him to sleep.

He stood up and sat back down just as quickly, hoping the action would release just enough adrenaline to keep him awake until what he assumed would be the receptionist's predictable offer to get him an espresso or some other hoighty-toighty caffeinated beverage to sip during the impending conversation. A best-case scenario for grilling David Miller would have Charlie in and out within minutes and on to the next idyllically decorated sanctuary of powerful white men. While he waited for the receptionist's nod, he silently practiced the words and phrasing he'd employ during his mini-interrogation in order to get the preferred end result as speedily as he desired.

I just need this slob to phone his lawyer. If I'm lucky his council is here amongst all these other shit-grins. If I go in hard he'll use the goddamned sixth amendment, and that's exactly what I need. Once he does that, his lawyer calls Alicia's lawyer, and I'm out and on to the next.

The receptionist spoke. Charlie's eyelids popped open and his spine went erect. "Detective Johnson, David is wrapping up a phone call. It'll be just another five minutes. Can I get you something to drink while you wait? Espresso, maybe a double?"

Charlie smiled back at her, but before he could answer in the affirmative, David Miller strolled into the lobby from behind the modern marble wall that served as the thick delineation between those with power and those in need of those with power. Charlie recognized him immediately. Miller was every bit the profile description that had accompanied the member picture Chris had given him. Tall, fit, and not far off from his own self-assessment of a manlier looking version of Brad Pitt.

The five extra minutes he'd supposedly needed to wrap up his phone call had gone by awfully fast, and Charlie chalked it up to the bush-league type of tactics one might employ to keep a mind guessing—afford it zero time to hone in on a last-minute game face. The early phases of a perp's interrogation back at the station often involved the very same misdirect. One investigator tells the offender he'll return to the room in a few, maybe even offers to grab the subject a beverage before disappearing. Then, right as the suspect begins to believe he might have a little alone time to think, the second detective barges through the door demanding an immediate answer to a question meant to rattle.

Without hesitation, Miller approached Charlie with a strong stride and then extended his hand.

"Detective Johnson?" he said as Charlie stood to return the firm grip David had already begun before Johnson could find his legs. "I'm David Miller. I'll have Lillian bring your drink back to my office. What was it you wanted?"

"Black coffee is fine."

"Of course it is," David replied. "Lillian, one black coffee for the detective and if you'd be so kind, please bring me a Jasmine Green Tea." He turned his attention back to Charlie as he led him past reception. "They say that the aroma of Jasmine alone produces a significant reduction in heart rate that results in a sedative effect on mood and nerve activity—a natural stress reliever, I swear by it."

Charlie felt the eyes of the entire office doing their best to pretend that they had little interest in his visit. Heads stayed engaged with the screens directly in front of the very owners working so hard to employ the wonders of peripheral vision.

"The only thing that's ever worked for me, David, isn't as socially acceptable during the daylight hours."

David forced a laugh as he waved an arm to direct Charlie into his office.

"Fun and games detective, what's life without them?" he asked rhetorically as he closed the door to the sprawling space with views up and down the Hudson.

Charlie stepped slowly towards the floor to ceiling windows to fake interest and an appreciation for the panorama and the man who *owned* it.

"You picked a good day to find me," David continued. "That view is always at its best after a storm blows through."

"It's something else," Charlie said as he finished pretending to care.

He walked toward the two vacant oversized chairs situated in front of the desk that was seemingly afloat within the space despite its own overtly oversized existence. David followed Charlie's lead, and instead of seating himself at his desk, joined the detective in the second chair in an attempt to keep things casual.

"Detective Johnson, as lovely as that heavy scent of some second rate body scrub that followed you in here is, I hope you don't mind if we forgo any additional pleasantries and cut right to the inspiration behind your visit."

"You're a busy man, I'm sure," Charlie said sardonically.

"Truthfully, I could push aside everything else I've got lined up for the day if our conversation dictated that kind of time. But we aren't here to be friends, are we?"

Charlie left David's question unanswered.

"Would it surprise you at all if I told you I know the exact reason why you are here?" David prodded.

"I guess it shouldn't, but indulge me."

"Oh come on now," David chided. "You've a brotherhood of your own. I'm certain that if some cunt was running around town accusing you of rape, your own people might tip you off."

"I'm afraid I don't follow," Charlie lied.

"Alicia's own counsel is a good friend. And no offense, but I know enough about you to feel insulted by this act of ignorance you've decided upon," David spit with a mockingly shameful nod of disapproval.

"Fair enough," Charlie begrudgingly admitted. "Let's discuss your raping of two of Alicia's clientele then."

"Christine and Julie," David sighed.

Charlie nodded along in the affirmative.

"Detective, I've nothing to hide."

"Fine, why don't we start with Chris then."

"Let's," David brazenly insisted. "She's a hot piece of ass, no doubt. And believe me, I've tried to fuck her—I've long tired of the act of trying actually. Frankly, I think drugging and raping her might be the only way any man *could* achieve that."

The conversation wasn't going in favor of Charlie's plan. He decided to play along in order to buy himself some time for the necessary improvisation that'd be required to ensure it got back on track. He made a silent commitment to himself, a refusal to leave until he'd turned the tables.

"So you drugged her then?"

"I was speaking hypothetically Detective. What kind of man would I be if I had to drug women into submission?"

"What kind of man are you?" Charlie asked. The question

sounded as dumb leaving his mouth as it had in his head, but he needed David to spin about—needed time for a new angle to present itself.

"Oh, I see."

"I'm glad one of us does, because this time I'm not faking confusion."

"Are you making some sort of insinuation about my manhood? Perhaps you are wondering why a successful and attractive fella like myself would *need* to join a dating service at all—clinging to some old school notion you have about how real men pick up chicks."

"Am I?"

"Elite Two Meet is a fuck club detective." The playfulness from the first ten minutes was no longer living in David's voice. "If I was looking to meet Mrs. Right, I'm quite certain I'd go through more legitimate channels."

Charlie recognized the shift in David's tone. He'd dealt with plenty of ego—educated ego at that—and he sensed he was dancing near some hot button, though he still hadn't pinpointed exactly what subject might cause David to implode.

"Maybe you've got a small pecker, that it?"

"Please," David stood up. "This isn't the schoolyard Charlie."

Johnson had barked out that juvenile slight with no expectations—it was just another question posited in the name of time. The use of his first name didn't go unnoticed.

"Okay then. It's a... like you said, a fuck-club. But you've never had sex with Chris."

"Have you been listening to me?"

"Every word."

"She's a dyke, Detective."

"Maybe she's just old fashioned."

"Maybe."

"You've had sexual relations with many of Elite Two Meet's other female members though?"

"My fair share. Alicia has got a knack for picking them."

"How so?"

"Most of the women she brings aboard are that magic combination of incredibly beautiful but pathetically desperate—clinging to some childhood dream, a power couple—their success uncompromised... land the husband who already understands the trials and sacrifices it takes in order to be filthy rich. Have the kids before it's too late, before that biological clock ticks out." He paused. "I'd venture a guess that sleeping with the likes of me must seem like the quickest way to achieve that fantasy."

"And you've been involved with Elite Two Meet for how long?"

"Since nearly its inception."

"And during that whole time, you never sexually assaulted a one of them? Never forced yourself on any of them—you know, just a wee bit in order to close the deal? Not had a single woman in that two years say 'no' before you shoved her head into your groin? Exploiting that very desperation—the existence of which you just admitted?"

"Not to the best of my recollection, no."

Charlie stood up, confident he'd finally accomplished his objective. He didn't need a confession; he just needed this cocksure playboy's cooperation. His visit and the exchange they'd had would be enough to at least warrant an additional phone call to Alicia's counsel, and David's new demeanor was all the evidence he required to happily excuse himself.

"I've grown tired of waiting for Lillian, Counselor. I

appreciate your time, but I'm a man in need of caffeine. I'll show myself out," Charlie said as he turned to do just that. "Oh, also, I'll be sure to let you know how the best of recollections fare with those 'incredibly beautiful and pathetically desperate' women you mentioned. Have a good day."

CHAPTER THIRTY

Is it a crime, to fight, for what is mine?

—Tupac Shakur

An early afternoon commute on the subway from East New York back into Manhattan was no less lengthy than Chris' previous return trips, but at that hour the train's cars were sparsely populated. It had been a quiet, almost peaceful return to the city—a stale air ride with a repetitive click and hum that had produced an almost ideal meditative state.

Earlier, she'd contemplated handling a new arrangement with Swoopes via payphone or even by using Randy's cell—she still wasn't sure how to handle Randy. The train trip out to the White Elephant had her beating herself up about all the day's time it was eating. Her own indecision before finally choosing to race out and back to Brooklyn had her uncharacteristically nauseous on that first leg. But, by the time Chris resurfaced from the tunnels underground just shy of a few hours later, she felt vindicated for having made the decision to commit to delivering her new proposal to Swoopes and his people first hand, face to face. She was confident that it'd been all business, and that her offer to double their payout if they'd deal with Lisa's body meant one less errand on her already overloaded plate.

Once Chris reached ground level, her cell found its legs and unloaded several vibrations. Tucked amongst numerous benign requests from coworkers and clients, urgent attempts at flagging her attention and demanding her whereabouts by way of text, were the only two messages that mattered. Both were delightful combinations of words, the proverbial icing on the cake.

One down, one to go. Headed to Jeff Dufour's now.

Charlie's admission of obedience was a welcome relief—a sure sign that things were going to work out just fine and second only to Alicia's own admission.

I've been a bad friend. Ring me today, absolutely anytime.

Chris pocketed the device and kept up her brisk pace. She'd have plenty of time to ring Alicia after she dealt with Randy and Julie. Traversing through the hordes of aimless pedestrians clogging the sidewalks, she imagined a scenario in which fate had done her a huge favor: Upon her return to Randy's, she'd find him face down and dead, having choked on his own vomit—the victim of a self-inflicted overdose of booze, heroin, and painkillers. In that narrative, she'd have to finish Julie herself, but at least she'd have a silent and dead Randy to pin it on. Upping the absurdity on her fantasizing about exactly what she'd find when she arrived there, Chris toyed with the notion that before Randy had offed himself, intentionally or accidentally, that he'd gone ahead and ended Julie's life on her behalf. After all, Randy was already in a very dark place when she'd left him outside his building right after dragging his ass out of the bar—wasn't any of this possible? The warmth of the high-noon post-storm sunshine coupled with the meaning behind those two texts had Chris feeling like anything very well might be.

What at first had arrived disguised as a euphoric sense of

optimism tightened its grasp on Chris' psyche with each increasingly heavy step towards Randy's neighborhood. The weakness of body that might have normally resulted from living on the backend of too-little sleep had been temporarily shelved by the couple of bumps she'd snorted on the train ride back into the city. Lightheaded, Chris lost her focus long enough to momentarily believe she'd already forced Randy into that overdose. The same bright sun overhead was no longer pleasant, instead it felt blinding and the oft forgotten noises of everyday traffic became excruciatingly painful—each new honk, the whine of poorly maintained breaks, and the spoken words of others seemingly shouting into their phones was unbearable. In that moment, she was unable to mentally reconstruct significant chunks of time—the memories of that morning's facts began to bleed with the fiction.

I already killed Randy. Why am I headed back there now? Because you didn't, and maybe you don't need to off him. You've got to call the office, the last thing you need is those worrywarts sending someone over to make sure you are okay. I'll phone them when I get home. I'm not headed home, I'm headed to Randy's. Jesus Christ Chris—quit fucking around! Make an anonymous call to 911—let Randy try and explain his actions to the police. That isn't going to work you dumb bitch, as preposterous as his story might sound they'll still come searching for me to at least verify that he's delusional. Focus. Did you already kill him or are you headed over to handle it? And, if you didn't and you are headed over there, you better be goddamned ready to act quick—tonight's your night. You've come this far. If you haven't killed them both already, Lady, there's precious little time to get it done. Lady. Lady. Lady.

"Lady!" A booming voice shouted, reverberating within

Chris' skull and bringing her out of her head, straight back into the high-noon sun where she found herself frozen and staring forward from the middle of an avenue's crosswalk. "Lady! Wake the fuck up!"

The traffic heading her way showed no signs of slowing. Instinct did its best to will her into taking the necessary steps forward to get out of the way of the approaching vehicles. With its first step, her leg buckled underneath her weight and the city's buildings amplified the bone-chilling sounds of screeching brakes as her body tumbled to the ground.

"Fuck me," she chided herself right before her head violently made its acquaintance with the scorching hot asphalt below.

CHAPTER THIRTY-ONE

Behind every great fortune lies a great crime.

—Honoré de Balzac

Charlie needed to believe the text he'd sent Chris might buy him some time—even as he remained unsure of the exact reason he needed the extra ticks. He'd left David Miller's office feeling sick to his stomach and disturbed, with absolutely no intent on heading over to pho-interrogate the other "assailant." If his instincts about where the day might be headed were dead wrong—fine, he had no business loitering outside of Lisa's apartment building. The job he'd done on David would still be more than enough to keep the blackmailing of Alicia on track—but he found himself questioning whether that'd ever been Chris' intent.

He'd considered reaching out, confident that in even a brief phone call he'd be able to uncover the truth behind Chris' motives by evaluating where he thought the situation might be headed against whatever new lies she fed him. Pacing outside Lisa's walk-up while trying to decide upon his next action, Charlie questioned whether there was a payday of any kind at the end of their charade. The money—it was still a possibility regardless of Chris' true intentions. Any clear-cut attempt at doing the right thing in this situation would almost certainly leave him holding life's booby prize.

The more his tired brain allowed him to replay bits and pieces of past interactions with Chris, the more certain he became that any actual conversation with her would only lead to additional manipulations meant to minimize his involvement. Claiming to be diligently on his way to pressure the other schmuck was the only sensible option, and he theorized Chris would believe it wholeheartedly as his subordination was something he was positive that she believed she owned after last night, if not all along. It'd been hours since he'd hit send, and she'd not responded with any indication of appreciation or disapproval, and until she got around to it, a visit with Jeff Dufour could wait.

David Miller had called Chris a dyke, and initially Charlie had chalked up the derogatory term as little more than the petty name calling employed by a bruised ego. Miller was clearly a man used to getting his way—what he wanted, when he wanted it—throw in Charlie's own accusations, and it wasn't uncommon to have perps resort to immature blame-gaming. Nonetheless, the label had stirred Charlie's recollection of the previous evening: the intensity behind Chris' eyes, her energy, and the twitch of muscle underneath his heavy hand. She'd been as difficult to budge as an attack dog whose whole being is dead set on lunging at its victim to grab it by the throat with only the kill as an acceptable outcome.

A half-hour earlier he'd had no clue what unit Lisa called home, but his shield had worked its predictable magic on an elderly tenant back from an errand run who was all too happy to squeal.

"You here about the music?" she'd asked.

"Ma'am?"

"The music—that girl had her music blaring all damn night.
I'd hoped someone would phone you guys. Bit late aren't you?"

"It's a big, busy city, ma'am."

"Must be Detective. Noise complaint seems a bit below your
pay grade, ask me. She's in 3F."

"Thank you ma'am."

The old biddy concluded their conversation with a narrow
squint and an intentionally suspicious-sounding "Mmm-hmm"
before heading back inside. Charlie had declined her gestured
invitation to follow with a cockamamie excuse about waiting on
his partner.

"Oh please," she'd spit before disappearing into the shadows
behind the building's closing glass door.

3F. Rational thought gave way to sixth-sense. Charlie's own
attempts at dissuading himself from heading up to see Lisa failed.
The timing of another tenant's exit from her building was all the
extra incentive he needed to commit.

CHAPTER THIRTY-TWO

My one regret in life is that I am not someone else.

—Woody Allen

Randy sat through the last of four straight episodes of *Saved By The Bell* on E! Entertainment Television. Jessie Spano had gotten hooked on caffeine pills—fell victim to the pressures that her friends, family and society would likely portray as compulsions she'd laid on herself. They'd take no credit for having driven her to a premature demise, had Zach not arrived in time to prevent her next step towards that eventual destination. Even in his drug induced stupor, Randy drew some hard parallels between Elizabeth Berkley's plight and his own.

He turned his heavy ogle toward Julie's disarranged form lying beneath his apartment's only window. The sheets he'd been trying to pass off as curtains were drawn, but her lifeless body was still visible thanks to the television's brilliance.

No longer in control of the introduction of his thoughts, Randy wondered if Zach had only stepped in to help Spano so that he might get into her pants somewhere later down the road.

"You're dead," he said hushed but aloud before swigging the last of what remained in the bottled fifth of whiskey he'd been clutching during the episode marathon's duration.

Chris' ultimatum had been explicit.

"Let me take care of this, or you go ahead and fuck it all up—I'll be the first to point a finger."

What exactly Chris had meant when she assured him it'd all be fine was unclear, but he very much understood that any additional deviations from her instructions wouldn't benefit him. Even so, not long after Chris had left, he'd gone ahead and stuffed a solid black duffle bag with all the clothing it could handle. He'd packed just minutes after the realization that Julie wasn't just passed out, sleeping or some combination of both.

The duffle bag was on the couch with him. Pennsylvania was not all that far away, and the Canadian border easily reachable before that day's end. The urge to flee had surrendered to the intoxicating effects of some illicit combination of Xanax, Valium and Johnny Walker Blue. The latter had been a top-shelf addition to Randy's liquor cabinet, a special occasion beverage for an event that had never arrived.

Making a run for it no longer seemed a worthwhile commitment—far easier now to ruminate on the whereabouts of Elizabeth Berkley. The last performance Randy could remember was the few episodes she'd guest starred opposite Jennifer Beals on Showtime's *The L Word*. He reached for his phone to put its browser to good use, typing the words "where is Elizabeth Berkley now" in conjunction with episode five's reprisal of the show's theme song as it announced the network's commitment to a third hour of more cautionary tales of teen hi-jinx.

Before the search engine had a chance to return the results of his query, Randy had already laid the device back down in front of him. Under the guise of needing bladder relief, he willed his muscles to walk him to the kitchen to look for another bottle of booze that he was almost certain didn't exist.

"You're dead and this shit is fucked up," he informed Julie on his way past.

After a thorough search of the only two cabinets and three kitchen drawers his unit possessed, he tried to keep his mind straight on the promise he'd made to stay put until Chris returned. Snorting another couple of lines wasn't going to cut it—not on its own—his physical craving demanded it be partnered with more liquor. He considered the consequences of not returning from the corner store quick enough in order to be present and accounted for the very minute she opened his front door.

Temporarily back in the moment, his mind flooded with violent snapshots of the twisted proceedings he'd been a part of the night before. The images of torn flesh, a tapestry of pulverized features resulting from Chris' unrelenting series of blunt force traumas on the body of a woman whose name he didn't even know—for a split second the memories seemed real enough to cause his stomach to contract, catapulting what little it was carrying onto the kitchen floor. The endorphins that accompanied the retch were a welcome phenomenon, and Randy's nausea left as quickly as it'd arrived. When he looked up he could swear that Julie's face had managed to form a contemptuous grin.

The burning only anger can orchestrate overcame Randy's whole being. The television show's characters' inane prattling on about their next dilemma became an unwitting score to the series of violent blows he unleashed upon Julie's defenseless corpse. The crack of delicate bone under each punishing strike unearthed one lost memory after another—a lifetime of having been the obedient muscle misused by weaker intellectuals promising him the world and posing as friends.

Julie's face remained the image of Chris' until Randy's rage gave way to a crippling self-loathing that left him shaking and confused. Kneeling beside her, he stared at his trembling fists, the huge hands were blood soaked and speckled with bits of flesh, hovering over the backdrop of the nearly unrecognizable physiognomy split to pieces underneath. Tears did their best to form, but the hypocrisy of the situation prevented them from traveling any further than deep behind Randy's eyelids. Try as he might, any attempt at true remorse was thwarted by his very nature, or stunted by the effects of the various pharmaceuticals that remained snaking through his soul—perhaps some combination of both was the culprit behind his feeling hollow.

He stood quickly, nearly losing his balance as he backed away from the crime upon the crime he'd dutifully executed. The television program's canned laughter used to punctuate every new ridiculous one-liner underscored Randy's own disoriented actions. Scrambling to make his way to an undecided destination, he quickly rinsed his hands before scurrying about his bedroom in a desperate attempt to collect the very same belongings he'd already shoved into the black duffle bag hours earlier. He caught a man's reflection in the full-length mirror that hung precariously to the front of his one closet door. The blackness under as well as deep within the eyes of a face absent of color didn't immediately register as his own. The instant it did, the sight sent him panicking back to the living room where he nearly tripped his way to the coffee table, falling to his knees to inhale the remainder of the cocaine he'd so deftly collected into sharp little lines.

The drug did its best to kick-start his focus, and made just enough of an impact that when he fell backwards into his sofa he reacquainted himself with his black duffle bag. He grabbed at it, catching sight of hands still unkempt, and stood to pursue the act of flight over fight. After one last look at what he'd done to Julie, he turned and raced out of his unit, leaving her there to suffer through the sixth straight *Saved by the Bell* episode that'd just begun.

CHAPTER THIRTY-THREE

For no one—no one in this world can you trust. Not men, not women, not beasts.

—Conan the Barbarian

Charlie tapped lightly on the dimly lit door labeled 3F. There was no verbal response from within, but the faint sound of scrubbing was audible when he leaned in to press his ear to the thin piece of laminate on its front side. The pungent scent of vinegar registered, its molecules binding with Charlie's cilia set the hairs on the back of his neck on end. He put his hand to the knob in order to determine whether it was locked while contemplating the end results of either a quick-burst entry or a more delicate introduction to what lied behind the door. A subtle twist suggested there'd be little resistance, it was unlocked and he committed to the latter action and some sense of decorum even as his instincts had led him to believe nothing good was waiting for him on the inside.

The towering building that sat nearly on top of and directly behind Lisa's allowed for very little in the way of interior sunlight. Her unit's windows were wide open with their curtains pulled aside, even so, the contents of her living room dwelled mostly in shadows. The fresh air wafting through the meager openings, laced with subtle but putrid hints of the smoldering summer garbage of the city's alleys below, was doing little in its efforts to mask the smell of chlorine bleach. The humming world outside was faint, and besides the repetitive allegiance of a small brush scrubbing in short, focused back and forth movements, the only other sounds were the barely perceptible thud of bass trapped by headphones and the deep wheezing of someone's strained physical efforts.

Charlie drew his firearm from the holster on the small of his back as he took a few steps forward. The words "Lisa, are you okay" were just about to emerge from his mouth when his third step permitted vision beyond the backside of the couch occupying the center of the studio. Though the moving mass had its back to him, Johnson recognized Fat Man immediately.

Unaware that he had company, Fat Man remained uncomfortably seated on the hardwood floor in some mangled version of what one might refer to as Indian style. His attention was on the task at hand, and any notifications of the impending disruption were drowned out by the blare and boom of the music pumping from the oversized headphones that straddled from ear to ear atop his very undersized head. He paused and withdrew the brush from the bloodstained floor in order to dip it again into the small bowl sitting next to the bottle of vinegar. Other cleaning supplies, some opened and others still wearing their tamper-proof seals, were strewn about on either side of him. Various towels, paper and cloth, cluttered the area, already filthy from their efforts to help restore the hardwoods back to some semblance of their former evidence-free glory.

As he firmly pressed the newly soaked brush down into the wood's exposed grain to begin scrubbing again, he felt the muzzle of Charlie's gun sink into the fat on the back of his neck.

He left his hand heavy on the brush, and refrained from making any motion, while the excess vinegar puddled around the tool.

Charlie ripped the headphones off of Fat Man and tossed them to the ground.

"Fuck, I thought T-bone locked that shit."

"Where's Lisa?" Charlie said as calmly as he could while processing the implications of all the toxic cleaning paraphernalia in front of him.

"Charlie?" Fat Man said with a hint of relief in his otherwise panicked voice. "What the hell you doin' here?"

Fat Man started to turn his head to address the detective, but Charlie forced his gun even deeper into the nape of his neck, encouraging him to reconsider.

"The girl who lived here, Jackass. What did you guys do to her, and where is she?" Charlie demanded with a volume meant to infer business while keeping nosy neighbors uninformed.

Fat Man let out a big sigh, and tried to find enough breath to make a coherent sentence. "Aw fuck man, you know dat girl? Lisa's the girl lived here?"

"I'm asking the questions, *Lionel*," Charlie barked. "Should I be at all concerned that your crew is gonna come back through that door anytime soon?"

"Fuck nah man—motherfuckas wuz supposed to help, but it's always my ass ends up dealing with the shit end of the stick. And in this case, there was shit too, *actual* shit."

Fat Man didn't need the blunt pain delivered by a swift pistol-whip to regret having made an attempt at levity—the millisecond the words left his mouth he realized it'd been crass.

"I got an idea, *Lionel*," Johnson offered as he delicately swung around Fat Man to confront him face-to-face. "How about we skip ahead, past any additional rituals of bad guy versus good guy back and forth, and you just own up to her whereabouts."

"You look anxious my man, how unusual—I ain't recall ever seein' yo' face so contorted." Fat Man grinned in spite of the piece pointed at him. "What happens here now? I tell you that bitch is dead and you shoot me?" He was pleased to see the additional panic his words had inspired in Charlie's eyes.

"Is she?"

"Take a look around motherfucka, this shit here look survivable to you?" Fat Man laughed.

Charlie put all of his weight into the boot he had resting atop of Fat Man's wrist. The grin the bloated sack of shit was wearing vanished, and when the scaphoid and lunate bones buried deep within the blubber gave in under Charlie's stomp, Fat Man let out a squeal unbecoming of the swine it resembled.

"Shit Charlie, ain't nothing you gonna do to me gonna change facts," Fat Man coughed on his own accelerated breathing. "I ain't the doer—Swoopes neither—I'm just the asshole gets the privilege of cleaning up some other cunt's mess."

Charlie stayed silent. His right arm began to lower on its own will, his piece still pointed at Fat Man but with less intent, as his mind tossed around the inevitable. The rushing noise of the city's traffic felt distant, almost nonexistent, and the myriad of smells that had been wafting around the room since his arrival overloaded his olfactory lobe, causing a sting that immediately blurred his vision. He'd not seen Lisa an adequate number of times for his brain to bring her face to the forefront of his memory, as it tried, even Charlie had to acknowledge that the image of a beautiful woman—and now dead woman—he stood their pining for might not be an entirely accurate depiction.

"You want to pay yo' last respects, I suggest you get to gettin' hoss."

"Hmmm?" Charlie stumbled his way back to the conversation, retrained his piece directly at Fat Man's head.

"Fool, I don't have to tell you how fast Swoopes is gonna have that body M-I-A."

Charlie could feel his trigger finger dancing about. There was no logical reason to end Fat Man right there. Even if ultimately it might be considered some favor to society-at-large, there'd be paperwork to fake, more lies to tell, and a whole host of other East New York assholes ticked off that'd he'd taken it upon himself to excuse this one—usher him to the other side the way only the authoritative wallop of his Glock Seventeen could. The gunshot itself would be difficult to ignore as well, a single muzzle blast might normally be blamed on the backfire of a passing vehicle, but the old lady who'd tipped off Charlie to Lisa's apartment number would likely think otherwise.

Fat Man was wearing bright yellow rubber gloves. A second set was still in the freshly opened package beside him. Choking him to death would be difficult. His name wasn't a misnomer, and Charlie knew the blob had some strength living beneath the appearance, but it didn't completely squash the surging urge he had to at least give it a try.

"Where'd they take her body?" Charlie asked.

"Man, I don't keep tabs on the final restin' place of every Dick and Jane who crosses us, even in this case, when they ain't crossed us. Could be any number of locales."

Charlie knew a legit answer would hardly matter—any effort to catch up wouldn't bring Lisa back—but he still decided in favor of applying his boot to Fat Man's face with a jaw-snapping kick.

Fat Man recoiled, found his balance and barked up at Charlie, "You so curious, text Swoopes yo'self. I'm sure he'd love to hear from yo' delinquent ass, ring 'im! Hell, I'll ring 'im."

Charlie ignored his sincere offer and asked a final question, looking for an answer he was sure he already knew.

"Who set this all up, Lionel? Who's paying?"

"Don't know her name—that's the truth. But dat blonde bitch ain't someone you never wanna cross. I could see that shit in her eyes the first time she came to say 'how-dee-doo.'"

Charlie had his answer. Fat Man could see the proverbial click of understanding behind the detective's eyes.

"We done here?"

Charlie grinned down at Fat Man, firmed his grip on the firearm in his hand and swung it into his face with an intense energy only available to those with unadulterated wrath, delivering the very justice Dante had once described as perverted to revenge and spite.

"We're done," he said as Fat Man fell to the floor either unconscious or pretending to be. Charlie put his gun back in its holster and turned to leave. "Thanks for your time, *Lionel*."

CHAPTER THIRTY-FOUR

Three things cannot be long hidden: the sun, the moon, and the truth.

—Buddha

It had been a typically busy pre-event type of day for Alicia, though the reasons behind the accelerated blurring of that morning and afternoon's hours were anything but typical. Four o'clock came and she'd still not left her apartment, yet Alicia had never been more confident in her belief that that evening's soirée would be every bit the success the last two years' gatherings had all been.

The previous evening had morphed into morning in front of open eyes. She'd promised herself a couple of hours sleep after leaving the office, but she never committed to making them materialize—too much to do, too much on the mind, and an unprecedented excitement about an unsure future. If there were any physical signs of exhaustion, Alicia would only come to know them when she finally got around to assembling herself for what she'd decided would be her last attended event—maybe not forever, but at least for some significant period of time.

"Bean, I'm fine—*you'll* be fine. The party will be fine."

She'd uttered some combination of the assurance to Bean

repeatedly throughout the day, and again and again to anyone else Bean had put in charge of ringing her to discuss the supposedly urgent last minute details. From the comfy confines of a home, all of the usual pre-party fires—the very same and sometimes self-inflicted complications that might normally have had Alicia and her crew racing about and shouting amongst each other at the top of their lungs—seemed more like molehills than the mountains she'd taken pride in moving so deftly in the final ticks leading up to previous events. While Alicia's focus lay elsewhere, she hadn't completely bailed on her enthusiasm for managing every last detail. Solely blaming Bean for the patterned interruptions would be hypocritical, and so Alicia had taken to showering her with an unusually verbose amount of gratitude at the end of each and every call.

They probably think I'm nuts, and maybe I am.

An earlier phone call with her attorney hadn't done much to faze Alicia either. Nothing George said was enjoyable to hear. Try as he might to push her to the brink of unsound judgment, she'd kept what she'd often described as her father's tolerance and cool for unfortunate and unforeseen consequences.

"If, in some way, my creation has played a part in fostering or even encouraging the despicable acts of violence and abuse Chris described, I've got to acknowledge that, deal with it, and move forward."

George unfurled his vision of a future in which Elite Two Meet's success and profitability was severely damaged by the media frenzy that was sure to ensue once the sycophants to an audience that celebrates misery caught wind of the company's involvement in a double-rape investigation. His own small stake in the upstart aside, he truly wanted to believe that he was acting in Alicia's own best interest.

"There are other ways to proceed, Alicia," George prodded in an uncharacteristically hushed tone. "As your council I'm advising that we get in front of this situation. If anything, I've failed you in not doing so already."

Alicia played dumb. "What are you suggesting?"

"Some sort of agreement. Let me arrange a meeting with Chris, Julie, their attorney—if they have one—and the two of us."

"Money in exchange for shut mouths, you mean?"

"Resolve the situation to the mutual satisfaction of both parties is what I'm suggesting—for your benefit, and theirs."

"What's the going rate on rape-accusation-removal these days?" Alicia quipped.

"Stop being a child."

"I'll think about it, George," Alicia concluded. "Good-bye now."

George had continued arguing in the affirmative of a preemptive out-of-court settlement via emails and texts throughout the remainder of the day. Alicia desperately wanted to permit herself to remove that option from the table completely, but had yet to come down from the fence on it. In between checking in on her team's progress, she argued with herself, presenting opinions in favor for and against green-lighting George's efforts to put an end to the Chris situation quietly and on the company's dime.

An earlier effort to gauge her own devotion to either legal scenario by way of communicating with Chris via text had gone unresolved. She'd sent the message just after noon and had been surprised when each new vibration of her phone hadn't been the alert announcing Chris' reciprocation. Alicia's empathy for Chris went toe-to-toe against her frustration with the new reality her organization found itself in thanks to Chris' predicament. With each passing half-hour a new emotion led the battle for Alicia's full attention, but by early afternoon the lack of a response from Chris altogether hadn't aided in the creation of a mental state comprised of total understanding and possibly even true forgiveness.

Against her better judgment, Alicia had also crafted three separate texts to Lisa, unintentionally delivered with considerable gaps of time between each.

I'm sorry about last night.

This might sound strange, but I'm grateful to have met you.

I'm planning on getting away from here for a while, any chance you'd meet with me tomorrow for a quick sit? I understand if you'd rather not.

Alicia was confident in her belief that Lisa wasn't going to join Elite Two Meet nor show that evening. There was little point in continuing to try to coerce her into doing otherwise. That much was certain after Alicia's flop of a last-ditch pitch the night before, the failure of which likely hadn't hinged solely on Chris' odd behavior. Alicia ruminated on their exchange and the vision of Detective Johnson appearing seemingly out of nowhere to snatch Chris away from the café. It made very little logical sense to be angry with Chris given what she'd claimed to have lived through, but some small part of Alicia couldn't help but want to believe that things might have played out differently with Lisa had Chris not shown.

Lisa hadn't bothered to respond. Bean's final check-in with Alicia before she and her crew headed to the event's location wasn't unwelcome. At the very least, her benign intrusions had done well at helping Alicia not feel completely and utterly alone.

If she intended on sticking to her plan for the evening, time was no longer on Alicia's side. The day's worth of destination exploration and financial rejiggering she'd engaged in while pretending to care what Bean, George, or anyone else had to say had left her staring down one last commitment. The final page of pre-purchase flight information on her computer's screen looked no different than it had at the end of each other time she'd bothered to enter the very same travel variables. She rolled the cursor back and forth over the airline's confirmation button—still unable to convince herself unequivocally that whatever her new future had in store would begin with a quick trip back home. She'd never had any issues with the act of buying round-trip tickets there before, but that was likely because each and every time she knew she'd ultimately cancel her visit under the guise of living deep in the weeds of her profession. She convinced herself—for just long enough—that none of it really mattered and allowed her thumb to push into her laptop's track pad in order to process the charge for the trip to her credit card.

She closed her browser and finished off the remainder of the caffeinated beverage that'd lived by her side for the day's duration. She hoped the concoction would be just enough of a spark to force her out of yesterday's clothes, into the bathroom, through the labor of a shower, and on to the dinner party. Its effect in the name of her forward progress was debatable, but the adrenaline jolt she'd needed to simply stand up from her desk came by way of her phone's specific contact ringtone.

Chris had finally decided to call. As Alicia watched her device ring-out, fully aware that phoning at any time had been her earlier suggestion, she did her best to believe that she'd absolutely dial Chris right back, just as soon as she was put together, out the door, and on her way to the restaurant.

CHAPTER THIRTY-FIVE

If you don't design your own life plan, chances are you'll fall into someone else's plan. And guess what they have planned for you? Not much.

—Jim Rohn

The emergency room physician stood over Chris as she decided against leaving Alicia a voicemail message of any kind.

"Not picking up?" the doctor asked.

"Nope."

"You don't want to leave a message for your friend?"

"Nope."

"Do you have another friend you'd like to try?"

Chris attempted to end the asinine nature of the conversation. "That's really none of your business."

The physician reached out to take back Chris' phone, holding his open palm in front of her with an expression worn on his face that was meant to ensure its obedient return.

"Alright, maybe you'll want to try again when I come back to review your blood work with you. I'll need your cell until then."

"Why?" Chris asked if only to delay the inevitable.

"That's just the way it is back here."

"Right," she said while still refusing to place her phone into his hand. "And why exactly am I back here again?"

"We just had that conversation, are you unable to recall it?"

"Humor me."

"Well, I'm still not absolutely sure. You arrived here unconscious and I suspect the fall you took was likely the culprit. You've a rather large contusion on the back of your head, but you also arrived with many symptoms of severe dehydration. I'm guessing the latter led to the former, but I'd prefer to have a bit more information before we decide for sure."

He hadn't removed his hand, and Chris reluctantly placed her phone into his palm.

"How long is that going to take?" she asked with an intentional demure.

"Not long," he replied. "Not long at all."

Chris watched as he disappeared into the commotion and chaos surrounding her.

Prior to that moment, none of the emergency room's other activity had registered. The dissonance amongst the beeps, pumps, and whirrs of various machines under the barked authoritative orders among the animal like moans of those in pain rose to an almost unbearable level. She put her hands to her side, pressed deep into the foam, and propped herself up from her gurney to take in the spectacle behind the belligerent cacophony.

The subtle sting of the needle delivering some electrolyte concoction into her arm was the only indication that the scenes playing out before her weren't the fiction of some hyperactive dream. She felt uncomfortably fuzzy, but at peace, despite the throbbing sensation the emergency room's hustle and bustle was inflicting upon her head. Unsure of whether the emotion was the direct result of something they'd administered while she was out cold, or the cumulative effects of her own dosing and the unscheduled rest her fall had insisted upon, she decided to lie back down and dwell in it. For a few moments, the pseudo-affection of strangers caring for perfect strangers kept her mentally drifting contentedly atop the stretcher parked haphazardly in the middle of it all. The anger and confusion she'd initially felt upon opening unsure eyes was buried deep beneath the analgesic relief her own surrender to the world had rewarded—not dead, but only an ember of the rage that'd previously consumed her still existed.

Chris' innate drive to control the situation was lost to the Gods, even as she mediated on all of the week's prior transgressions, their implications, her roll in them and the woman who was the impetus behind their history.

The moment itself felt like a rebirth. An opportunity to begin anew, despite the insistence of persistently solid reasoning that foreshadowed a future filled with many difficult hurdles. Calm but unsure, Chris instructed herself to accept that anything she'd done could be undone—to believe in the existence of solutions that while likely unpleasant to her own immediate wellbeing, might carve out a life worth living at some distant point down the road. Lying there, as her eyelids refused to remain open, she felt she'd made an admission to herself, and acknowledgement of her role in a future scandal and a not-yet-heard confession to the unsuspecting world outside the ER's doors that had barely ever bothered to know the frail train wreck she'd become.

An unfamiliar but only recently recognizable voice broke the spell of her tranquility, "Good news."

Chris found the strength to open her eyes. The attending physician had returned with her phone in hand and was hovering over the gurney. His optimistic intentions were betrayed by a genuine demeanor; wearing an overly eager smile that served in extending Chris' euphoria until he concluded revealing his noteworthy development.

"Looks like your friend is trying to contact you," he said as he presented Chris' cell. "Can't say for sure since I'm unable to unlock it, but looks like you've got a new message."

With a hand weakened by the first few moments of waking from an unexpected slumber, Chris grabbed the device and rested it against the swell of unconditional love growing from inside her chest.

"Thank you," she whispered.

"You got it. You can read it or listen to it, whichever, but don't make any calls, okay?"

"*You* got it," Chris answered as her eyes surrendered to the backs of their lids once more.

"I should be back shortly to go over your lab work," he finished with an attempt at reassurance, placing a gentle hand to her shoulder.

Surprisingly, Chris floated in the intent of the gesture. As he walked away she felt herself breathing easier and deeper than she had in some time. She cocked one eye open just long enough to watch him disappear a second time among this unusual sea of true despair mixed with genuine human bonding. She wondered if he'd keep a similar attitude towards her when he finally got around to seeing the results of the blood work. She assured herself that he'd almost certainly seen worse, and that no matter the trace amounts of narcotics left coursing through her system from the previous few days, it wouldn't be reason enough to discredit her authentic need to be there under his temporary care.

The emergency room was lacking on indications of time,

clocks didn't hang from the walls and while plates of curtained glass created boundaries all around Chris, none exposed the world outside. Until she propped her cell up with its base against her robed chest, the day's hour had seemed inconsequential. Exhaustion made even the simple task of unlocking its screen a three-attempt process—one last misguided digit and she'd be unable to hear the voicemail from Alicia that the device's alert box tantalizingly indicated was awaiting. Chris made a concerted effort in using her pointer finger with care, focusing on each digit intensely through the haze of blurred vision. The final tap on the last of a string of numerals unveiled the phone's home screen. There was the day's actual hour, floating above a cherished photograph of Alicia and herself at an event she'd co-authored almost a year ago. It was a quarter to seven, and before even holding the phone to her ear in order to listen to Alicia's message, the calm in her belly bowed out to the sting of sensing exactly what unwelcome news might be forthcoming.

Chris, I saw that you phoned. You didn't leave a message, are you okay? I'm assuming you aren't coming tonight, given the situation… which I think is for the best. I'd tell you to ring me back straight away, but as you can probably guess I'm headed to the event, and I'll be beyond indisposed for the next couple of hours. I'll try you again late tonight or first thing tomorrow morning. Maybe we can grab an early coffee before I catch my flight home. I hope we can connect before I go.

The replay of each recorded word incited what had been the nearly dormant collection of ill emotions Chris still had bundled within. Living among the hurried breaths of Alicia's rushed journey to a destination that wasn't the hospital was either an intentional or unintentional string of thoughts laced with meaning that might be undetectable to most, but not to Chris.

It'd been absolute, a firm refusal to accept reality, followed by disingenuous posturing meant to indicate concern and caring— all crafted in the guise of an off-the-cuff communication made by a body too professionally dedicated to give thought to anything but their own selfish ends.

By the time Chris listened to the voicemail a sixth straight time, she found herself already standing outside of the hospital's exit. The rush to admit new casualties of life's daily grind left her relatively undetected by any of the staff or medics zipping back and forth between the ER and their ambulances. She'd unwittingly grabbed the clear plastic bag containing the wardrobe she'd worn when she arrived there earlier. She was clutching it with a grip that left a self-inflicting pain—she stood still, almost dazed.

As she put her phone down to her side, Chris caught the curious look of a young child seated across the way. Her eyes bright with naiveté, the little girl's bewildered expression instigated Chris' own quick examination of her current state. A small pool of blood had formed on the inside of her arm opposite the elbow where the needle had recently lived. Tiny drops had spilt down her arm, still fresh and glowing brightly atop her pale, ghostly complexion. Barefoot in only her underwear and the hospital issued robe, she felt an uncontrollable laughter swarming inside. Before it had a chance to escape and possibly alert those souls within earshot, she swallowed it. She looked back towards the toddler, and a broad smile came over her face. With a gentle wink meant to buy the continued silence of the little girl, Chris put one finger to her lips to confirm and seal the secret between them.

The little girl responded in kind and put her tiny digit to her lips to close the pact between them, then watched as Chris stepped into the pedestrian traffic of a heavy home-time commute that had done little to indicate that they were at all aware of her unusual participation.

CHAPTER THIRTY-SIX

I gave up love and happiness a long time ago.

—Richard Ramirez

Two Truths and a Lie. It wasn't the only icebreaker employed by Elite Two Meet, but it'd always served Alicia's guests well. Facilitating conversation amongst a large group of professionally powerful men and women that went beyond their own practiced and perfected daily rhetoric couldn't fall on the shoulders of a boozy cocktail hour alone. There were few events in which at least one or two of the participants didn't already show up buzzed or full-on drunk, and, more often than not, their being there worked in favor of quickly igniting a good time. On occasion, Alicia found herself playing the role of bouncer, having to quickly create diversions in order to remove unruly members not quite up to the task of holding their liquor. Those awkward instances with the more boisterous of the offenders often served as an unscheduled tension buster for the group though—something, someone, and a situation for all to have in common, a shared experience to riff off of in real time. Few of the icebreakers Alicia had used over the years had ever rendered a similar sense of ease among her groups as auspiciously as serving up a common enemy for their quips, gossip, and shared speculation.

Forty-five or so minutes into the evening had passed, and the lack of a human spectacle to sacrifice in that way, for the good of the group, coupled with her own quick evaluation of the mood and demeanor of that night's men and women, led her to pick Two Truths and a Lie. Lying was fun. Lying was easy. And though far too many of her members were abysmally bad at presenting truths that might be perceived as lies, there were usually enough far-fetched fibs to get the group rollicking into their second and third drinks.

The game appeared to be working wonders with that evening's crowd, though for the first time, Alicia acknowledged that the act of having fun might in and of itself be the biggest lie perpetuated by any one of her guests. Who among them was actually having a good time? It was possible that the extraordinary distance she felt from the activities was hers and hers alone—a feeling one might describe as the observational complacency of a bored theatergoer, except she'd scripted the performance, hundreds of times, and watched it almost always play out virtually the same, therefore unable to pin its banality on anyone other than herself.

The final official lies and the truths that accompanied them came and went while Alicia tried to keep herself present enough to keep things on schedule. Other than the very first few month's events she'd thrown, these gatherings were orchestrated to have a deliberate ending. In those earlier experimental days, her unseasoned approach had her believing that people knew when to call it a night on their own, possessed the good sense to see their opportunity with another soul and take their fledgling connection elsewhere for it to flower. She'd been wrong of course. Even amongst the assembly of a big city's most confident movers and shakers, the time-honored tradition of manipulating one's courage with drink against the later ticks of an evening's darkness was practiced by most. Without an official ending to an event, there'd been far too many a night in which Alicia found herself sitting across from belligerently intoxicated and hysterically disappointed members who'd let booze get the better of them. Their failure to make a connection blamed squarely and repeatedly on her, all to the tune of additional dollars spent keeping the establishment and its gratis bar open into the wee hours of a weeknight. Depicting the cutoff time for her events as something other than rampant frugality had been no harder than ending each of them with what had become one of many Elite Two Meet signature catch phrases she or one of her staff delivered in a final toast—"To endings. Because tonight's is just your beginning."

Alicia caught herself reminiscing on the creation of that signature toast, and doubting it had any substantive value, even as it had served her well in getting bodies out a seemingly infinite number of bar, restaurant, and event hall doors. She wondered if the same could be said about the way she'd left things with Lisa the night before. Maybe their evening's ending, as tragically uncomfortable as it'd been, was only the first step towards something far more gratifying. She'd not heard from Lisa since, and was under no illusion that at any minute she would come bouncing into the scene, newly eager to be an Elite Two Meet member or anyone else to Alicia for that matter. Her acceptance of an immediate future sans Lisa left Alicia in the throes of some bizarre combination of tormented optimism—comfortably frightened with the possibilities that tomorrow might hold.

"Alicia, perhaps we should start seating."

The stares of an uninformed but attractive group teetering on the verge of an awkward silence accompanied by Bean's gentle vocal nudge brought Alicia out of her own head.

"Yes, please everyone—why don't we move this to the dining tables?"

With that, and a casual flick of her wrist, the twenty members began their short pilgrimage from the bar to the four tables each set for five individuals in the adjacent room. A sixth chair with no place setting lived at one end of all four tables though, and, in fact, the only truly new wrinkle to tonight's event was that odd clustering of bodies. Several weeks ago, Bean had made a compelling case for how having an uneven number of people at each table with an empty chair for rovers might instigate a more natural way for the members to cut their losses with one another if things weren't working out. At the time, Alicia had only green lit the implementation of this novelty to prove it a failure, possibly make an example of Bean. Yet as she watched the group take their places with the curiosity of children playing dress-up, she felt a tinge of actual excitement about what might result from Bean's intuition.

He may have been in the restaurant for quite some time, but it wasn't until the bar lay nearly empty that Alicia realized Detective Johnson was sitting on the stool furthest from it all, looking fixedly at the group as it moved to the other room, his eyes scrutinizing either the attendees themselves or their collectively bizarre participation.

He finally looked away and met Alicia's admonishment.

"Detective," Alicia said firmly. "Neither David nor Jeff are present this evening—nor Chris. You have no real business here, none that I can condone anyway."

Charlie picked his drink up from the bar, and while bringing it to his lips replied, "You might be right." He polished it off in a single gulp. "The city of New York would likely disagree though," he added while patting the badge he'd placed on the bar in front of him.

Before Alicia could interject he continued, "I won't pretend to understand why the folks in there pay you boatloads to arrange these things." He took another quick glance at the menagerie of interesting but uniquely attractive faces in the distant room and offered his assessment, "They all seem pretty capable."

Alicia intentionally kept her distance, determined to make any additional conversation with him as difficult as possible. "Loneliness knows no socioeconomic boundaries," she pontificated.

"Indeeth," Charlie slurred as he motioned to the bartender. "Give me another."

Alicia made eye contact with the server behind the bar, "He's not with us—make sure the detective pays for his own drinks please."

The bartender nodded compliantly as Charlie rolled his eyes and spat, "Not good enough for the club, no doubt about that."

"Is it your intention to sit here and get liquored up?" Alicia asked as pleasantly and sincerely as her angered and trembling vocal chords would allow. "Is that what the city is paying you to do tonight?"

Charlie abruptly slid forward semi-intentionally as he went to put less distance between them. "Two Truths and a Lie, huh?"

Alicia didn't quite know what to make of his intonation so she left unanswered what seemed less like a question and more of a drunk puzzling over recent events. She shot a quick look to the group still arranging itself behind her, and caught Bean motioning for her to join everyone just before she reengaged with Johnson.

"I've got a lie," Charlie said.

He'd taken the liberty of positioning himself even closer to Alicia, near enough for her to take in the caustic aroma of whiskey and heated breath.

"We *all* do," she replied.

He snatched the fresh drink from the bartender's hands and repeated himself. "I've got a lie. And it's a real doozy."

"I couldn't pretend to care, Detective."

Her quip incensed Charlie—and his eyes sobered up long enough to deliver a glower that hurried Alicia's pulse and summoned an immediate chill within.

"See," Charlie growled, "that's part of the problem—part of *my* problem anyway. None of your kind—of this kind, Chris' kind—ever do," he continued as he used his drink hand to point to the increasingly raucous group behind Alicia. "Fucked up thing is, I'm here to *help* you."

"I haven't the faintest idea what you are getting after."

"Missy, no. You definitely don't."

"Well, I'd ask you to leave, but you seem certain that you are well within your rights to be here, so, tell you what…" Alicia said productively, trying to buy herself enough time to figure out what exactly, if anything, she could do with him.

"What's that?" Charlie asked.

"The drinks are on me until you make yourself a burden. If and when that time comes, I'll surely not hesitate to have some of *your* own kind come and remove you."

"That's awfully kind of you, Alicia," Charlie nodded. "Awfully kind."

"Good. Now if you'll excuse me, I'd like to get back to my event."

"But of course," Charlie said, faking a courteous bow before reseating himself on the next nearest barstool. "Waiting on a friend is all."

The detective continued prattling on behind Alicia as she walked past the dinner party towards the washrooms. She casually signaled to Bean to keep things moving, though it hardly seemed necessary as the first item from the tasting menu had already arrived.

Until it vibrated, Alicia had only faintly realized she'd been clutching her cell the duration of the event thus far. Though hardly surprised, she was stung by disappointment when her initial glance indicated it was a text from Chris and not Lisa. She opted to leave it alone for the moment as she found the staircase to the bar's lavatories. She'd no designs on using the facilities, hadn't participated in much of the drinking thus far, but the flush of anger brought on by Detective Johnson's presence there had demanded she spend a few moments with herself.

Alicia descended down the steps, into the cooler air collecting amid the orange flicker of numerous oversized candles that hung delicately from the black walls of the halls below. The pungent smell of one too many cleaning products kept the attempt at luxurious ambiance paltry at best, and she noted that if she'd any intention of continuing hosting events in the future that this little detail would have single handedly struck the restaurant from repeat consideration. Her phone pulsated into her hand a second and third time, and then again right on the heels of those. The number four now stood between the parenthesis under Chris' name, but Alicia felt no obligation to unlock her phone because of it. As she came to the base of the second flight of steps the unpleasant odor of Lysol gave way to the sour stench of cigarette smoke riding a wave of funk generated by the heated August city trash wafting through the sliver of a slightly opened back alley door.

A rambunctious laughter rang out from the floor above, leaving Alicia to speculate that one of her guests must have been holding court with the lot of them. Her phone made several more attempts at grabbing her attention, but she didn't bother with confirming with her eyes what she surmised would only be additional pleas from Chris, insisting that Alicia reach out immediately.

Another gust of cigarette smoke blew through the gap the back door's propping had created as Alicia searched for a letter W among the six other closed black bathroom entrances. The scent's strength indicated that the culprit was just on the other side, puffing away, amid all the rancid throwaways from that eatery and those around it. While Alicia was sure it was likely a busboy or some other kitchen hand and not one of her members, she couldn't let go of the annoyance of their inconsideration— would not tolerate what she perceived to be an imperfection to the evening, even if it was working capably at camouflaging the remaining and also less than pleasant fumes of toxic bleaches and scouring powders that'd been used to prepare the lavatories earlier that day.

Alicia caught a glimpse of herself in a dimly lit hallway mirror. It reminded her of exactly who she could be—who she had been most of her adult life, or pretended to be at least. The thoughts that had swirled within her the past twenty-four hours, the upcoming betrayal she'd conduct on her own persona, none of it had yet altered the image of the successful all-business no-short-cuts perfectionist she still projected. Whatever anger she'd felt towards the detective on her way down had refocused its zeal around the idiot whose smoke break was unraveling the otherwise flawless execution of another Elite Two Meet event.

Livid, Alicia marched straight towards the backdoor armed with the practice of hundreds of similar tongue-lashings she'd delivered in kindred situations over the years. She could shut the door on the poor slob, leaving him with very little options other than inconveniently circling back around the block and to the restaurant's patron entrance, or she could burst through the door and unleash a week's worth of continually building intense frustration unabashedly onto that same poor slob.

Before Alicia could weigh the pros and cons of either action, she'd already committed to the latter. She swung the exit door open, and with the swift and hollow crack of a steel bat making contact with her skull, collapsed instantaneously to the ground, halfway in and halfway outside of the threshold. She tried to make sense of her assailant through the sting and pain, but her vision was momentarily too blurry to discern anything other than a figure towering above her, the offending cigarette still in hand.

"You fucking cunt! Don't you know how to answer a goddamned text?" Chris shouted.

Alicia's brain sent the word "Chris" to her mouth, but it escaped into the world as nothing more than a barely audible sloshing of spit mixed with blood.

The rattle of the bat's exterior hitting the ground echoed throughout the skyscraper-made canyon, climbing into Alicia's brain to only further accentuate the throbbing pain on her left temple. Before any attempt to lift herself could materialize, Chris grabbed Alicia by the arms and had begun dragging her out of the doorway and a bit further down the back lane, then propped her from the small of her back up against the bricks, their heat still palpable from that day's unrelenting sun. Alicia's phone had landed a few feet away, and Chris went to retrieve it in order to cement her point.

"You see, Alicia," Chris said as she kneeled down beside Alicia's unresponsive posture, "had you bothered to unlock the damn thing, you'd have seen the digital version of me politely asking you repeatedly to kindly come meet me outside. I believe I even used the word favor—please do me a *favor* I'd typed."

Chris paused as if she were expecting a response. When none made its way forward, she clutched the phone like a brick and whipped it against Alicia's face, bashing the already bat-weakened bone under her skin repeatedly. Alicia could hear herself screaming for Chris to stop, but if the words had been realized it'd done little in the way of curtailing the violence. Through pooling blood she thought she caught the movement of another human being approaching from behind Chris, but when she dared to open her eyes again after a few seconds passed without receiving another crack to the face, she saw no one else there with them.

"Alicia," Chris said with an entirely new and caring lilt. "What are we going to do with you?"

Systematically, a few things synced up within Alicia's brain, and moderate speech became achievable again. She was positive that when she said, "I don't understand," that the words had actually left her mouth in an intelligible fashion. If they had though, Chris was slow to acknowledge they'd been heard as she walked away momentarily to reclaim the discarded bat.

"What's to understand? Girl sees girl. Girl falls for girl. Girl gets girl," Chris said as she kneeled back down beside her. "In this case, the girl gets the girl with an unfortunate brute force, but…"

Chris was tickled by her own attempt at levity.

In a bid to stave off any additional physical punishment, Alicia did her best to acknowledge the twisted humor behind the sentiment with her own blood soaked grin. For a moment, the reciprocation behind Chris' eyes mistakenly signaled a possible end to the assault.

Chris began to stand. She pulled a cigarette out and tossed the pack to the ground. She lit it and continued.

"I'm going to have to kill you, Alicia." Chris' tone had turned dark again as quickly as it'd reverted to pure Pollyanna. "But I love you. I always did. Even after I caught you with that bitch, Lisa." In between puffs she mused, "Had it not been for her, I honestly believe you'd have come around on me. I went to an awful lot of trouble to get your undivided attention you know."

Chris squatted back down abruptly, and grabbed Alicia by the hand, she squeezed it lightly and with the butt still hanging from her mouth practically cooed, "I killed her too. Hadn't ever planned on having to murder anyone to get through to you, but c'est la vie." She then exhaled as insult into Alicia's face.

Alicia's eyes began to tear again. Pain, fear, confusion and the misguided realization that Lisa's death—even if she chose not to believe the words coming amid Chris' tirade—was somehow on her own head now.

When Chris saw the sorrowful streaks forming, she reiterated, "That's right. Killed your gal pal." And then she gave Alicia's hand one last comforting squeeze before discarding it and then erecting herself above her again. She tossed the butt to the ground, and put the bat's thin handle into both of her hands. "I'll be the first to admit, this all kinda sucked, but I love you."

Chris raised the barrel overhead with the express intent of bringing down a single blow strong enough to end Alicia's existence right then and there.

Any physical effort to thwart the bulk end of the bat's destruction wouldn't have mattered, and so Alicia focused what little strength she could muster into a countenance she tried to direct at Chris' eyes before she eked out the words, "I love you too."

Chris paused, holding the weapon in a circular hover over the already slightly mangled body of the only person she'd ever loved—she smiled timidly, trying to swindle herself into believing Alicia's last words might possibly be true. But she couldn't.

"Fucking liar," she spit softly.

Chris moved to bring the bat down, Alicia's eyes shut with an uncontrollable flinching of useless preparation for its impending and brutal connection. In the darkness and pseudo-safety that the backs of eyelids provide, her ears registered two quick and muffled popping sounds, followed by a repeat performance of the reverberating echo created by the clang of the bat dropping to the ground again. The unsettling shrill ping was accompanied by the heavy thud of Chris' body as it spilt forward and onto the pavement beside her. The force of Chris' body's collision with the ground sent a quick burst of air into her face.

Alicia opened her eyes. After a rapid succession of blinks cleared the pain induced haze over them, she was finally able to make out the shooter. Detective Johnson stood just a yard or so in front of her, on the other side of Chris' body, whose petite crumpled mass lie bleeding out into the cobbled street as the finality of death crystalized over her face. He took his time coming towards them and then thrust his booted foot into Chris' abdomen two times, while never removing the aim of his gun from the head atop her lifeless body.

Charlie took another step forward, put his gun back into the holster behind his back as he knelt down, and held out his hand in an attempt to help Alicia get onto her feet. She summoned the strength to move, trying to influence an arm to place her trembling hand into his, then saw another shadow emerge behind the detective as her fingers finally found their grasp.

"Charlie Johnson, guess it looks like you won't be collecting my money after all."

Charlie went completely still. Cursed himself under his breath for having not thought through his actions—for having ignored his gut, or rather for having recklessly liquored his gut into an ambivalence about what future tragedy might arise on the backend of his decision to put Chris down. He damned his gastronomical former fortune teller for coming way late to the party to let him know that he'd another's gun trained on him at that very moment.

"Nope. Guess not," Charlie said aloud.

"Shame that," Swoopes teased.

"Isn't it."

"You don't know the half of it my old friend."

"Do tell."

"That little chee-kah you was sweet on?" Swoopes instigated.

"Lisa?" Charlie asked.

"Yeah, she still alive. This must be some sorta Shakesperian shit here."

Charlie's relief to the news was greeted by the sparkle that returned within Alicia's eyes upon hearing the same information. It warmed his soul, he felt vindicated, if for only a moment. He knew she'd no idea that they'd both be dead soon.

"You gonna let Lisa live?"

"Don't see why not, I got no beef—besides, ain't looking like I'm gonna get paid for dumping her body no more thanks to you," Swoopes declared as he came up closer on them, eyeing the accuracy of the kill shots Charlie had achieved in offing Chris.

Alicia's hand squeezed Charlie's tight, then she intentionally let go, freeing it for the possibility of defending them both, but the opportunity never came.

"Some sense of humor on her too for a girl who had just got beat within an inch by this crazy bitch, you know?" Swoopes noted as his pointer finger made its final preparations to execute them both with two quick squeezes.

"Yeah, I know," Charlie conceded.

"Pity."

(END)

ABOUT THE AUTHOR

"So, why *are* you the way you are?"

Peter Rosch is what happens when a Polish drag racing varsity bowler and a beautiful but über paranoid French Canadian Air Force Brat get together on a disco dance floor in glorious Albuquerque, New Mexico. He's a recovering alcoholic who favors the run-on sentence—the one thing for which he offers no apologies. Eighteen years in New York City, Boston, and Los Angeles as an award-winning Writer, Creative Director, and Commercial Director have left him moderately famous in an industry filled with the very best kind of people—lunatics.

This is his second novel.
For more information please visit: peterrosch.com

Made in the USA
Lexington, KY
08 July 2014